Now Laban had
two daughters; the
name of the older was
Leah, and the name of the
younger was Rachel. Leah had weak
eyes, but Rachel had a lovely figure
and was beautiful.
Jacob was in love with Rachel and
said, "I'll work for you seven years in
return for your younger daughter
Rachel."
Laban said, "It's better that I give her
to you than to some other man. Stay
here with me." So Jacob served seven
years to get Rachel, but they seemed

like only a few days to him because of
his love for her.
Then Jacob said to Laban, "Give me my wife.
My time is completed, and I want to make
love to her."
So Laban brought together all the people of the
place and gave a feast. But when evening came, he
took his daughter Leah and brought her to Jacob,
and Jacob made love to her. And Laban gave his
servant Zilpah to his daughter as her attendant.
When morning came, there was Leah! So Jacob
said to Laban, "What is this you have done to
me? I served you for Rachel, didn't I? Why
have you deceived me?"

—GENESIS 29:16–25 (NIV)

Ordinary Women of the BIBLE

✦

Ordinary Women of the BIBLE

THE RELUCTANT RIVAL

LEAH'S STORY

MESU ANDREWS

Ordinary Women of the Bible is a trademark of Guideposts.

Published by Guideposts
100 Reserve Road, Suite E200
Danbury, CT 06810
Guideposts.org

Cover and interior design by Müllerhaus

Cover illustration by Brian Call and nonfiction illustrations by Nathalie Beauvois, both represented by Illustration Online LLC.

Typeset by Aptara, Inc.

ISBN 978-1-961442-07-8 (hardcover)
ISBN 978-1-961442-08-5 (softcover)
ISBN 978-1-952959-00-4 (epub)

Printed and bound in the United States of America

Ordinary Women of the BIBLE

❖

THE RELUCTANT RIVAL
LEAH'S STORY

Dedication

To Charlasu (Susie) Hunt, my precious sister,
who has always been favored by Yahweh and faithful to Him.

Acknowledgments

As I write this, my elbow is leaning on a stack of amazing books in the Ordinary Women of the Bible series written by other authors. I'm so thrilled Guideposts Books has offered a biblical fiction series to its readers, and it couldn't have happened without the tireless efforts of Susan Downs. This skilled and passionate editor was determined to bring the very best authors in Christian fiction to Guideposts to participate in the project, and she made the offer hard to turn down! Thank you so much, Susan, for your tireless efforts to find tried-and-true writers as well as debut authors to carefully weave creative fiction into the unchanging foundation of God's Truth.

I'd also like to thank my agent, Tamela Hancock Murray, who first spoke with Susan about this idea and pulled me into a meeting back in 2018. What a joy to see the incredible fruit this project has borne.

Three beta readers helped me with the first draft of *The Reluctant Rival*. Thanks to Meg Wilson, Kristen Watkins, and fellow biblical fiction author Carol Ashby. And, as always, my family has made this book possible. Without their help, I truly couldn't do what I do. From cooking and cleaning to editing and proofreading, my sweet family does it all! Thanks especially to Roy and Emily for last-minute proofing. I love y'all deeply!

CHAPTER ONE

*During wheat harvest, Reuben went out into the fields and
found some mandrake plants, which he brought to his mother Leah.
Rachel said to Leah, "Please give me some of your son's mandrakes."*
~ Genesis 30:14 (NIV) ~

Harran, Paddan-Aram

Leah waved dust and chaff from the air as she bent to gather
another bundle of wheat then pulled a leather string from
around her neck to bind it. Straightening, she stood the bundle
on end, making a neat row behind the servant she'd been
following all morning. His wide, smooth sweeps with a scythe
felled the golden, knee-high stalks, and each time Leah felt
weary, one glance at her younger sister's increasing stacks
urged her forward. "Looks like you and Bilhah will be cooking
the evening meal all week."

Rachel glanced at Leah's bound stacks and hurried her pace.
"It's barely past midday. Your age will slow you down by day's end."

"Ha! We'll see who's built for endurance, little sister." Leah
kept her tone light, but both knew this was more than a game.
They'd always been competitive—too much perhaps.

The volley of words was a momentary distraction from the
endless rhythm of harvest. Bend, bind, stack, bend, bind, stack.

Leah kept watch over her four young sons, who followed her closely. Reuben, Simeon, Levi, and Judah—all age five and under—played more than they worked, but they also helped the gleaners pick up the loose heads of grain.

Five-year-old Reuben was an old soul. Simeon came a year later and Levi less than a year after. Leah had been so grateful for three sons—the number of completeness—that when Judah was born, she felt compelled to name him *Praise*.

Bend, bind, stack, bend, bind, stack.

It had been two years since Leah had conceived. Why?

Bend, bind, stack, bend, bind, stack.

Granted, Jacob didn't visit her tent as often. Had the same God who matured the heads of grain caused her womb to lie fallow?

"*Imma*, look what I found!" Reuben bounded toward her with three unripe mandrake apples. "Are these the ones you boil to make *Abba* like you?"

Her cheeks warmed when the scythe-wielding servant grinned over his shoulder. "Shhh, Reuben." She knelt and took the precious find from his hands. "Yes, you've done well, sweet boy." He was the only one of her sons who woke when she cried in the night, often falling back to sleep with his arms around her neck.

"May I have one or two of your mandrakes, Reuben?" Rachel knelt beside them. "My little boys aren't yet big enough to join the wheat harvest and find treasures."

Leah bolted to her feet, nudging Reuben behind her and clutching the mandrakes. "*Your* little boys?" she said, incredulous. "*Bilhah's* boys are near the age of Judah and could be in

2

the fields if you wanted them with you. *Saying* they're your sons doesn't make it so, Rachel."

"Just because I refuse to work them like slaves when they're barely weaned doesn't mean I ignore—"

"You *dare* instruct me on raising children?"

"Shall I instruct you on pleasing Jacob instead?"

Leah flinched. There it was. The competition she could never win. "Isn't it enough you stole my husband? Now, you would steal my son's mandrakes?"

Rachel's jaw tightened, looking down at the unripe fruit in Leah's hand. "You know I could bear Jacob a child with the mandrakes' sweet-smelling balm and Inanna's power."

"I refuse to be drawn into the same argument, when you know we'll never agree." Why must she cling to Abba's gods? Jacob's household should serve his God.

"Fine!" Rachel stomped her foot. "You can sleep with Jacob tonight if you give me *all* the mandrakes."

Leah had proven by the wedding deception that she'd do anything for a night with Jacob ben Isaac. She shoved the three green mandrake apples into her sister's outstretched hands. "Jacob may have chosen you, Rachel, but his God favored me."

The younger sister stuffed the prizes into her shoulder bag and sneered. "I'll take Jacob over his god any day."

Bilhah and Zilpah had prepared a tasty meal by the time the wheat harvesters returned to camp. Deborah, Rachel's childhood nursemaid, took charge of the children during the meal, but as soon as it was over, she and Rachel disappeared— as they often did. Leah helped the two slave-wives put the children to bed and clean the dishes. It mattered little that Leah had bound the most stacks of wheat or that she'd hoped to have time to bathe in the river before Jacob returned from the flocks. Her little sister had always been and would continue to be favored and spoiled without anyone to hold her accountable.

On nights like these, when Leah pitied herself for Rachel's many slights, she need only think of Bilhah's life to feel better. Abba had mistreated Bilhah before giving her to Rachel as a maid, and then Rachel gave her to Jacob so she could bear children counted as Rachel's. At least Jacob gave her full wife status. But then Leah's dear maid Zilpah felt overlooked after Bilhah had children. She was a daughter of Laban from a concubine and felt she should be Jacob's wife too since Bilhah was counted so. Leah offered her to Jacob, hoping he would decline. He didn't. Now, both slave-wives had two sons, and Jacob had four headstrong wives.

"I'll finish cleaning the dishes." Leah tried to take a bowl from Bilhah's hand, but she held it tightly, pushing Leah's hand away.

"I'd rather clean." Bilhah's dark eyes glistened. "Did you and my mistress fight in the fields today?"

Avoiding the question, Leah removed her apron and tossed it in the basket of soiled laundry. "I'm going to meet Jacob when he comes in from the fields." Bilhah and Zilpah looked at her like she'd grown a second head. "I'm saving him the embarrassment of having to leave Rachel's tent and come to mine."

"So you did fight," Zilpah said. "Why did Rachel agree to let our husband visit your tent tonight? Hasn't it been months since—"

"I hired him with mandrakes that Reuben found in the field." It sounded vulgar, but it was the truth.

Bilhah's smile brightened her dreary mood. "So our husband will visit only you tonight, not us?"

"You seem relieved." Leah knew Jacob hadn't visited the slave-wives after their second conception, but she thought it was his choice, not theirs. "You don't want more children?"

"Why would we?" Zilpah answered, rubbing sandy dirt over a plate and setting it in the clean stack. "Our husband barely notices the sons we've given him, and with each child we bear, Rachel hates us more."

Bilhah remained silent, already grinding grain for tomorrow's bread. She never spoke ill of her mistress.

"Must our whole lives revolve around Rachel's emotions?" Her sister's absence fueled Leah's resentment.

The question lifted Zilpah's perfect brows. "Aren't we all driven by emotions to do things we later regret?"

The maid's not-so-subtle reminder stung. Fear had convinced Leah to comply with her abba's plan to deceive Jacob on his first wedding night. As Laban's older daughter, she'd been betrothed from birth to the elder son of Abba's sister. Decades before, Abraham's servant fetched *Doda* Rebekah, who was taken to marry Abraham's son, Isaac, in Canaan—promising the future betrothal of any offspring to join Isaac's house with Laban's. Leah, as the elder, was betrothed to Esau—Doda Rebekah's firstborn twin—and Rachel to Jacob—the second-born. But when word of Esau's pagan cruelty reached all the way to Harran, fear caused Leah to do the unthinkable.

"Take a bowl of stew to Jacob's tent," she called over her shoulder, walking toward the fields. "I don't wish to leave my husband tonight to retrieve his food." Leah couldn't risk that he'd slip out of his tent and into Rachel's.

Zilpah caught up and turned her around for a hug. "I'll make a sacrifice to Inanna on your behalf, Mistress. May the mother goddess open your womb and give you as many sons as you wish." Before Leah could correct her, Zilpah hurried back to the cook fire. Oh, how she wished Jacob's other wives would embrace his stories of Abraham's God.

Heaviness wrapped her in gloom as dusk settled over Harran. She scanned the endless, rolling plains and strode toward the fields where Jacob had charge of Abba's flocks and herds and the undershepherds who guarded them. With a quick glance over her shoulder, she noted with pride that Jacob's camp was settling into its bedtime routine. In the distance, the sun's last rays warmed the tan, clay-domed houses of Abba's estate. How different her life was in Jacob's humble tents than the life she'd lived as a child in Laban's feigned wealth.

By the time Leah and Rachel were grown, Rebekah's sons were much older. Esau had already married Canaanite wives, and Jacob seemed married to the study of Yahweh. Though

Abba inherited land and houses when *Saba* Bethuel died, the honor Bethuel had earned died with him. Whatever Abba didn't spend on wine and prostitutes, he owed in gambling debts. And when it was clear Isaac would never send bride prices to unite their houses, Abba ranted that his sister in faraway Canaan had married a liar and thief.

Leah hurried her pace as memories grew darker. A childhood spent hiding from Abba's rage and tending her imma's wounds sent gooseflesh rippling down her arms. Jacob showed favoritism toward his more beautiful wife—as Abba had toward Rachel's imma—but at least Jacob didn't beat those he deemed lesser. Leah slowed, approaching the wishing tree where they'd buried her imma after one of Abba's beatings went too far. She stopped and let her fingers brush the long, thin strands of bark on the plane tree.

Closing her eyes, she could still see Imma's light-colored eyes, a perfect reflection of her own. Their Mitanni heritage chained them to a people now dispersed, slaves and exiles. Their light eyes were like an iron collar. Declaring them weaker. Inescapably less than. *Yahweh, why couldn't Abba have told Imma of You before she died?* But to Laban ben Bethuel, Yahweh was simply one god among many, and his cruelty meant Leah would never see her imma again. *Yahweh, forgive me. I still hate him.*

Sighing, she opened her eyes and wiped her cheeks. "I must be grateful he taught me how to read." Her whisper carried on the breeze as she sniffed away more tears and pinched her cheeks, trying to clear her sadness. Abba had manipulated her enough. Why allow the past to taint this hard-won night with her husband?

Hurrying toward the giant rock at the edge of Abba's pastures, she glimpsed Jacob's form silhouetted in the sunset. Her heart did a little flip. Still broad-shouldered and handsome, her husband now had streaks of gray in his shoulder-length brown hair. She had loved him the first moment she saw him.

He's Rebekah's youngest, Rachel had whispered. *My betrothed!* Leah tried not to love him, but the fear of marrying Esau made loving Jacob both easy and practical. She agreed to Abba's plan though she knew Jacob might hate her after their wedding—after she'd pretended to be Rachel, his beloved.

Would he reject her tonight?

She smoothed her robe, tightened her belt, and tried to appear pleasant. Confident. But how could she explain why she was waiting for him? Her mouth went suddenly dry. He was fifty paces away. She dared not tell him she'd hired him with Reuben's mandrakes. How long had it been since he'd visited her tent? Weeks? Months? Maybe three months ago. Had he stopped coming to her because Rachel forbade him, or because she was displeasing? How had she imagined this night could go well?

Jacob drew nearer. Squinted in the waning light. Raised his hand in greeting.

Trembling, Leah smoothed her robe again. Hadn't Yahweh confirmed her as Jacob's rightful bride by giving her four sons? But why had she stopped bearing? Had she somehow angered

Jacob's God? Or had Rachel's sacrifices to Inanna kept Leah from conceiving? *Yahweh, I've served You faithfully and taught my sons about Your Covenant....*

"Leah?" Jacob reached for her shoulders. "Is Rachel well?"

Rachel. Always Rachel. "She's well enough to sell you for three mandrake apples. You sleep with me tonight."

CHAPTER TWO

God listened to Leah, and she conceived and bore Jacob a fifth son.
~ Genesis 30:17 (NKJV) ~

One of Laban's house slaves ran toward the flock, scattering the sheep in every direction. Jacob's shepherds shouted at him, and the dogs barked, but the man seemed deaf to all scolding.

"You have another son, Master! Another son!" He halted three paces from Jacob, bracing hands on his knees while he panted. "Mistress Leah waits in Master Laban's guesthouse to present her fifth son to you."

Thank You, Yahweh. "Return to my wife, and tell her I can't come while the ewes are lambing. Perhaps in a week or two I'll—"

The young man shot up. "But Master Laban is waiting with a freshly opened wineskin."

Laban would most likely drink it all by the time Jacob reached the estate.

"Please, Master Jacob." The servant turned to show the whipping scars on his back. "If I return without you, my consequences will be severe."

Jacob sighed, massaging the back of his neck. Did the man realize what consequences Jacob risked by leaving his ewes with lesser shepherds? Laban cut his wages for every lamb or ewe that died in childbirth. Surveying the flocks and undershepherds, Jacob decided to go. At least those on duty this morning were capable men he'd hired and not Laban's incompetent sons.

"Go back and tell Laban I'm on my way," he said. "I'll follow after I've given instructions to my undershepherds."

"Thank you, Master Jacob." The man ran toward the estate while Jacob told his men he'd be gone most of the day. Laban wouldn't let him give a quick greeting and leave, and once he saw Leah, he'd want to spend time with her. *A son.* She'd done it again. He let his head fall into his hands, exhaling a relieved sigh. The woman he hadn't wanted had become a wife of great worth.

After helping a ewe complete a twin birth, he raced across the gaping plains and entered camp. Nearly deserted, it felt eerie without the life and joy of his wives' voices and his sons' laughter. The boys were undoubtedly at the estate with Laban's wife and maidservants.

His women had adjusted well to life in tents after Laban had cast Leah and Jacob out of his compound following their wedding night. If Jacob had meekly accepted Leah instead of Rachel, would Laban have allowed Jacob's family into the sprawling complex of mud-brick cone-shaped houses?

No. Laban was a heartless conniver. Jacob had worked seven years to earn Rachel and lived in a tent since the first day he arrived. No doubt it was punishment for his parents' failure to honor the betrothal agreement sooner. Laban never forgot a slight.

Bawdy laughter erupted from the central dome, leaving no doubt about where Laban and his sons were celebrating. But where had Leah given birth? As much as he hated to, he'd have to join them and ask.

Crossing the threshold, he matched their volume. "Greetings, and good day!" Being the aggressor worked best when dealing with Laban. "Time for some wine to celebrate before I meet my *ninth* son!"

Laban's three sons gripped Jacob's wrist and offered the mandatory congratulations, but invisible daggers launched from their eyes during conversation. Patting his stomach after the midday meal, Jacob said, "I'm grateful for your hospitality, Laban. Now, I'm anxious to visit my wife and new son."

After a few more feigned pleasantries, Laban summoned the servant who had fetched Jacob from the field. Exhausted, Jacob followed the young man through the winding system of conical huts, halls, and bricked archways.

"Don't leave me," he said. "I'd never find my way out of here." Jacob's wry smile declared it only partly jest.

"Just ring the bell when you're ready to leave." The man bowed.

"You may go," Jacob whispered, but nothing could tear his gaze from his wife. Leah lay cradling their newborn at her breast. She always fed them the first day—before the wet nurse took them. *Yahweh, she is a wonder.* How his heart had changed toward her since they woke together for the first time. When dawn's glow cast its revealing light on her, he'd let out a feral wail at the sight of those bright blue eyes.

"You came." Leah's weary smile beckoned him. "Come. Meet our fifth son, *Issachar.*" The confidence on her face today was a stark contrast to the fear he'd seen that first morning.

"You named him *wages?*" Jacob crossed the threshold, chuckling, and sat beside her on the straw-stuffed mattress. "Because you hired me with mandrakes?"

"Actually, he's my wages for giving Zilpah to you." She reached for his hand and squeezed gently. "I'm sorry Abba summoned you from the flocks. I know they're lambing. I don't expect you to stay long."

Always practical. If it were Rachel in the bed, she'd expect him to stay until summer—and he would, gladly. Two sisters had never been more different. Did he love them both? What was love? On the morning Leah became his wife, she'd declared her love for him. He didn't care. He wanted Rachel. *Thank You, Yahweh, for giving me both.*

Leaning forward, he kissed his first wife. Issachar protested at being squeezed between them. Laughing, Jacob took him from her. "I'm glad I came to see this noisy gift from Yahweh." He held him up to see the adorable, pinched face. "You are an opinionated one already, Issachar, but you must let Imma rest tonight on this soft mattress before she returns to camp tomorrow."

He offered the babe back, but Leah averted her eyes. "Thank you for coming. You should probably get back to your flocks."

Leah was never in a hurry to be rid of him. "What aren't you telling me? Where are your sister-wives?"

"They've gone back to prepare my tent."

"But they always stay with you the first day after a birth."

Crimson rose in her cheeks, proving she was upset.

"What happened?" he pressed. "Have the four of you been fighting again?"

She looked up, forcing a smile. "Abba said he might welcome guests tomorrow, and he needed this room."

The full impact of Laban's cruelty took a moment to absorb. "Your abba won't allow you to stay in his house for even one night after you've delivered his ninth grandson?"

"Jacob, it's fine—"

"No!" He shot to his feet and started pacing. "I've lived here long enough to know Laban's only guests are townspeople who bring their own food and wine because he's too miserly to feed them." He stopped pacing and shouted at his wife. "I won't stand for it, Leah. If you get an infection or have complications in the night, it will take twice as long for the midwife to reach our camp than if you were here and—"

"Jacob!" She shouted over his ranting, causing Issachar to wail.

Silenced by the pain etched on her features, he felt like a rabid dog that had attacked its own sheep. He pulled his fingers through his hair and sat down beside her. "I'm sorry. I'm not angry with you. I'll speak to your abba, and you'll remain here—"

"No, Jacob." She pressed her hand against his cheek while trying to reassure their son. "I'll rest better in my tent anyway, and at least one of my sister-wives will stay with me all the time."

She leaned forward and brushed his lips with a gentle kiss and then lingered in a second kiss that promised more sons. "Go, Husband. Tend your sheep, and let my sister-wives tend me."

Jacob obeyed Laban's daughter, the woman with whom he'd reluctantly finished a wedding week so long ago. Were it not for her persistent questions about Yahweh, he might never have spoken to her at all. It was her inquisitive mind, indomitable spirit, and the love in those intelligent blue eyes that finally won his respect. His affection for her grew as her loyalty to Yahweh increased, and he had no doubt that with Leah leading his household, his sons' inheritance in Canaan was secure.

If only he could take the best features of all his wives and roll them into his beloved Rachel—but he'd still have to work for her surly abba, Laban.

CHAPTER THREE

Leah conceived again and bore Jacob a sixth son.... So she called his name Zebulun. Afterward she bore a daughter, and called her name Dinah.

~ Genesis 30:19–21 (NKJV) ~

The faint smell of hyssop entered Leah's consciousness. Before she was fully awake, she grabbed a slop bucket and emptied her stomach.

Issachar's wet nurse stirred. "Are you all right, Mistress?"

Leah peeked over the bucket's rim in the dawn's half light. "I'm fine," she lied. "I think last night's pistachios were a little moldy."

The woman nodded and turned over, her deep, even breaths proving she'd fallen asleep almost immediately. They'd both been up half the night, the nurse with two-year-old Issachar, and Leah with eight-month-old Zebulun. Leah's sensitivity to smell usually signaled pregnancy, but how could it be? She'd decided to feed Zeb herself, forgoing a wet nurse except when Jacob called her to his tent, hoping to give her body a rest from birthing. She hadn't even experienced a full cycle yet. *Yahweh, please. Not another baby so soon.*

Besides the exhaustion, she couldn't bear the thought of Rachel's wounded expression when she told her of another pregnancy. That particular competition had lost its glory to the overwhelming compassion Leah felt for her barren baby sister. By midmorning, when Leah could barely drag herself from her tent and she'd emptied her stomach contents three more times, Rachel came looking for her.

"You're as gray as Jacob's favorite donkey." She stood beside Leah's sleeping mat, unpacking her basket of clay pots.

"Thank you, dear sister. You always know how to make me feel better." They both grinned. "I'll be fine." Leah had been using the word *fine* all morning. It quickly cut off most conversations—except with Rachel.

"You're not *fine*." She started mixing herbs into a cup of steaming water.

"I can't—" The smell made Leah reach for the bucket.

Rachel's eyes rounded. "You're pregnant again!"

"Not necessarily." Leah couldn't look at her. "It could be moldy pistachios."

"He slept with you once since Zeb was born, and you're still nursing!"

Leah felt like a child being chastened. "I'm sorry, Rachel." *Wait!* Why was she apologizing? Her head snapped up, meeting her sister's glare. "No. I'm not sorry. He's my husband too, and it's not my fault you haven't gotten pregnant. If you'd ask Yahweh for help instead of praying to the silly teraphim hidden in your tent, perhaps you'd conceive."

"They're not silly!" She began putting the clay jars back in her basket. "Harran's gods listen when Deborah and our sister-wives pray. Why don't they listen to me?" Her voice broke, and she squeezed her eyes closed, pressing a stream of tears down her cheeks.

Leah suddenly felt worse than she had all morning. She reached for Rachel's hand and offered the only comfort that mattered. "Our husband's God is the God of all creation, and He has a plan that includes us all. Yahweh has something for you, Bilhah, and Zilpah even though you don't yet serve Him."

"I wish I could believe you." She lifted Leah's hand to her lips, kissed it, and left.

Five weeks later, Rachel and Leah were both vomiting in slop buckets—and it had nothing to do with moldy pistachios. Jacob had never seemed so happy or Rachel so awed. Finally, the wife Jacob loved would bear his child.

"I prayed to Yahweh." Pride tinged Rachel's tone while she worked the grindstone one morning. "He answered me, Leah, just as you said. Jacob's God is real!" By the third month, her awe abated. "Why is Yahweh punishing me? Will I ever feel like myself again?"

"Yahweh isn't punishing you." Leah rolled her eyes and offered a piece of yesterday's dry bread. "Eat this before you rise from your mat each morning. You'll feel better."

Leah sat down beside her as mourning doves cooed outside Rachel's tent.

She ate a few bites. "Every time Jacob comes near me, I attack him like a lioness."

"I saw the claw marks." Leah tried not to laugh but failed.

"It's not funny." Rachel swatted her, unable to hide a grin. "I feel awful about my tantrums, but I can't stop them."

Abba's spoiled daughter, born of his favorite wife, had never been able to curb her tantrums, but Leah wouldn't dare say it. She pulled Rachel into her arms instead. "All the suffering will be worthwhile the moment you hold your baby. Jacob loves you, and he'll adore you even more when you give him a son."

Leah swallowed the lump in her throat, aching at the truth she'd just spoken. When Rachel's child came—be it son or daughter—Rachel would again be called to their husband's tent every night, her foul moods and fear of losing the baby forgotten.

Leah—ignored.

She was a first wife who would always be second, but she'd spent every night in Jacob's tent for the past two months. Though he'd never said the words, Leah hoped she might have at least a portion of his love. They shared deeply about Yahweh's Covenant and what it meant for their sons, feeling closer than she imagined possible.

"I'm sorry for my part in our feuding." Rachel released her, startling Leah from her thoughts. "If I stopped fighting for Jacob, I thought your fertile womb would win him over completely." Her dark eyes glistened with tears.

In that moment, the weight of Leah's great wrong against her sister felt like a millstone around her neck—and a torrent of tears loosened the eight-year burden of guilt. "I'm sorry too, Rachel. I was so frightened of Esau. Everything I'd heard about him from traveling merchants made the betrothal feel like a death sentence."

"I know—"

"No! You don't know the half of it!" Leah shook her. "Abba said Esau married Canaanite women who worship gods by burning their children. Those could have been *my* children. My sons! He's a murderer, Rachel, but I would still have been forced to honor the betrothal covenant."

"No, no." She shrugged off Leah's hands. "Abba wouldn't have made you marry someone like—"

"Yes, he would have." Leah held her gaze and watched the facade fall away. It was time for truth between them.

Sighing, Rachel looked at her hands before speaking quietly. "I didn't know of Esau's wicked wives. I thought you agreed to Abba's plan to deceive Jacob because you were tired of waiting and anxious to marry. I felt betrayed by both my sister and the abba who loved me."

Leah's heart ached, realizing for the first time the depth of betrayal Rachel felt. "Looking back, I realize Abba's motivation for offering me as Jacob's bride was far less noble than saving me from Esau. During the seven years Jacob worked for your bride price by shepherding Abba's flocks and herds, he increased Abba's wealth more than any bride price from Isaac and Rebekah. Since he knew Jacob wanted you, he was convinced Jacob would serve seven *more* years and pay the second bride price he lacked."

Rachel looked startled, lips parted as if on the verge of a question that she couldn't quite form. Finally, she choked on a humorless laugh. "I always thought Abba loved me." She shook her head, but her eyes remained focused on Leah. "The wedding switch wasn't your idea at all, was it?"

Leah shook her head slowly. "When Jacob arrived, I knew then I never wanted to marry Esau. So I had asked to remain in Abba's household and never marry."

Rachel lifted her chin, a shadow darkening her features. Did she realize Leah loved Jacob at first glance? "Why wouldn't you let Abba find you another husband?" Words from a dark-eyed beauty to a pale-eyed outcast.

The memory of Abba's words still stung. "He said I'd wept so much over a betrothal to Esau that I was too ugly for any man to love. So he taught me to keep his business records—so my weak eyes could at least be useful."

Shame bowed Leah's head, but Rachel lifted her chin. "Abba has stolen too much from us, Sister, but we can restore the loss by fighting *for* our relationship instead of fighting each other."

Deep emotion radiated from Rachel's dark eyes—but would it last? "I've missed you, little sister." Leah wanted to be close, as they'd been before Jacob ben Isaac arrived in Harran.

During their pregnancies, Rachel allowed Leah to enjoy Jacob's full attention at night while the sisters enjoyed deepening their friendship all day. It was the sweetest time of Leah's life—until she gave birth to her daughter.

Their precious Dinah changed everyone's lives.

CHAPTER FOUR

*Then God remembered Rachel, and God listened to her
and opened her womb.*
~ Genesis 30:22 (NKJV) ~

L eah refused to request Abba's guesthouse for the birth of
her seventh child, preferring instead the familiar sur-
roundings of her tent. Her bag of waters broke just after the
evening meal, and rather than call for Harran's midwife, Leah
placed herself under the tender care of her three sister-wives
and their four maids. The relaxed atmosphere of early labor
deepened their sisterhood, and the camaraderie was as different from her other six births as fresh milk from moldy cheese.

As dusk changed to darkness, the camp outside grew silent.
Shepherds and servants cared for Jacob's sons while Jacob himself scurried to the fields, making some excuse about checking
on Laban's flocks. Zilpah wiped Leah's brow with a wet cloth,
grinning. "How can our husband—a shepherd who's delivered
thousands of lambs—get skittish at the twinge of his wife's first
contractions?"

Leah wanted to laugh, but the time for humor was over. No
matter how many times she'd given birth, the pain was as real
with her seventh labor as with the first. She sat perched on the

U-shaped stack of bricks, leaning back against Rachel's rounded belly. A contraction tightened like a belt across her middle, building and building....

Leah released a low groan, but the pain pushed her past dignity. "I need to push! Get him out!"

Rachel stroked her forehead. "Push, if you feel ready."

But she'd already started. Rachel would soon discover a woman's body dictated the process.

"That's it," Bilhah coached. "Keep pushing." She and Zilpah were positioned at Leah's knees, ready to catch the baby when it slid from the womb.

The tightening ebbed, and Leah sagged against Rachel's belly, exhausted and desperate for relief.

"You'll deliver the head with the next big push," Zilpah said, patting her left calf. "This baby wants to greet the sunrise."

"Leah?" A male voice shattered their private world. Jacob stood at the tent's entrance, framed in dawn's dim light with eyes as wide as the full moon. "Are you all ri—"

"Oooh—" Leah's body demanded she push again. Bearing down, she could think of nothing but how atrocious she looked to her husband. *Will he ever want to bed me again?* "Aaahhh!" The fiery pain made her hope he wouldn't.

"The head is out, Leah!" Bilhah cried.

"Gentler now," Zilpah said. "Gently, so I can ease out the shoulders."

Leah obeyed and kept her eyes closed, trying to ignore Jacob during one of the most humiliating—and beautiful—moments of her life. She focused her whole being into a final, controlled push....

"It's a girl!" Bilhah announced.

Leah wilted against Rachel, releasing a torrent of tears at the sound of her daughter's lusty cries. "You did it," Rachel whispered. "We have a girl to raise."

Zilpah placed the squalling babe on Leah's belly. "She's so tiny compared to the boys." Leah did a quick count of fingers and toes—ten of each. *Thank You, Yahweh.*

"Look at her tiny hands." Jacob leaned over them, offering his forefinger to the infant and kissing Leah's forehead. "Well done, Wife," he whispered. "I pray Yahweh gives her your character and loving heart."

Leah saw only admiration in his eyes, not the revulsion she expected. "I'm glad you were here," she said, surprised that she meant it. "Someday, you can tell her you witnessed her first breath."

Jacob nodded and turned an adoring gaze on Rachel. "Witnessing my daughter's birth has convinced me to do as you've asked, my love. I'll stay with you for our child's birth."

"Oh, Jacob!" Rachel threw her arms around him, elated, but exhaustion and despair weighed on Leah like a boulder. Bilhah and Zilpah exchanged silent dread. No one wanted a man in the world of women.

Without warning, Rachel released their husband and whisked the baby away from Leah.

"What should we call her, Sister?" She hurried over to Deborah, showing off the infant like a prize, then settled on a reed mat. Jacob followed, as if under a spell, and looked over her shoulder.

"Her name is Dinah." Leah's voice sounded like a wounded cow, so she gathered her courage and spoke with authority. "She will be *Dinah*, because Yahweh judged me worthy to raise a woman of my own."

"Shouldn't you wipe that off?" Jacob asked Rachel, ignoring his daughter's name.

"We don't wipe it off because it's a natural moisture coating from the mother goddess." Rachel massaged the waxy, cheese-like coating into the baby's skin. Jacob watched intently while she sprinkled salt on a wine-soaked blanket, moved Dinah to it, and continued massaging the salt and wine into her coated skin. "The wine and salt protect her from any ill effects of the Evil Eye."

Jacob's dark brows drew together, but he didn't scold Rachel for her superstitions or devotion to Harran's gods. Dinah squalled at the gritty massage, and Rachel cooed at the protest. "You'll have four immas to teach you Inanna's ways and—"

"No!" Leah sat up, nudging Zilpah and Bilhah aside. "*My* daughter will serve Yahweh alone." She met her sister's startled expression. "Do you hear me, Rachel?"

"You must lie still." Zilpah nudged her back against Bilhah's chest. "Your bleeding hasn't stopped yet." Leah had been clear-headed after delivery, but she felt a little dizzy now, seeing waves like a stream above Zilpah's head. Breathing deeply, Leah tried to regain calm.

Bilhah brushed hair from her sweaty forehead. "Surely, Dinah should learn the ancient traditions of the mother goddess. How else can she know the joys of womanhood?"

Leah's eyes slid closed, too weary to argue—especially if Jacob remained silent. "You've heard my decision." Activity swirled around her, but Leah focused on the sound of Dinah's whimpers. Her daughter would need to nurse soon, but Leah would wait until Jacob left. She wasn't ashamed of the unique way Yahweh provided for immas to feed their infants. In fact, she'd nursed all her babes on the day of delivery and Zebulun until she discovered she was pregnant with Dinah. She believed it a holy moment, a precious bond shared between imma and child. She would nurse Dinah too, but she'd employ a wet nurse for the nights Jacob called for her to his tent.

Opening one eye barely a slit, she peered at Jacob and Rachel cooing over her daughter. How long until he called her to his tent? She shook the thought from her head and relaxed, determined to focus on anything but her aching heart and body. Recalling the dream she'd experienced in Jacob's arms one night, she conjured the beautiful woman with straw-colored hair who was plowing a field with a team of six oxen. She'd awakened with a mixture of excitement and dread, knowing the child in her womb was the flaxen-haired beauty and the oxen were her six brothers—whom this girl would command with a will as strong as iron.

With a deep sigh, Leah let the cacophony of whispers rise around her baby's cry. In Jacob's camp, secrets were as plentiful as bread and manipulation as fine as flour. Would Baby

Dinah become a weapon in Abba's schemes and Jacob's defense? Would Leah's stance on Yahweh cause more division? Did Jacob approve—or even notice—her faith, since his eyes were so full of Rachel?

Yahweh, I don't want to fight over a husband who doesn't love me. Why can't I be content with You alone?

But what about her sister-wives? Could she ever be content to leave them to their pagan gods now that she knew the truth? With the effort of pushing a boulder, Leah opened her eyes and focused on her sister-wives. Zilpah, preparing Leah's mat. Bilhah, washing out the birthing rags. Rachel, seated on a mat with Jacob beside her, holding Dinah in her arms. During the eight months Leah slept in Jacob's tent, she'd challenged his tolerance of their pagan practices. He'd waved off her concern, calling the pagan rites "women's superstitions." His reassurance of Yahweh's pleasure in Leah—shown by her many sons—hadn't lessened the longing she felt for her sister-wives to know the truth.

"Oh no!" Rachel's shout drew everyone's attention. She plopped Dinah into Deborah's arms and struggled to her feet. "My bag of waters—it's breaking!" The wet stain on the mat beneath her confirmed it.

Jacob jumped to his feet, supporting her. "Bilhah, take the baby from Deborah so she can accompany Rachel and me to the guesthouse."

His words hit Leah like a slap. "You're taking her to Abba's house? He'll no doubt let Rachel stay more than a day."

The guilty expression on three faces proved it was true. Jacob, Rachel, and Deborah had planned the birth in advance—and kept it from Leah. She turned to measure Bilhah's complicity, but she had taken Dinah in her arms and turned her back while Rachel's old nurse hurried out of the tent.

Zilpah stepped to Leah's side, pity etched on her features. "I didn't know either," she whispered. "I'm sorry."

Leah offered her hand to Zilpah. "Help me to my mat. I want to feed Dinah." Zilpah supported her elbow, and Jacob flanked Leah's other side as they walked.

"Your abba insisted Rachel deliver in a guesthouse." His tone was almost pleading.

Leah couldn't look at him. Bilhah waited at her sleeping mat with Dinah and gently transferred the warm bundle to her arms. Leah looked down at her gift from Yahweh and worked to control her breathing—though she couldn't control her tears. "Leave, Jacob. Be with Rachel."

"It's my first birth, Leah." Rachel sounded indignant. "Abba wanted Harran's midwife to oversee the birth in case there were complications."

Leah glared over her shoulder. "Of course, he wanted only the best for you, Rachel. And how long will you stay in the guesthouse after the birth? Two days? Three?"

Rachel lifted her chin. "With my first birth, I could be more susceptible to infection."

Leah shifted her gaze to Jacob. "How long?"

He stared at his sandals. "A week under the midwife's care."

"And you'll stay with her the whole week, of course." If Leah's eyes could have shot fire, Jacob would have turned to ash.

He paused a heartbeat before looking into her eyes. "I'll check on you and Dinah every day."

But he would *live* with Rachel and her child in a guest house. "Don't bother."

Leah dozed throughout the day in the half haze of an exhausted new imma. Later that night, when the whole camp slept, Dinah's lusty cry drew Leah from her mat. She lifted the baby into her arms, positioned a mat beside the tent flap, and swaddled her newborn. Lying on her side, she let the night breeze cool them and stroked her daughter's cheek as she nursed. A brilliant full moon glowed in a clear night sky.

"Jacob, how I wish you were lying next to me in Abba's pasture with a flock of goats so we could praise Yahweh together." The stillness itself was a chorus of praise to the One Jacob had taught her to worship. Had she been too harsh with him when Rachel's labor began? Had she rekindled a battle that need not be fought?

The sound of hurried footsteps interrupted her thoughts. Jacob suddenly pulled back the flap. Startled at nearly stepping on them, he gasped. "Why are you lying so close—" He noticed the babe at her breast, and his features softened. He knelt beside Leah and stared in awe, placing his hand on the baby's downy-soft head. "This may be my favorite sight in the world." When he looked at Leah, moisture lined his lower lashes. "I'm happy you have a daughter to enjoy."

"She'll bring us *both* joy, Husband."

He nodded and cleared his throat. Removing his hand from Dinah's head, he sat on his heels and stared at the full moon. "Rachel delivered a little boy—Joseph—our firstborn."

"Your *firstborn*?" Heat raced up Leah's neck into her cheeks. "You have only one firstborn, Jacob ben Isaac. Or have you forgotten? His name is Reuben." She removed Dinah from her breast and swaddled her, scuttling to her feet. Placing the sleeping newborn in a sling held between two tent poles, she was careful not to wake their two youngest sons, Issachar and Zebulun.

"I meant *her* first—"

"Shhh!" Leah said, rushing past him. She slapped open the tent flap and led him toward the pastures where they could speak privately. Still weak from Dinah's birth, she stumbled and nearly fell over an exposed tree root.

Jacob's strong arms slid around her, making her feel as safe as Dinah's swaddling cloth. He whispered against her cheek, "It was your abba's decision to put Rachel in his guesthouse. Please don't make Joseph and Dinah part of your private war."

"Private war?" Anger stoked her strength. She pushed him away, leaning against a tree instead. "It's never been private, Jacob. My humiliation was public from the moment Abba saw the color of my eyes. Reuben will not be humiliated by favoritism as I have been."

His features hardened like flint. "You may buy me with mandrakes, woman, but you will never dictate my sons' inheritances."

She swiped at angry tears, knowing he was right. A woman had few rights, and she hadn't won Jacob's respect with angry demands. Perhaps a softer tone and his own words would penetrate his heart. "For eight months, I've lain in your bed, and you've said I'm the wife of Yahweh's favor. It's *my* womb our God has blessed. Reuben is your only firstborn, Jacob. *My* son. *Our* son."

He stepped closer, relentless. "If you believe yourself favored by Yahweh, Leah, then trust Him—and me—to do what's best for this family." Seeming satisfied, he raised his chin as if he'd used Leah's faith as a clever trap.

Had he forgotten she was raised by the man who outwitted him? "All right, Jacob." Leah matched his smirk. "You've seen what choosing favorites did to your family and mine. Let Yahweh deal with you ever so severely if you cheat your *true* firstborn out of his inheritance."

CHAPTER FIVE

As soon as Rachel had borne Joseph, Jacob said to Laban,
"Send me away, that I may go to my own home and country."
~ Genesis 30:25 (ESV) ~

Leah lay on her mat, enjoying the last morning of her week-long seclusion after Dinah's birth. The baby cooed beside her, content after drinking her fill from Leah's breast. Dinah's newborn eyes were the color of a midnight sky, dark and indistinct, yet with a hint of blue. Had she inherited the same curse that stared back at Leah in every polished bronze mirror?

She traced her finger across Dinah's forehead. "I would give my life to spare you the heartache those weak eyes bring." In Harran, light-colored eyes bespoke one of two things: either the gods' displeasure or a lineage of slavery. Leah's imma had been Abba's prize for a victory in a game of Hounds and Jackals against a traveling merchant. Abba vowed that he gave her status as a wife, as Jacob had done for Bilhah and Zilpah, but Abba had always treated her like the blue-eyed Mitanni slave of a merchant.

Leah lifted her baby's hand to her lips and whispered, "You are Yahweh's gift—no matter what color your eyes become. With you alone I will share my heart, a daughter I will love and who will love me more than any other." Even as the words left her lips, Leah felt uneasy. Would her daughter choose lovely Rachel over her as Abba had chosen Rachel and her lovely imma?

"Leah?" Jacob slipped into her tent. "I must speak with you."

Heart in her throat, she could barely croak, "Of course." She hadn't seen him since her tantrum over Rachel's firstborn, Joseph. After covering herself, she also wrapped Dinah and stood to offer the baby. "Would you like to hold your daughter?"

He smiled but his arms remained at his sides. "I can't stay long," he said. "I've come for your wise counsel."

Pulling Dinah to her heart, Leah inhaled a sustaining breath. "How may I help?"

He led her away from the entrance, looking over his shoulder as if someone might have followed. "I've asked your abba for permission to return to Canaan with my wives and children."

"I can guess how that was received."

He nodded, acknowledging her insight. "Rachel seemed surprised when I told her your abba had learned through divination that Yahweh had blessed his flocks and herds."

"Abba will believe in any god that serves his purpose." A spark of hope lit in Leah's chest. "Do you think Rachel believes Yahweh's power is greater than Abba's gods?"

Pausing a moment, he focused on Dinah rather than meeting Leah's gaze. "Your sister believes the same as Laban. Yahweh blessed his flocks because of me." He looked up, sighing. "Your abba asked what gifts he could offer that would make me stay, but we all know Laban promises one thing and gives another."

His eyes pierced her. Rachel had been the once promised gift and Leah the *other* Laban had given. Dinah squirmed, and Leah realized tension had tightened her grip. Relaxing her arms, she kept her defenses high. "How did you answer him? You know if Abba casts us out, we own nothing. Even the tents are his."

"Two seasons without me or my shepherds, and your abba's estate would be as broken down as it was twenty years ago." His wry smile replaced her angst with hope. "Laban knows it too, which is the reason he agreed to my proposal."

"What proposal?"

His smile dimmed. "It may not sound profitable at first."

Her angst returned. "Jacob, what was your proposal?"

"I've asked for all my wages to be paid in spotted and speckled lambs and goats." He said it quickly as if she might not realize the horror of it.

Leah swallowed hard then repeated the sticking phrase. "*All* your wages?"

"Yes, but listen." He grabbed her shoulders, desperation in his eyes. "My undershepherds are already separating the flocks, removing the speckled and spotted sheep so we can shear them quickly and sell the wool."

"No one wants that wool!" Her shout woke the baby, who began wailing, and Leah fought tears of her own. "How could you give up your grain and garden wages? How will we feed our camp?"

"You must trust me, Leah." He matched her pacing step for step. "Our camp's women create the most beautiful woolen garments in Harran. If we begin using *only* speckled and spotted wool to make uniquely patterned cloth and garments, the value of our flocks will soar."

Leah stopped abruptly and squeezed her eyes shut. *Think, Leah. You must think.* Familiar with the up-and-down emotions after each birth, she feared saying something she'd later regret. Endure the next few weeks' tempestuous moods, reclaim her role as household manager, and she would prove at least useful to Jacob—if not desired. The real test would come later today when Rachel returned to camp with Baby Joseph. Could she maintain a calm, healthy camp for everyone's benefit? Could she return to Abba's estate and continue keeping his records? Would he trust her now for record-keeping of Jacob's separate flocks and herds as well?

With a deep, calming breath, she regained enough control to look at her husband again. His brows scrunched together and lifted. He looked like a frightened boy. "Have I ruined us, Leah?"

"I've been saving some of your wages each month, exchanging it for silver and hiding it in a hole under my sleeping mat. We'll use that silver to buy supplies until we can earn enough from the speckled garments."

"You've saved enough silver to feed the whole camp?"

"I would never trust Abba for the welfare of your household, Jacob."

He couldn't have appeared happier if she'd birthed another son. "You're not the only one your abba betrayed. When Yahweh blesses the speckled and spotted flocks to rebuild our savings, we'll return to Canaan." Jacob's expression softened, and he opened his arms. But Leah stepped back, rebuilding walls around her heart.

"Today, Jacob, you focus on Rachel. She'll need your help moving back to camp with her son."

His eyes lingered on her. Was it regret she saw? Pity? She dared not hope for love. "Thank you, Leah." He inclined his head in a respectful bow and left.

One Week Later

Leah stood beside Rachel in Jacob's tent, both women bouncing wailing infants while their husband shouted. "He's cheated me again! He's not a man—he's a serpent!"

Rachel turned to Leah with a panicked whisper. "Do something! I don't want Jacob and Abba fighting."

What exactly did she expect Leah to do? On the very day Laban had promised Jacob the off-color flocks as wages, he'd ordered Rachel and Leah's brothers to remove every streaked, speckled, and spotted goat and all dark-colored lambs. By the time Jacob realized his scheme and sent his undershepherds in pursuit, they found Laban's sons three days away with most of the flocks butchered and the silver spent.

"Have you consulted Yahweh on the matter?" Leah asked when Jacob drew a breath.

Back turned on his wives, Jacob stared at his tent wall. "What if Yahweh is keeping me under Laban's thumb?" He whispered the awful possibility. "What if He's punishing me for the deception I inflicted on my own family?"

"It could be." Rachel passed Joseph to her nurse and stepped closer, moving her hands over his broad shoulders and muscular back. "But the gods of Harran reward cunning. I'm sure my brothers acted on their own. Both Abba and the gods will reward you if you find a way to retaliate."

Leah remained silent, watching her husband fall under Rachel's spell. *Please, Jacob. Tell her that Abba is a thief, and Yahweh is the only God you will worship.* But Jacob turned into her embrace without a word, letting Rachel's honeyed lies overshadow the truth.

"Jacob ben Isaac," Leah declared in a voice reserved for chastising. Both he and Rachel were startled and turned toward her. "You are Yahweh's Covenant bearer—born a miracle of miracles as Abraham's seed. The one true God has promised our descendants will one day possess the whole land of Canaan, and your goal is to return there someday."

Dinah's wailing ceased, and she looked up at Leah as if listening. Feeling overwhelmingly blessed, Leah ignored the sickening tenderness with which Jacob held Rachel's waist. "Think of all Yahweh has given you since coming to Harran—four wives, eleven sons, a daughter. You've acquired under-shepherds and maids for our household, and Yahweh has multiplied Abba's flocks under your care. And you're respected among all the shepherds in Paddan Aram." She glanced at Rachel and reminded them both, "Even when Abba practiced divination, his gods confirmed it was *Yahweh* who blessed his household through *you.*"

Familiar anger lit Rachel's eyes. "Yet *Yahweh* allowed our husband to be cheated."

Why must everything become a contest between them? After inhaling deeply, Leah captured angry words and ignored her sister's gibe. "Please, Jacob. I beg you. Seek Yahweh's guidance. Alone. It's the only way our family will return to the land He promised."

Jacob held Leah's gaze, lips pursed into a thin line, while Rachel snuggled closer to his side. Leah turned away. Imagining their closeness at night was torture enough. She need not witness it.

Baby Joseph whimpered in Deborah's arms. Hungry, no doubt. Rachel was determined to forgo a wet nurse when she saw Leah nursing Dinah, but Rachel found it hard to cease activities when her son demanded to eat.

"Give him to me," Leah said. She had started feeding both babies at least twice a day. Rachel's nurse looked from one sister to the other, waiting for direction.

"I'm going to the fields." Jacob exited the tent flap before his wives could object.

Deborah still held Joseph, his whimpers erupting to full-throated cries. "I'd be happy to feed him," Leah offered. The baby turned his open mouth toward Deborah's arm, searching for his next meal, while the three women stood in awkward silence.

Sniffing drew Leah's attention to the tears streaming down Rachel's cheeks. "Why are you crying?" She transferred Dinah to Deborah's other arm and gathered Rachel into a fierce hug.

"I'm a terrible imma," her sister wailed. "My nipples are too sore to nurse. I want to sleep more than I want to care for my child. I have no idea what he wants when he cries. And my son likes you better than me." She wiped her leaky nose and eyes on Leah's shoulder. "And I feel guilty saying it, but I liked my life better before I had a baby."

Leah rubbed her back, trying to be compassionate while hiding a grin. "I remember feeling those same things when Reuben was born, but you'll feel more like yourself in a few weeks."

"A few weeks? Aahh!" Rachel spiraled into more wailing. Perhaps silent comfort was better. Leah simply stood while her sister gripped her like a lifeline. When Rachel's weeping finally slowed, she released Leah and spoke with a timid and shaky voice. "Will you be Joseph's wet nurse, Leah?"

Stunned, she searched her sister's face for hidden motives. "Why not ask one of the young immas in camp?"

"Because you're the best imma I know," Rachel said without hesitation. "Dinah hardly ever cries, and her cheeks are as rosy as apples." Mischief sparked in her eyes. "I think you produce mostly cream like Abba's prize cow."

Leah gasped playfully and shoved her shoulder. "Call me a cow again, and I won't help you."

Rachel smiled but quickly sobered. "I'm truly grateful for all you do, Leah. Our household would collapse without you."

Leah looked away. She could almost hate Rachel until she said things like that. Her sister had enough of Abba in her to sound convincing. "Of course I'll nurse your son." Leah turned, meeting her sister's gaze. "We'll raise Joseph and Dinah like twins, born from two mothers."

CHAPTER SIX

The angel of God said to [Jacob] in the dream…
"I have seen all that Laban has been doing to you."
~ Genesis 31:11–12 (NIV) ~

J acob sat upright on his mat, rubbing sleep from his eyes. *Could it work, Yahweh?*

"Another dream?" Rachel sat up beside him and placed a hand on his shoulder.

He nodded. Was it truly Yahweh's instruction or the result of an overly spiced meal?

"Was it the same dream as last night?" she asked.

"Yes. And the night before." Not likely spicy stew.

His wife rose from the mat, lit a lamp, and went directly to her shoulder bag. "I brought this—in case the dream returned." Producing a stone statue no larger than her hand, she said, "It's Dumuzi, the shepherd god."

"Where did you—"

"I borrowed it from Abba's shrine."

A stab of panic propelled Jacob to his feet. "I don't need your abba's god to tell me what Yahweh's dream means." He wrenched the stone from her hand and shoved it back into the bag. "Besides, if he realizes you took it, he'll find a way to blame me."

She retrieved the god again, her jaw muscle working as Laban's did when he was angry. "If you're certain your dream is from Yahweh, why are you so disturbed?" Pulling out a small clay plate, incense, and two flint stones, she then knelt and set up a small altar. "I see no harm in seeking guidance from Dumuzi, the god whose protection over shepherds has proved effective for generations." When she'd finished arranging the elements, she looked up with a single brow raised—he recognized the silent challenge to kneel.

He could refuse and endure another lecture on Harran's gods. Or he could kneel beside his beloved and let her call on her silly god, knowing Yahweh was the only One who could deliver him from Laban's schemes. He knelt and tried not to roll his eyes while Rachel lit the incense on the altar.

"We call on you, great Dumuzi, son of Enki, consort of Inanna." She waved the smoke toward them as she prayed. "Come to us now, that we might use your power to overcome the evil used against us. Come, oh great Dumuzi. Come." Eyes closed, Rachel began to sway and hum.

Jacob sighed, wondering how long he should wait before leaving for the fields.

The altar fire suddenly flared, and Rachel's expression changed from reverence to delight. "Dumuzi is here, Jacob. Ask for anything, and it will be yours."

Hair rose on the back of his neck and gooseflesh on his arms. "Stop this, Rachel!" He jumped to his feet and stomped the altar fire.

"No!" she shouted, grabbing the idol to save it.

"Your abba's gods have no place in my household."

Rachel stood to face him, panting with fury. "You've disrespected Dumuzi, Jacob. You've disrespected *me*!"

Staring into the beautiful eyes that captured him the first moment he saw them, he shook his head. "I stepped on your fire, your clay dish, and a few herbs, my love. For this, and this only, I apologize." He grabbed his robe from the basket beside the mat and left her fuming.

"You must sacrifice to Dumuzi or pay for your affront!" she shouted. "Please, Jacob! Don't anger—"

Her last words were garbled by the sounds of early-morning activity in the camp. "Shalom," Jacob greeted a maid already working at the central fire. "I'd like to break my fast in the fields this morning." They both ignored Rachel's continued shouting while the woman wrapped bread and cheese in a cloth and handed it to him. "Thank you."

He started toward the fields for a quiet day with his flocks. Rachel's ranting faded in the distance, and the brisk morning air chilled him—or was it his wife's pagan worship that raised prickly flesh on his arms? Perhaps it was the herbs that flared in the fire.

Yahweh, I believe only You can give me the same dream three nights in a row.

Leah was right. He needed time alone to work out the plan Yahweh revealed in his dreams.

Jacob's stomach rumbled like thunder, and his undershepherds exchanged a conspiratorial grin. They too had heard Rachel's morning tirade. Who hadn't? She'd likely awakened the whole camp. The other wives had brought the shepherds' midday meal when the sun was overhead, but Jacob was still waiting as the sun descended into the western sky. Rachel was punishing him.

A shepherd's whistle gained Jacob's attention. The man nodded toward a feminine figure on the horizon. *Leah.* At a distance, he could differentiate Laban's older daughter only by her plain robes. Her height, weight, shape—even her voice— were so similar to Rachel's, it had been easy for Leah to deceive him on their wedding night. How would life have been different if Laban had given him Rachel as promised—or if Jacob had been content with Leah alone?

When she was only a few paces away, he saw her blue eyes were cautious, roving his face like a shepherd's hands roamed a newborn lamb for defects. Jacob smiled, hoping to reassure her. "I hope the basket on your arm has food in it."

The tension around her mouth relaxed. "It does, but what makes you think it's for you?" She offered a smile and joined him under the shade of a scraggly acacia.

He kissed her cheek and slid two waterskins from her left shoulder and a skin of watered wine from her right. "I was beginning to think Rachel would rather see me starve than forgive my affront to her idol."

"She might." Leah offered him the basket while she spread a blanket under the tree. They sat down together, and Leah began unpacking his meal. "When Zilpah and Bilhah sent word that Rachel hadn't brought your midday meal, I thought you might need something to hold you over until evening."

"Hmm." So all three wives might pay the price of Rachel's wrath when she returned to camp. "Thank you." He stilled her hand, capturing it under his own. "And thank your sister-wives for me."

She kept her eyes averted. "Rachel said you've had dreams— or should I say *a dream*—for the past three nights. Is it from Yahweh?"

He was fairly certain *this* wife no longer used Laban's idols to chant and pray. He tipped up her chin and searched her mesmerizing blue eyes. Moisture had gathered on her lower lashes. "Did you ask Yahweh to speak to me?" She nodded almost imperceptibly. "Then perhaps the dreams are His voice. An answer to your prayer." Jacob gently pressed his lips against hers. She smelled of cinnamon and cloves. Thinking his meal could wait, he pulled her closer—and his stomach growled.

She laughed, nudging him away. "Your stomach seems the more persistent urge right now, Husband."

"For now." He reached for a few almonds and enjoyed watching her unpack.

His wife's cheeks grew pink like a maiden's. Part of her charm. "Would you mind telling me your dream?"

"I believe Yahweh gave me a lesson in shrewdness." He pointed at the pile of fresh-cut branches he'd worked on all day. "I peeled back the bark on poplar, almond, and chestnut branches to create white stripes on them. In my dream, I placed the peeled branches in water troughs when the strongest ewes were mating with the healthiest rams, and they produced spotted and speckled lambs for our wages."

Leah laughed. "Do you really think it will work?"

"It sounds like madness, but maybe it's similar enough to pagan practices that your abba won't challenge it."

"It's wondrous madness!" She kissed his cheek. "I trust your judgment."

Jacob halted midbite and set aside his cup. *I trust your judgment.* Leah's simple affirmation felt like cool rain in summer.

"Have I said something to offend?" Leah sobered.

"Just the opposite." He brushed her cheek with the back of his hand. "Your words are more nourishing than this midday meal."

She captured his hand, turned a kiss into his palm, and released him so he could return to his meal. As usual, his first wife had created a feast with the simplest of fare. Almonds, dates, raisins, bread, and soft cheese were served with respect, care, and encouragement. Jacob ate like a ravenous dog, and after a few long draws of water, he noticed his wife's fidgeting.

Leah never lingered.

Now it was Jacob who avoided her eyes. "Is something bothering you?" Something was always bothering at least one of his wives.

She picked at her nails. "I realize the flocks are your responsibility and the household is mine, but I believe our sons—at least the four oldest—are well past the age of training in the fields." He looked up then and saw determination had replaced her angst. "Reuben is eight, Jacob."

Shoving a large bite of cheese-slathered bread in his mouth—to give himself time to think—he pondered how his eldest son had grown so quickly. *Reuben is eight?* Simeon, Levi, and Judah weren't far behind. But if he began training Leah's four oldest in the field, wouldn't the slave-wives expect their sons to be trained as well? He loved his sons, but he knew nothing of raising children. Perhaps he could manage one boy, but six—or eight?

"How old are Bilhah's and Zilpah's boys?" He reached for more almonds, but Leah stopped his hand before he tossed them in his mouth.

"Dan is six," she said, "the same age as Judah, and Naphtali is five. Zilpah's sons, Gad and Asher, are four and three—too young to leave camp. But Jacob, I—" She clamped her mouth shut. Her lips pressed into a white, thin line, while her cheeks flushed.

"Tell me what has upset you."

"Only *my* sons should join you in the fields at first, Jacob, because I have taught them of Yahweh. They know of His Covenant with Abraham and Isaac and the inheritance that awaits you in Canaan. The other boys' immas…" She shook her head, again trapping words behind a gate of restraint. But her intense blue eyes were stormy and dark.

If only Rachel could give Leah more words and Leah share with Rachel more silence—he'd have two perfect wives and a far more peaceful household. "Why is it important the slave-wives teach their sons of Yahweh before they tend flocks with me?" Jacob smiled, trying to lighten the moment. "Would they teach them better than I?"

Without a hint of humor, she raised a brow. "Will you teach them at all?"

The accusation in her tone sparked his anger. "How dare—"

"An abba may teach his son many things, my lord, but an *imma* teaches her children to eat, sleep, walk, and talk. We teach them the very foundation on which they build their lives—including which god they must serve. Your other wives have taught your sons to build their lives on Harran's gods. If you want Dan, Naphtali, Gad, Asher—and *Joseph*—to serve Yahweh, you must give your wives an incentive to teach them." She inclined her head in a respectful bow. "Every boy seeks time with his abba, Jacob, and every imma works to give her son that gift. Didn't your own imma, Rebekah, find a way to secure Isaac's blessing for you?"

Jacob's cynical laugh lifted her eyes to meet his. "You can't compare Imma's conniving with your request, Leah. Yes, I wished for Abba's approval all my life, but it was Yahweh's Covenant blessing I fought for. Esau would have squandered it. He cared nothing about Yahweh or His Covenant."

"Is it really so different?" Leah lifted her chin, as determined as he'd ever seen her. "If you don't command your wives to teach their sons of Yahweh, will your boys realize their inheritance in Canaan is as important as the air they breathe?"

Appetite suddenly lost, Jacob shoved away his wooden plate and scrubbed his face. *Yahweh, have I ruined my sons? Am I a terrible abba?* The boys had come in quick succession, and he'd been consumed with uncovering Laban's latest plot. Other shepherds in Harran sometimes brought their sons to the fields, but Jacob's men never asked to bring theirs. He dropped his hands and frowned at his demanding wife. "I'm still not sure Reuben is old enough to train in the fields. None of my undershepherds who have sons Reuben's age bring them."

"Would they dare begin their training when you haven't started with Reuben?"

Looking away, Jacob pretended to scan his flock. Leah had thought this through far better than he. "All right. I'll bring our four oldest sons tomorrow. I'll begin their training."

"And you'll talk with the other three wives tonight?"

His gut rumbled again. Not hunger this time, but dread. "I'll speak with Bilhah and Zilpah," he said, still not meeting Leah's gaze. "Rachel will hear of it and understand what's expected of her." At least he hoped she would understand. He couldn't let her teach Joseph—possibly their only son—to worship Harran's gods.

But neither could he bear the thought of another confrontation like this morning's.

CHAPTER SEVEN

When Laban had gone to shear his sheep,
Rachel stole her father's household gods.
Moreover, Jacob deceived Laban the Aramean
by not telling him he was running away.
So he fled with all he had....
~ Genesis 31:19–21 (NIV) ~

Six Years Later

Leah leaned forward, eyes wide, matching the anticipation of her two six-year-old listeners. "Abraham lifted his knife overhead to slay his son Isaac, but the Angel of the Lord called out from heaven, 'Abraham! Abraham!' And Abraham—"

"And Abraham stabbed Isaac!" Joseph jumped to his feet, grabbed the wooden spoon from his bowl of gruel, and started toward his sister.

Dinah jumped to her feet and ran. "That's not how the story goes! Imma, tell him." Fury turned her around, and she tackled her brother.

Laughing, Leah let them wrestle on her favorite rug before she stood and grabbed each one by the arm. "All right, that's enough for this morning." She hauled them outside. "Joseph, tell Imma Leah the *true* story of Yahweh's blessing on Abraham's family."

He exchanged a precocious grin with his almost-twin sister and began, "The Angel of the Lord said to Great Saba Abraham, 'Don't harm the boy. Now I know you fear Me because you didn't withhold anything from Me, not even your only son.' And Yahweh provided a ram, caught by its horns in the thicket, for Abraham's sacrifice." Joseph folded his arms over his puffed-out chest, beaming.

"Very good," Leah said and turned to Dinah. "Can you recite the parts your brother left out?"

Dinah stuck out her tongue at Joseph and began. "Abraham named that place Yahweh-Yireh—the Lord will provide. Then the Angel appeared a second time and said, 'Because you have not withheld your only son, I swear by Myself that I will surely bless you and give you as many children as there are stars in the sky. Your children will conquer their enemies and bless all people everywhere.'" She looked at Leah quizzically. "Why did Yahweh want Great Saba Abraham to kill his son?"

"It was a test," Joseph replied. "Abba said sometimes Yahweh requires hard things to see if we trust Him."

Leah knelt between them, gathering both in her arms, fighting the warring emotions that had started early today. "You're such a smart boy, and I'm glad your abba takes a special interest in teaching you about Yahweh." If only Jacob had taught his other ten sons about Yahweh. Perhaps they wouldn't treat Rachel's only son with such disdain. But Jacob's favoritism proved itself in many more ways than a lesson or two on Yahweh.

"There's my boy!" Rachel's open arms beckoned Joseph to the camp's central fire. He ran to her. "How did you sleep?" she asked.

He looked back at Leah first and then up at Rachel. "You should probably ask Imma Leah because, well, I was asleep."

Both Rachel and Leah chuckled, despite the tension between them. Leah's inkling that Joseph and Dinah would be twins from two immas became reality when she'd agreed to nurse Joseph years ago. She hadn't realized Rachel intended her to raise him completely. Not that Leah minded. Joseph was bright and cheerful, the perfect playmate for Dinah, and Leah loved them both as her own. But Rachel carried an unspoken burden of the imma she wished she could be—and it had driven a deeper wedge between Laban's daughters.

Rachel chased Joseph into Deborah's arms, and her little boy squealed with delight. Dinah ran toward Bilhah and Zilpah in the shade of a craggy old oak, where Jacob's slave-wives spent most of their day weaving garments with the now-prized speckled-and-spotted wool. Another day in an endless flow was beginning.

Leah dressed and fed Joseph and Dinah, taught them of Yahweh's faithfulness every day of their young lives, and then left them in Zilpah's and Bilhah's capable care. Rachel would soon be on her way to apprentice under Harran's midwife. Leah grabbed a handful of almonds to eat on her way to Abba's estate, where parchments and ink were as familiar as sheep and goats were to Jacob. She'd kept Abba's records since he'd taught her to write and added Jacob's flocks to separate scrolls when his peeled branches yielded the hoped-for speckled and spotted animals.

Pausing on the dusty trail between their camp and Abba's estate, Leah scanned Abba's property amid the Harran plains. Now, most of the goats and sheep were speckled and spotted, belonging to Jacob, and even some of Abba's cattle had shown signs of change from their solid-colored coats. A wry grin curved her lips as she resumed her morning walk. Rachel's threats of Dumuzi's vengeance had proven false, and Yahweh's clever instruction quickly increased Jacob's wages. Panicked by the change, Abba continually scoured Leah's records for errors. When none were found, he decreased Jacob's wages, but with every change, Yahweh increased the flocks in Jacob's favor.

"Even Harran's gods choose my sister's son over me," Abba had said yesterday. He'd get no sympathy from his elder daughter.

"Shalom, Dacina." Leah greeted Rachel's imma when she stepped into the courtyard.

"I suppose my daughter will ignore me today like every other day." The woman's small black eyes flitted nervously like a bird's. "I'm terribly lonely with Laban and my sons away for sheep shearing. The least Rachel could do is—"

"She's extremely busy," Leah interrupted. "Learning the various herbs and incantations from the midwife is complex, but you should be proud. She's doing well." Why must Leah defend Rachel to her own imma?

"Pfft. My daughter comes only when she wants something." Dacina whirled abruptly and walked away.

It was true. Rachel visited the estate only to ask for favors or something of worth. She and Dacina had never been close since both competed for Abba's attention. *Maybe the only way Rachel shows love is through competition.* It was a strange thought, but it might explain the widening chasm between them when Joseph and Dinah were near. Leah and Rachel had been so close as children, relied on each other completely as girls. But they often felt like enemies as women.

"Mistress! Mistress!" Leah had just entered Abba's library when one of the shepherds hurried toward her. He scurried across the room and peered over his shoulder, as if ensuring they were alone, before whispering, "Master Jacob wants both you and Mistress Rachel to meet him in the fields right away!"

"Is he hurt?"

"No, Mistress." He shook his head wildly and looked over his shoulder again. "Too many ears here or in our camp."

With only a nod, she followed him, keeping pace as they retraced her steps through the halls and buildings. Finally emerging into nature's greater privacy, they marched across the expansive plains to where Jacob waited alone under his favorite tree, watching his speckled and spotted flocks grazing nearby. The messenger whistled to alert him to their approach. Jacob turned, but his attention was stolen by something behind her. Leah looked over her shoulder and spotted Rachel with a second messenger, not a hundred paces away. Instinctively, Leah increased her speed and reached Jacob first. Breathless, she bent to rest her hands on her knees.

"You may go, Tobiah." Jacob dismissed her messenger and laid a hand on her shoulder. "I'm sorry for the urgency, but we must leave as soon as possible."

She stood, meeting his gaze. "You're scaring me."

Before they could say more, Rachel's voice split the morning air. "What is this about, Jacob? I should be at a birth right now!"

Jacob winked at Leah and mumbled, "If I didn't love her so, I might be tempted to leave her behind."

"Where are we going?" Leah's question trailed unanswered behind Jacob, who had already hurried to meet Rachel.

After dismissing her messenger boy, he led Rachel to the shady spot where Leah stood. "Let's sit down," he said, supporting Rachel's elbow as she folded her legs beneath her. Leah sat beside her, and Jacob took his place across from them. "What I'm about to say might be difficult to hear, but it is the truth. Before your abba and brothers left to shear their sheep, I heard your brothers complaining that I'd cheated your abba out of his flocks. When they return, I fear they'll somehow harm our family or flocks."

Rachel shot a panicked glance at Leah. "Abba wouldn't harm us." But her words held little conviction.

Leah studied her hands, believing it best for Jacob to address his favored wife's concerns. Jacob reached for Rachel's hand. "Laban might not harm *you*, my love, but you've seen how his attitude toward me has changed since our wealth has grown. He's changed my wages several times, yet each time Yahweh has worked in the flocks to counter your abba's cheating."

Rachel removed her hand and looked away, but rather than plead for her approval, Jacob turned his attention to Leah. She nodded and offered as much silent encouragement as her smile could give.

He sat a little straighter and spoke to Rachel's bowed head. "At first Laban offered all the speckled and spotted livestock as my wages. Do you remember, Rachel?"

She nodded but still didn't look up.

"When I followed Yahweh's instructions and placed the peeled branches before the mating ewes, they produced abundant offspring. Your abba has changed my wages with the passing of every season—yet still, Yahweh builds my wealth over his."

Finally, Rachel met Jacob's gaze, her perfect brow furrowed. "Why wouldn't Abba want his daughters and our children to prosper?"

"Because he knows Jacob will take us back to Canaan," Leah answered before their husband had to speak the hard truth. "It's the land Yahweh has promised to give us and our descendants forever, Rachel."

"I don't understand." Rachel alternated accusing looks between them. "How can either of you be sure your god will do what he says?"

"Because the Angel of the Lord appeared to me last night in another dream—as vividly as twenty years ago in Bethel on my way to Harran." Jacob stared into Rachel's shocked features.

Had he glimpsed Leah, he would have seen awe. She placed a hand on his arm. "What did He say, Jacob?"

Slowly, eyes filling with moisture, he turned from Rachel to the wife who trusted the dreams. "Yahweh said, 'I've seen all Laban has done to you. I am the God of Bethel, where you anointed a pillar and made a vow to me. Leave this land *at once* and go back to the land of your relatives. I will be with you.'"

Prickly excitement rushed from Leah's head, down her neck, and through her arms. "Did you hear that?" She looked at her sister but found her usually expressive features stony.

"Rachel?" Jacob straightened further, as if bracing for a blow. Tears pooled on her bottom lashes, but she revealed little else. Jacob pulled her into his arms, eyelids sliding closed. "I'm sorry, my love. I know the thought of leaving your home and your abba is difficult."

For several heartbeats, she let him hold her. Leah felt like an intruder. Perhaps Rachel would respond better if she and Jacob could talk alone.

Leah started to rise, but Rachel wriggled from Jacob's embrace. "Stay." She pressed firmly on Leah's arm. "I'm ready to leave Harran if you believe Abba has truly excluded us from any share of his inheritance."

"I have never had a share in his inheritance," Leah said without malice, "but even your share was excluded when you gave Jacob a son. You're no longer Abba's responsibility or concern, Rachel."

Her red-rimmed eyes nearly bored a hole in Leah. "He sold us to Jacob and then squandered the bride price our husband earned. He's regarded us all as strangers." She turned to Jacob then. "Your God took Abba's wealth and gave it to us. I suppose if your God speaks to you, we should listen."

Rachel's uncharacteristic calm sent a shiver up Leah's spine. What thoughts lurked, silenced now by caution, that would later become ranting? What emotions, currently hid by restraint, would unpredictably spew?

Jacob, seeming oblivious to the danger, offered Leah a triumphant smile. "Can the household be ready to leave by dawn?"

A gasp escaped before she could stop it. "Dawn?"

Jacob's features darkened. "When Laban returns after shearing and finds us gone—along with everything I own—he'll chase us, Leah. We need to put as much distance as possible between our camp and him."

Rachel stood and offered Leah her hand. "We'll be ready. Won't we, Sister?"

Leah nearly laughed. Rachel had no idea what such a move required. She spent all her time in Harran with the midwife. But Leah accepted her sister's hand and help to stand. "We'll be ready."

Jacob stood and pulled Leah into a tight embrace. "Thank you," he whispered against her ear. "With your faith—in Yahweh and me—our household can do anything."

"Let's go, Sister." Rachel tugged on her arm. "We shouldn't waste time."

Dazed by Jacob's confidence, Leah stumbled away with her sister but looked back and found her husband waving. She waved in return, murmuring, "I hope we don't disappoint him."

Rachel made no comment. Leah glimpsed her features as they marched like soldiers toward Abba's compound. Still hard. Determined. When they neared camp, Leah turned to the right, but Rachel turned toward the estate. "Where are you going?" Leah called after her.

Rachel stopped, turning to face her. "I need to visit the estate before I can help you pack."

Of course, she'd need to say goodbye to her imma. "I don't envy your farewell to Dacina. Do you want me to come with you?"

Rachel rushed to her side, voice low. "Why would I tell Imma we're leaving? She'd send a messenger to Abba immediately."

"Then what *business* could you have at the estate?" Leah's fury raised her voice.

"Shhh!" Rachel peered all around them. Two servants worked fifty paces away, but she still leaned closer to whisper. "I'm taking Abba's gods."

"What? No!"

"You don't understand." Rachel stormed toward the estate, but Leah matched her pace, keeping her voice low.

"You're right. I don't understand. Why would you jeopardize our family by *stealing* from Abba?"

"He owes me those gods." Rachel stopped, hissing the words. "If he hadn't betrayed the mother goddess by betrothing us as children to foreigners who worship an unknown god, we could have married men who respected our traditions."

"Jacob is Doda Rebekah's son—not a *foreigner*." Leah's voice carried to the courtyard, causing the servants to turn. She dropped her voice to a whisper. "How can you complain about a God who has provided riches and blessings like Yahweh has given Jacob? Our husband came to Harran with nothing, but he returns to Canaan a wealthy tribal chieftain."

"He dishonors our gods," Rachel said through clenched teeth. "And you betray the gods who have protected us all our lives."

"Protected?" Leah choked on a bitter laugh. "No god cared for me until Yahweh showed me favor." She leaned close enough to see the flecks of gold in her sister's eyes. "Maybe that's why you hate Him so."

"Harran's gods were my only protection when you and Abba betrayed me." Rachel ground out the words between clenched teeth. "Only they can keep me safe when Abba discovers we're gone."

CHAPTER EIGHT

Then Jacob put his children and his wives on camels,
and he drove all his livestock ahead of him,
along with all the goods he had accumulated in Paddan Aram,
to go to his father Isaac in the land of Canaan.
~ Genesis 31:17–18 (NIV) ~

Twenty-Six Days Later
Mizpah, Gilead

Leah wrapped Joseph's head in a piece of white linen and placed a band of braided hemp around his forehead to secure it in place. "It will keep you cool while you ride in my camel basket." She pointed at Jacob, who was mounting his camel's saddle. "You see? Abba is wearing a keffiyeh too."

"Head coverings are for girls." He tried to pull it off, but Leah held it in place. He should know Imma Leah didn't tolerate the misbehavior Imma Rachel allowed.

"Stop!" He slapped at her hand.

Leah pulled him into her lap and wrapped him in a constrictive hug, pinning his arms at his sides. He struggled while she whispered, "Do you see your abba's caravan moving without us? Look, Joseph. Because you refuse to obey, you won't be at the front of the caravan this time."

His little body stilled, and he began to whimper. "But I want to be with Abba."

She loosened her grip to a loving embrace and kissed the skewed cloth on his head. "And your abba wants you there, but he'll only allow an obedient son at his side. Parents are given to children on earth so they'll learn to obey God in heaven. It is a mighty responsibility your abba and I have been given. You must obey us so you'll grow up to obey Yahweh."

Dinah sat beside Leah, eyes wide. "I'm wearing my head covering, Imma."

"Yes, Love." Leah pulled her into their circle of three. "You've obeyed well today. We must all obey those responsible for our care."

"Imma, hurry." Reuben stood over them. "You and the babies need to get on your camel before the rest of the caravan can proceed."

"I'm not a baby!" Joseph jumped to his feet, protesting, but Dinah opened her arms to the big brother who spoiled her. Reuben carried her to Leah's dear camel she had named Willow. She'd hoped the sassy dromedary would soak up water like the willow trees Jacob had described from his journey twenty years ago.

Now, nearly to Canaan, Leah had seen the lovely willow trees, but there was little time to admire them. Fear of Abba's retribution kept them moving at a harrowing pace. For Joseph and Dinah to travel quickly, Zilpah concocted a double basket that hung over their immas' camels, Rachel's and Leah's saddles holding the apparatus in place. As long as the baskets on both sides were filled with equal weight, a camel didn't care what cargo it carried.

Leah watched Jacob lead the caravan up a distant hill, Rachel on her camel at his side. The familiar pang of loneliness returned. With a little envy. Anger too. For twenty-six days she'd ridden beside her sister. Willow carried Dinah in one basket with supplies in the other, and Rachel's camel carried a double basket with Joseph and supplies. They'd ridden closely enough for the almost twins to entertain each other, but as days turned into weeks, the hot, active, complaining six-year-olds grew too much for Rachel to bear.

"Enough!" Rachel's early-morning shout drew Leah's attention—at the moment her hand struck Joseph's cheek.

"Rachel!" Leah cried.

Both imma and son stared at each other in shocked silence before Joseph curled into his basket and disappeared. Rachel's ashen countenance met Leah's. "I've given him dates and nuts, but he won't be quiet."

That was the moment Leah decided Jacob's "twins" would finish the journey together on her camel. If it had been only a matter of Rachel's discomfort, she would have let her sister learn the inevitable lessons of every imma. Children disobey. They complain. They even rebel. But when she struck Joseph, well... No child deserved that lesson.

"Come, my big boy," Leah said to Joseph after she'd helped him from his basket. "You can help me onto my saddle before you climb into your basket."

"I'll help you, Imma Leah." He accepted her hand, puffing out his little chest. What was it about some males who instinctively needed to protect their women?

"Are you all right?" Jacob shouted. Leah looked up and found him galloping toward them. "What's the delay? Why is Joseph riding with you?" He hadn't seen Rachel slap his favorite son. Slowing his camel as he neared, he studied Joseph.

"I'm obedient now, Abba." Joseph's sheepish grin drew a chuckle from his abba.

"I'm glad to hear it." But he glared at Leah. "We can't afford to wait."

"Go ahead," Leah said. "We'll catch up." Joseph would enjoy Willow's gallop. Rachel had been afraid of anything faster than a walk.

After hesitating only a moment, he nodded and turned his camel away. "I want to reach the Jabbok by nightfall." Then he swatted his camel, urging it toward the front of the caravan where the shepherds and flocks had halted—and Rachel waited. Bilhah and Zilpah rode camels mid-caravan, but their sons were with Leah's, driving the flocks and herds with the undershepherds. Poor Deborah rode in a wagon near the end. The journey had been hard on her, so Rachel relieved her of normal duties and paid her little attention. The rolling hills of Gilead were beautiful, but Leah would be happy to reach the safety of Jacob's family camp in Beersheba.

"Are you coming, Imma Leah?" Joseph tugged on her hand. "Or are you being disobedient to Abba?" The grin pushing up his rosy cheeks was too cute to ignore.

She growled and swung him into the air while hurrying toward Willow. "You're getting too big for me to carry."

He wrapped his arms around her neck. "Am I big enough for Abba to train as a shepherd?"

Her heart broke for the boy, sure neither Jacob—nor his sons—would ever treat Joseph like the rest. "Not yet, Love." She brushed her nose back and forth against his, their special sign of affection. "You must grow big and strong before Abba lets you shepherd his flocks."

Distracted, he pointed behind her. "What's that?"

Leah turned and noted a small column of dust rising over the hills. Her stomach clenched, and she broke into a run. Nearing Willow, she called out to Reuben. "Leave Dinah with me. Take Willow and tell your abba they're coming!" She watched color drain from her firstborn's cheeks. "Now, Reuben!"

He scooped Dinah from the basket and placed her feet on the ground beside Leah. Then he hurled himself onto the camel as it rocked to its feet. With a whack to Willow's rump, he urged her into a gallop.

Joseph stomped his feet. "But I want to go!"

Leah drew both him and Dinah into a fierce hug, forcing calm. "Your saba Laban has come to speak with Abba. We must hide for a little while."

"But why must we hide from Saba?" Joseph wriggled from her embrace, his intelligent brown eyes exposing her shaded truth.

Leah had no more time for subtleties. "Saba Laban wants to hurt Abba and may try to hurt others who took something that belonged to him."

"Like the idols in Imma's saddle basket?" The fear on Joseph's face pierced her.

"Come on." She herded Joseph and Dinah toward a copse of trees. "We'll hide in the ground cover until it's safe to come out." They followed her, silent as mice.

How much had Jacob's youngest children discerned of the danger chasing them from Harran? During the first two weeks of flight, every adult slept with a dagger and every child stayed in his imma's tent. Joseph, of course, slept with Rachel and Jacob. Leah's sons, old enough to carry daggers of their own, slept in front of her tent flap, swearing to protect both her and Dinah.

But who could protect them now, huddled behind bushes, while the rest of the caravan had already traveled west without them? Leah peeked at the eastern hill. The growing cloud of dust proved a caravan approached, and the ground shuddering beneath her feet proved it was large. Had Abba brought an army? Hired mercenaries? Would he kill his own family? Surely not his grandsons—but he didn't even know all their names.

"Leah!" Jacob rode into the clearing, halted his camel, and jumped off the beast before its legs folded for his dismount. "Leah, where are you?"

"Here!" She ran out of the thicket, Joseph and Dinah trailing behind her. "We're here!"

He hoisted Joseph into his arms, squeezed him tightly, and then placed the boy on his camel. He placed his arm around Dinah's shoulder and pulled her to his side. "Rachel is waiting with the caravan beyond the next hill. Take Joseph." He pulled her into a quick and fierce embrace. "I can't lose Joseph," he whispered and then released her.

Dinah waited beside her abba while Leah started to climb onto the saddle with Joseph. But she hesitated, practicality filling her with terror. "How will I hold both children while gripping the reins?" *Yahweh, what do I do?* But she already felt the answer in the deepest part of her. Placing both feet on the ground, she stared into Jacob's eyes, pleading.

"Please," he said. "I'll deal with Laban's retribution, but my sons *must* enter Canaan. Save Joseph, Leah, regardless of your feud with Rachel. He's my son."

She stepped closer to her husband and kissed his cheek. "He's my son too." She reached for Dinah's hand and tightened her grip. "Run toward the stream where we ate our meal, Jacob. Draw Abba away from us." She spoke with a calm not her own. When he hesitated, she shouted, "Go!"

Blanching at her harshness, he looked at Joseph once more before sprinting away from them. He only looked back once.

Leah kissed the top of her daughter's head. "I need to speak with Joseph for a moment. Don't move." Then she reached up to put the reins in Joseph's hands. "Hold on tight while leaning forward and back with the camel when she gets up." Leah tapped the beast's shoulder, pulling Dinah away with her, as the camel started moving.

"No!" Joseph shrieked. "I don't want to go alone. I don't know how—"

"Abba's camel knows the way," she soothed. "Dinah and I will find you." Her voice broke, and she slapped the beast's hindquarters. She swept Dinah into her arms and dashed toward the bushes for cover.

Within moments, Jacob stumbled back into the clearing, surrounded by horses and their riders. Dinah whimpered. Leah covered her mouth and whispered against her ear. "We must be quiet as butterflies, my love." Was Dinah trembling, or was she?

Abba and his sons surrounded Jacob. Pushed him backward. Taunting. "Did you think you could steal me blind and get away?" At least fifty camels carried armed men, and behind them twenty servants led donkeys with supplies. "You carried off my daughters in secret, Jacob ben Isaac. You didn't let me kiss my grandchildren goodbye or allow me to send you away with a celebration." Abba and four of his men walked their camels in a tight circle around him.

"Forgive my thoughtlessness." Jacob stumbled in the center of their intimidation. "I thought if I tried to leave while you were home, you would take your daughters and my children by force." Leah cheered silently, proud of her husband's courage to speak truth. It was his only weapon against Abba and his men, heavily armed with bows, spears, and short swords.

"What you've done is foolish." Abba lifted his fist, signaling his men to halt. "I could destroy you, but last night, the god of your father appeared to me with a warning. 'Be careful not to say anything to Jacob, either good or bad.' So I must let you return to your abba's household—unharmed."

Leah's breath caught. Could Abba travel so far and return home with no retribution?

Abba tapped his camel's shoulder, sending it to its knees. With two long strides, he met Jacob face-to-face. "I must know. Why would you steal my household gods?"

Jacob winced as if Abba slapped him and then leaned to within a handbreadth. "I've stolen nothing. Search my camp yourself. If you find anyone with your gods—they die."

"No…," Leah whispered.

Dinah pressed her small hand over Leah's mouth. "Butterflies, Imma."

Leah kissed her palm and led her precious girl away, crouching low and scurrying toward Jacob's waiting caravan. She must warn Rachel before Abba and his men found the gods that could kill her.

CHAPTER NINE

So Laban went into Jacob's tent and into Leah's tent
and into the tent of the two female servants, but he found nothing.
After he came out of Leah's tent, he entered Rachel's tent.
~ Genesis 31:33 (NIV) ~

When Leah and Dinah caught up to the caravan, Joseph was asleep in Deborah's arms and Rachel waved Leah away. How could she warn her when Rachel wouldn't let her speak? Thankfully, Abba demanded to inspect the flocks and herds before searching the camp for his gods, which gave Leah time to prepare for their uninvited guests. While tents were unfurling, she sent women to gather water and shepherds to decide which ewes to slaughter for the evening meal. If Abba was well fed, perhaps he could ignore Jacob's hasty vow. Surely, when he saw it was his favorite daughter who held the treasured idols, Abba's vengeance would be satisfied by simply reclaiming the worthless stones and returning home.

By the time Jacob led Abba and his men into camp, all four wives' tents were up, and Abba demanded to begin the search. The women worked together, preparing the evening meal—all the women except Rachel, who was hidden away in her tent with Deborah. Now that the camp was settled, Leah needed to warn her sister.

She set aside the hand mill. "I need to check on Rachel and Deborah. Today's excitement might have put too much strain on the old woman." Conversation around the central fire barely slowed as she rose and walked the twenty paces toward Rachel's tent.

If you find anyone with your gods—they die. Jacob's words still sent a chill through Leah's bones. Had Rachel discovered the vow and decided to hide from Abba in hopes he wouldn't search her tent? Tamping down her annoyance, she reached for her sister's tent flap. More likely, Rachel was using Deborah as an excuse to skip hard work. She barged into the tent without waiting for the invitation.

Deborah was lying on a mat, facing the wall. Snoring. Rachel looked up from spinning, looking as annoyed as Leah felt. "You have no right to—"

"Would you rather Abba search for his gods and kill you when they're found?"

Her cheeks lost their color. "He wouldn't *kill* me." It was more of a question than a statement.

"Jacob made a vow, Rachel. Anyone caught with Abba's gods will die." She waited for the full impact to change her sister's features.

Instead, Rachel waved her away again and returned to spinning. "He won't even search my tent."

Leah closed the space between them, grabbed the spindle, and tossed it across the tent. "Abba accused *Jacob* of stealing his gods! Our husband will have every tent searched to prove his innocence."

Deborah turned over, eyes still dazed with sleep. "What's this about stealing?"

Leah ignored her. "Consider how Jacob will feel when he must keep the vow he made. You will die today if Abba finds his gods in your tent."

Rachel rose slowly, a guilty stare focused on the double saddle basket two paces away. "They've been balancing Joseph's weight during our trip." The tremor in her whisper proved she finally understood her predicament.

"I'll start with Leah's tent." The sound of Abba's voice sent Rachel into Leah's arms. The sisters stood like statues, listening so hard it hurt. "It's your fault, you know, Jacob," Abba said. "You convinced Leah to worship only Abraham's God, so I'm sure she stole my gods to make a point."

"You'll start with my tent." Jacob's voice was a growl.

Shadows and footsteps passed by, and Rachel placed Leah in front of her like a shield. "You've got to take the gods out of here," she whispered. "Hide them somewhere else."

Leah pulled her sister into a ferocious hug. "We'll never get them out of here without Abba seeing." Leah's whisper felt like a shout. "I'll have them search my tent next. Maybe that will be enough time for you to think of something."

They could hear Abba and Jacob conversing next door, words indistinguishable but the search ending. Leah took a deep breath and stepped outside just as the two angry men emerged from Jacob's tent. "You see?" Anger simmered in

Jacob's voice. "You'll find nothing that belongs to you any-where in this camp."

One glance down the row of family tents, and relief surged through her. "Abba, you may search mine now, then Bilhah and Zilpah's tent. Deborah isn't feeling well, so you can search our sons' tents afterward." She tugged on Abba's sleeve. "By the time you've finished, I'm sure your tent will be ready, and you can refresh yourself before tonight's meal."

Abba pulled his sleeve from her grasp, but he followed Jacob into her tent. She ducked inside behind them and watched as Abba tossed clothes from her baskets and peered into every box and clay pot. He scowled as he marched toward the exit but stopped to glare at Leah. "I'll search Rachel's next."

"But Bilhah and Zilpah are waiting for you to search theirs so they can start meal prep—"

But it was too late. The tail of Abba's robe disappeared into Rachel's tent. Jacob scowled at her in silent question. He had no idea his world was about to end. She couldn't bear to watch his heart break or to hear her sister's death sentence, so she waited outside between Abba's guards. Praying. Listening.

"Forgive me, Abba." Rachel's voice sounded too calm. What had she done? "I'm sorry I can't greet you with a bow, but my red moon has begun—another month without conception." Her voice cracked with emotion, calmness devolving into snif-fling and whimpers.

Abba scurried from her tent, shaking his head. "Women."

Leah motioned again toward the slave-wives' tent. "This way, Abba." Disgusted, he followed, finding nothing in Bilhah and

Zilpah's tent but their statues of Inanna that looked nothing like Abba's gods.

When Leah moved to lead Abba toward her sons' tents, Jacob caught her arm. "Send Bilhah and Zilpah to help prepare the meal, but you should go back and check on your sister." His eyes pierced her with hidden meaning. "She seemed unwell."

He knows!

"Of course." Leah offered a curt bow and raced toward Rachel's tent. Her flow ended five days ago, and Jacob knew it. So did Leah because he always called her to his tent during Rachel's seclusion.

Slipping into her sister's tent, she found Rachel digging a hole in the ground with a wooden spoon. "What are you doing?" she hissed.

Startled, Rachel sat down hard on her saddle, face as pale as goat's milk. When she saw Leah was alone, fear turned to anger. "I'm burying them in case Abba comes back." Before Leah could tell her how pointless it was because he'd see the disturbed dirt, shouting erupted outside, drawing them both to peek out the narrow tent opening.

"What is my crime?" Jacob's voice rose in pitch and volume. "You've disturbed my wives, humiliated my servants, and pawed through all my goods."

Abba stood straighter, jaw set, but gave no answer. While he'd searched the women's tents, his men had searched the servants' tents and the shepherds' belongings. The whole camp lay in shambles, and Jacob was claiming his redemption— publicly.

"Let our relatives judge who has been wronged here." Jacob swept his arm over those gathered: servants, children, wives, and Abba's sons. "I've served Laban faithfully for twenty years. His sheep and goats did not miscarry, nor did I eat a single ram from his flocks. I bore the loss myself if an animal was killed by a wild beast. And if any were stolen, I gave him the repayment demanded from my own wages. Heat consumed me by day and cold at night. Sleep fled from my eyes."

"I gave you my daughters!" Abba's thunderous words deepened his humiliation.

"You *gave* me nothing." Eyes narrowed, Jacob stepped closer with unnerving calm. "I worked fourteen years to pay their bride prices and six more years to earn these flocks— even though you changed my wages ten times. If the God of Abraham and the Fear of Isaac had not been with me, you would have sent me away with nothing. But Yahweh saw your scheming and my hard work." A slow, satisfied grin curved Jacob's lips. "And last night my God rebuked you, Laban."

Abba's gaze fell to his hands. "The women are my daughters, the children my grandchildren, and the flocks mine as well. All you see belongs to me, Jacob. Yet what can I do because your God protects you?" He looked up then, eyelids hooding an angry stare. "Will you at least make a covenant to serve as a witness between us?"

"No, Jacob," Rachel whispered, though only Leah could hear. "Abba will break it."

"Gather some stones." Jacob pointed in their direction, and Leah's heart clogged her throat. Had he heard Rachel's comment?

But Reuben, Simeon, Levi, and Judah walked past them to obey their abba, and Rachel sagged against her. Their husband took one of the large stones they gathered and set it up as a pillar. Then others from both households piled rocks into a heap around the pillar until Abba raised his hand to speak.

"This place will be called *Jegar Sahadutha.*" He spoke in Aramean, the words for *heap of witness.*

"No, it will be *Galeed.*" Jacob used the Hebrew term instead. "We'll enter Yahweh's Land of Promise, and I'll name this place with the language of *my* people."

Abba leaned forward, scowling. "We'll call it *Mizpah,* for in both our tongues it means 'watchtower.' These rocks will testify that even when I can't see you, Yahweh sees if you oppress my daughters or take other wives besides them. And let this heap and pillar also be a witness that I will neither pass beyond it to harm you, nor will you pass to my side and injure me." He straightened then, scanning those listening before looking again at Jacob. "May the God of our fathers, Abraham and Nahor, judge between us."

Jacob stared at Abba as if he were a serpent and turned away, lifting both hands to the sky as he addressed the gathering. "By the God who struck holy fear into my abba, Isaac, I will sacrifice a lamb—from *my* flock—to seal the promise in blood. We will feast together, and Laban's household may spend the night as my guests. We break camp at first light." His arms fell to his side, and he offered Abba a barely discernable bow. "I'll send a servant to notify you when the meal is ready."

Jacob marched directly toward Rachel's tent. The two sisters scurried away from the opening. "He looks angry." Rachel clutched Leah's arm.

"Indeed." Leah couldn't agree more but had no time for an *I told you so* before their husband barged in.

Jacob drew a breath to speak but pressed his lips shut as his face reddened. Trembling from head to foot, he glared at Rachel and released his anger in a strangled whisper. "You stole his idols."

Rachel gripped Leah's arm tighter as she nodded.

Jacob's lips curved around bared teeth. "Destroy. Them."

"What?" Rachel released her protector. "No, I can't." She stepped toward Jacob, but he lifted one hand. She froze midstride.

"You will ride with the servants tomorrow since your *flow* has returned."

"But it hasn't really—"

Jacob took a quick step toward her and gripped her arms. "But you will act in every way as if it has because if your abba discovers you have those statues, I…" He released her with a shove. Leah had seen the same betrayal on his features once before—the morning after their wedding.

When he turned to her, his features softened. "I need you to help with tonight's feast. I'll choose the sacrifice, but I'd like you to help me prepare it."

Leah placed her hand on his arm. "I'm honored to help, but eight of your sons have been trained in the ways of Yahweh. If you include them in the covenant meal and sacrifice, you would show Abba that Yahweh protects all those who honor Him."

He stared into her eyes for a long moment. She startled when he cupped her face with both hands. Then his lips claimed hers, and he kissed her thoroughly. Passionately. Strong arms drew her against him and held her tight until it felt like the kiss would last forever. When he released her, she heard Rachel's quiet sniffling.

She couldn't look at her sister, but Jacob sneered. "You'll remain with Joseph in your tent tonight, Rachel. I'll consider what to do about your betrayal while we travel tomorrow."

"Of course, my husband." Her head was bowed.

Jacob turned to go, but first he captured Leah's hand. "You'll share my tent tonight and leave Dinah with the slave-wives."

Leah glimpsed Rachel's fury as both sisters followed Jacob out of the tent. There was a feast to prepare. A sacrifice to make. Leah must focus on Yahweh's blessing and protection. She'd worry about Rachel's wounded heart tomorrow.

CHAPTER TEN

*Jacob sent messengers ahead of him to his brother Esau
in the land of Seir, the country of Edom.*
~ Genesis 32:3 (NIV) ~

Leah lay in the bend of Jacob's arm, one leg possessively flung over him while he snored. She'd been watching him sleep since the moon began its descent. How could she sleep when the Creator of the universe had proven His love and favor for her husband again? She felt like dancing. Singing. Shouting to the moon and stars! Even when Rachel had so carelessly placed them all in danger by stealing from Abba, Yahweh had stepped in and rescued them.

Rachel. She'd been livid watching Jacob kiss Leah. Perhaps Leah should have been angry too. Wasn't his passion meant to hurt Rachel? But Leah felt a measure of satisfaction. Gratefulness, even. Was she wicked or pathetic? For years Rachel had taunted her with Jacob's affection. Now, she knew the twisting inside when the lips she longed to kiss offered passion to another.

Jacob stirred, turning toward her though sound asleep. Leah turned over and pressed her back against him, and he instinctively wrapped his arms around her. Her eyes slid shut, drinking in his nearness. She didn't care that he was unconscious.

This was her paradise. The place she imagined when life was too hard and she escaped into her thoughts. Even during childbirth, when the pain grew too intense, she had closed her eyes and imagined herself in this cocoon of Jacob's presence. Secure. Loved. Well, at least appreciated. He often called Rachel *beloved*, but it was Leah he called when in need.

Jacob sniffed. Opened his arms and stretched like an unfolding flower in spring. The moment was gone.

"Is it dawn?" he mumbled.

"Almost," she said, turning over and facing him.

He opened one eye and offered a lazy grin. "Today, we gain our freedom from Laban."

Leah rose on one elbow, tracing the line of his beard. "To hurry our freedom, I asked the women to pack our morning meal so *everyone* could eat as they traveled. We'll be ready as soon as tents are down and animals are loaded."

He pulled her against his well-muscled frame and rolled. Hovering over her, with gentle brushes of his lips, he explored her cheeks. "You are a good wife, Leah. Yahweh gave me a good gift when He gave me you. I—" He stopped, almost startled, and searched the windows of her soul.

Say it, Jacob. Say you love me.

"I'm glad you're mine." He kissed her forehead and shot to his feet like a stone from a sling.

She watched the tent flap close behind him and then pressed her palms against her eyes, stemming the tears that burned. *Why can't he say it, Yahweh?* She'd seen love in his eyes. Hadn't she? Maybe not. How could she recognize it?

The sound of a ram's horn brought the camp to life. Leah dressed quickly and rushed to Zilpah's tent to gather Dinah. Joseph was there too. Bilhah herded the other children into a semblance of order. Rachel sat with her saddlebags beside Deborah in a wagon while the rest of the camp scurried. In record time, every tent was folded, every basket packed, and every animal prepared for the day's travel. Jacob blew the ram's horn again, calling Laban and his relatives to the mizpah, the watchtower, between their two households.

Leah stepped forward, presenting Jacob's children in order of birth for Abba's farewell and blessing—without revealing their immas, of course, for fear he might scorn the slave-wives' sons. "First is Reuben," she said, "then Simeon, Levi, and Judah. Next is Dan and Naphtali, Gad and Asher." Abba kissed each on the forehead and moved down the line. "Here is Issachar, then Zebulun, and then—"

"Ah, I know who this one belongs to." Abba lifted Joseph high over his head. "Joseph, the little prince, belongs to my Rachel."

Leah shot an accusing glare at her sister sitting smugly with his stolen idols. She could end *his* Rachel by revealing her duplicity. Jacob slipped his hand into Leah's, squeezing it gently. She met his pleading gaze and felt a pang of guilt that her fury had been so obvious.

Leah pulled away and lifted Dinah into her arms. "This is Jacob's only daughter," she said to the man who taught her to hate. "She'll know only love from her parents—*all* her parents."

Abba set Joseph down and affixed a granite smile. "Do you mean her parents in Jacob's clan? Or those in Esau's household?" He moved closer, intimidating. Courage waning, she stepped back. "Mark my words, Daughter. The moment your caravan enters Canaan, Esau will snatch Dinah away to fulfill *your* broken betrothal."

Leah's camel kept pace beside Jacob's mount all morning through Gilead's gently rolling hillsides. Leah shared her husband's dark mood. Abba's sinister remark about Esau had rattled them both—enough that Leah asked Bilhah to carry Joseph and Dinah in the side baskets in case Jacob wanted to talk. The sun was nearly overhead, and he hadn't spoken a word.

She could bear his silence no longer. "Have you exchanged correspondence with Esau in the twenty years since you left Beersheba?"

"No." Jacob focused on the dirt path.

Why hadn't he made contact? Was his abba still alive? Had his imma written to him? Leah waited for more explanation, but he said no more. In fact, he'd told her nothing at all about Esau. "Does Esau still live at your abba's camp?" Silence lingered to the point of rudeness. If she had something to throw at him, she would have aimed for his head.

"No," he said finally.

She'd almost forgotten her question! "How do you know Esau doesn't live with your parents if you've had no contact?"

"I asked a merchant when we traveled through Damascus."
Leah's heart galloped as Willow lumbered up a grassy hill.
Jacob's family was wealthy. Merchants would know if the eldest
son had made a separate camp elsewhere. "So you've already
considered that Dinah and I may be in danger when we return
to Canaan."

He looked at her for the first time. "Laban knows only
Aramean traditions but nothing of my family's ways. Abraham's
intention was to marry one wife, and Abba married only one
wife. As *first* wife, Leah, you need fear Esau least of all." His
eyes spit fire. His cheeks flushed. But he returned his attention
to the road without further explanation.

"I don't understand, Jacob. Esau was betrothed to me. Are
you saying—"

Jacob looked over his shoulder and leaned closer, keeping
his voice low. "My abba may only recognize the first marriage
under Yahweh's Covenant." He clucked his tongue and Leah
urged her camel to keep pace. After glancing behind them
again, Jacob seemed to relax with the extra distance from the
caravan, but he still kept his voice low. "Esau and I were both
promised one of Laban's daughters. Since Abba may only
acknowledge the first marriage, Esau may believe he has the
right to—" He sniffed and straightened on his saddle.

"The right to take Rachel?" Leah murmured the unthinkable.

Jacob cleared his throat and swiped at his eyes before
speaking. "As you can see, Dinah is in no more danger than the
rest of us. If my brother still hates me for stealing his birthright
and blessing, my whole family could suffer."

"Wh—" No. She bit her lip, stopping the flow of questions before they pounded her husband into pulp. *Yahweh, You know my fears. You know Esau's heart. Give my husband wisdom, and keep my fear from stirring more in him.*

She'd barely finished her prayer when light, brighter than the sun, shot from the sky to the road, spooking the camels. Willow bellowed and retreated, but Leah reined her in a circle toward Jacob's roaring mount. Both animals halted like statues when they faced a fire-ringed being blocking their path.

"Jacob!" Leah cried. He extended his hand. She could only reach his fingertips. His touch proved the moment real and quieted her.

Then a roar shook the heavens, louder than any ram's horn. Leah covered her ears. Closed her eyes. Would they die before she saw the Land of Promise? *Wait! No! My children's inheritance!* Keeping her hands over her ears, she looked up and saw Jacob staring at the fiery Creature. He was talking to Jacob, but she couldn't hear his words over the roar. Jacob nodded reverently—and the roar ceased.

The animals in their caravan bellowed and bucked, as unnerved as the humans. Jacob stared at the scorched spot in the road, while Leah tapped Willow's shoulder to dismount. She must check on the children.

Jacob was somehow beside her when she stepped on solid ground. "This is the camp of God," he said breathlessly. "We, too, will camp here. Yahweh's Angel gave me the message I'm to send Esau. My brother lives in the land of Seir—a country called Edom, named after him."

Leah fell into his arms, trembling. "What message will you send?" She prayed it included an edict for Esau to stay away from them.

"Would you write it for me?" He held her at arm's length, brows tipped up.

She'd never seen him so vulnerable. "Of course." Leah took three hurried steps to Willow's saddlebag and retrieved the small box that held her writing utensils. Jacob's distinctive whistle called for his two most loyal messengers.

While Leah sat on a nearby rock, her husband dictated. "I, Jacob, your humble servant, have been with our *dohd* Laban all these years. Yahweh gave me cattle and donkeys, sheep and goats, male and female servants. I send this message to my lord, Esau, hoping to find favor in your eyes." When silence fell, Leah looked up. "That's all," Jacob said.

She nodded, folded the parchment, and gave it to one of the messenger boys—now a man of seventeen—who was born in their household. His abba was the first undershepherd Jacob hired at Abba's estate. "This parchment holds Yahweh's words," she said, "and could determine our whole family's future. Ride fast and return safely."

"Follow the merchants' road south," Jacob said, "to the land of Seir. Ask for the tribal property called Edom. My brother Esau has named it appropriately—*red*—and you'll recognize him as a giant man covered in red hair."

The other wives and children approached, pale and trembling, as Jacob finished his instructions to the messenger. Leah avoided their eyes, waiting for Jacob to explain his experience, but the moment he sent the messengers on their way, Rachel flew into his arms.

"Are you hurt? What was that fiery *thing*? Did it harm you? Did it speak? What did it say?"

"Shhh." Jacob soothed her with a low chuckle. "I'm fine. The Angel gave me a message that we've sent to Esau. We'll camp here at Mahanaim until we receive his reply."

"Mahanaim?" Leah asked, unfamiliar with the word.

Still holding Rachel, he looked over her shoulder. "It's what I've named this place. It means *Two Camps*—Yahweh's camp and ours."

Leah watched Jacob and Rachel exchange quiet whispers that swept them into a world of their own. Once again, Leah was left to settle the children and organize camp. "Zilpah, take the women and start the cook fire over there." She pointed to a level clearing less than a stone's throw to the east. "Bilhah, feed the twins, Issachar, and Zebulun from this morning's leftovers. And boys," she said to the eight oldest sons, "help the men set up camp. You'll eat with the rest of us when work is done."

She returned to Willow. "I'll unburden you of these baskets, and then you and I can wash in the river." Tapping the camel's shoulder, Leah grabbed her reins and turned to go— and bumped into Jacob's broad chest.

"I thought I'd help you." He tried to tilt her chin up, but she looked away. "What have I done?" he asked quietly.

Throat tightened by anger and envy, she shook her head, unable to speak.

"All right," he said, stepping back. "Perhaps we can talk tonight when you come to my tent." Leah looked up, certain the surprise on her face was the cause of his smile. "Does that mean you'll come?"

She bumped him with her shoulder as she led Willow past him. "When have I ever refused you, Jacob ben Isaac?"

CHAPTER ELEVEN

When the messengers returned to Jacob, they said,
"We went to your brother Esau, and now he is coming to meet you,
and four hundred men are with him."
~ Genesis 32:6 (NIV) ~

It had been three days since Jacob's messengers left for Seir. Why weren't they back?

"What happened next, Abba?" Gad tugged on his sleeve. "What happened when the raven didn't return to the ark?"

Looking into the inquisitive eyes of his eight oldest sons, Jacob tried again to push fear aside. "Noah sent out a dove next." He shoved the last bite of bread in his mouth, finishing the midday meal. "The dove returned that evening with an olive leaf."

If a dove can return in a day, why haven't my messengers returned in three days? They rode dromedaries that should have taken them to Seir in a day. They could have given the message to Esau and returned yesterday. Had the brute captured them? Tortured them? He was capable of anything. Jacob should have sent more men. He cursed under his breath.

"Imma says we're not supposed to say that word," Dan said with a wry smile.

"Is Noah's story true, Abba?" Reuben's dark brows knit together. "Did Yahweh really destroy the whole earth and all people with a flood?" Leah's firstborn was the thinker, the skeptic.

"Yes, son, it's true. Yahweh destroyed the whole earth because every inclination of the human heart was only evil all the time." *Like Esau's.*

"But how do you know it's true?" Little Asher, his youngest shepherd, asked while climbing into his lap and stuffing almonds into Jacob's mouth. Holding his beard while he chewed, Asher giggled. "Was Noah grumpy like you, Abba?"

The question stung and seemed to suck all the air from his older sons' chests. "Grumpy?" Jacob growled, swinging Asher into his arms as he leaped to his feet. "Who did you say was grumpy?"

Asher's delighted squeals pierced Jacob's heart. He'd spent most of the past three days with his sons under the tamarisk tree, telling stories of Yahweh. Even in the midst of his tension, Jacob had enjoyed learning his sons' unique qualities. It had been valuable, meaningful. But grumpy? Glimpsing his flocks and herds roaming Gilead's hill country, Jacob felt suddenly overwhelmed by Yahweh's blessings.

He kissed Asher's cheek and resumed his seat among the boys, keeping Asher on his lap. "I know Noah's story is true because his son Shem taught me Yahweh's stories himself." His sons exchanged dubious glances, but only Reuben—who had his imma's skill with numbers—counted the years on his fingers. Jacob laughed. "Remember, Reuben, Shem was Noah's firstborn son."

Reuben finally lifted his honey-colored eyes, cautious. "How could you know Shem, Abba? He lived hundreds of years before Great Abba Abraham."

"You're a smart boy, Reuben, and you framed your doubt with respect. I'm proud of you." The corners of a smile lifted with his son's shoulders. "I knew Master Shem only a few years before he died at the age of six hundred. His grandson, Eber, took over teaching responsibilities at the House of Shem, where Noah's descendants learned to worship and obey Yahweh, the one true God."

"We're descendants of Noah?" Gad leaped to his feet, dancing in circles.

"Everyone on earth is a descendant of Noah." Jacob motioned him to sit. The boy couldn't be still longer than a shooting star. "We're descendants of Noah's firstborn, Shem, and it's from his line that Yahweh chose a family to protect His Truth. For generations, each clan sent its firstborn to the House of Shem to learn the truths taught to humans in Eden's Garden."

"But you weren't a firstborn," Reuben pointed out. "Why did you attend the House of Shem instead of Dohd Esau?"

"Yahweh chooses the heir!" Jacob's insecurity erupted with a shout. Reuben wilted, and Asher crawled off Jacob's lap to cuddle with his oldest brother.

His sons' wounded stares pleaded for reassurance, twisting the dull blade of guilt. Jacob considered sending them away. He was no teacher. How could he explain his abba's inexplicable favor toward Esau despite his brother's disregard for Yahweh? How could Jacob make them understand Yahweh sovereignly chose him while still in Imma's womb—without tainting the story with his own pain? Suddenly a lesson learned at the House of Shem surfaced. Perhaps the teachings of Shem could continue through him in this small way.

Jacob snatched up a handful of grass and held it out to his sons. "What if you only have one handful of grass, but there are two lambs? One is a big, white lamb. The other is weak and spotted. Both are hungry." He met each one's curious gaze. "Which one gets the tasty meal?"

"I'd give it to the weakling," Judah said right away. "A few such treats might make him stronger."

"Pfft." Simeon waved off his compassion. "Give it to the strong lamb and make him stronger. Weak lambs breed a weak flock, right, Abba?"

Fascinated by his sons' differences, Jacob nodded thoughtfully. "You're both right. Sometimes Yahweh called the strong firstborn to learn at the House of Shem while other times He chose the weaker sons to learn His wise teachings." He aimed his next remark at Reuben. "Unfortunately, when Eber died at the age of four hundred and thirty-four, the House of Shem disbanded. Now, it's *my* responsibility and privilege to teach my sons of Yahweh."

Reuben rose to his knees in an informal bow. "And we thank you, Abba." He dipped his head and then met his abba's eyes. "Might I ask one more question?"

Jacob grinned. His eldest always had another question. "All right, but then you must all get back to your flocks." They nodded vehemently and gobbled up the remains of their meal.

"Why were you chosen for the House of Shem?" Reuben asked tentatively. "You're not a weak, spotted lamb."

The boy's kindness startled Jacob. "I…well…" *Yahweh, give me words.* "My brother Esau refused the training. When we were forty, Esau married two Hittite women to stop our parents' nagging." By the quizzical looks on his sons' faces, Jacob realized they didn't understand about the Hittite women. "Because Abraham was called to be Yahweh's Covenant bearer to all nations forever, our line must be kept pure and devoted to Yahweh alone. We must always—"

"Master Jacob! Master!" His two messengers rode galloping dromedaries toward him.

Jacob and the boys jumped to their feet. "Take your brothers back to camp," he said to Reuben. "Tell your imma and Rachel to meet me here right away. Go!"

All eight sons fled as the messengers slowed their mounts to a trot and approached Jacob. "What? What did he say?" Jacob shouted while rushing to meet them.

"He's coming." The first rider tapped his camel's shoulder to dismount.

The other man slid to the ground. "And he's got four hundred armed men!"

The report pierced Jacob like a red-hot sword. Panicked, he scanned his camp and the animals scattered over Mahanaim's hills. Rachel and Leah were running toward him. *My Rachel. He can't take her.*

He grabbed the first messenger's robe, pulling him close. "Tell the shepherds to divide *everything* into two camps. Servants and animals. When they're done, have them wait in the fields for my instructions." Then he shoved him toward the camels.

The man nodded and grabbed the other messenger, and Jacob fell to his knees.

"O God of my fathers," he prayed in a strangled whisper, "You told me to return and You would make me prosper. I'm unworthy of Your kindness and faithfulness. I had only my staff when I crossed the Jordan, and now I've grown to two camps." He looked up and found Rachel and Leah almost upon him. His pleading ended in silence. *Save me, I pray, from the hand of that devil Esau. I fear he'll attack the immas and our children. Remember, O God, that You promised to make me prosper and give me descendants like the sand of the sea!*

"Jacob?" Leah's voice was thready and weak.

He stood. Unable to look at Rachel, he focused on the strongest of his wives. "Esau is coming." In the periphery, he heard Rachel's cry. She stood two paces behind Leah, to her right. The thought of losing her was too much to bear. He stepped closer to Leah and grasped her head so their noses touched. He tried to steady his voice. "Esau is on his way with four hundred armed men. The messengers have gone to divide the animals and servants, but you must divide the camp in two. We'll send the first group across the river tonight with gifts to meet my brother before he reaches the second camp."

Her eyes jumped right to left, searching his soul. "Who are you giving Esau with the first gift?"

"The first gift will be two hundred female goats and twenty male goats, two hundred ewes and twenty rams, thirty female camels with their young, forty cows and ten bulls, and twenty female donkeys and ten male donkeys."

"No!" Rachel said, marching toward them. "That's half our animals, Jacob! We're not giving your brutish brother—"

He released Leah and grabbed Rachel's shoulders. "Would you rather he take you?"

Leah stepped between them. "Gently, Jacob. Tell her gently." Her blue eyes calmed him. "She knows nothing of what you speak."

Rachel trembled, her breaths quickening as panic rose. "What don't I know?" She glanced from her sister to him. "What haven't you told me?"

He heard betrayal in her voice. "I kept the truth from you," he said, stepping closer, "hoping to spare you the fear you feel now."

She shoved him away. "Don't touch me. Just tell me the truth now, Jacob."

Leah stepped aside, head bowed, leaving the hard task to him. He dragged both hands through his hair and began. "Both Abraham and Isaac recognize only first wives and their firstborns as Yahweh's Covenant line. There is a chance, Rachel—only a chance—that Abba may recognize Leah as my only wife." Color drained from her lovely face. "If Abba recognizes only Leah as my wife, Esau may exercise the original betrothal agreement by taking Laban's second daughter." Rachel covered a horrified cry and melted into a hysterical puddle.

Jacob bent to comfort her, but Leah pushed him back. "You don't have time," she said quietly. "Only you can organize the two camps and send the gifts immediately. I'll move the remaining camp into a tight circle around the central fire."

"But she needs—"

"I'll comfort Rachel until you return." Leah stood like a pillar between them. "Esau has more than twice the men, and our shepherds have only rocks and sticks for weapons. We can't afford *not* to send an extravagant bribe, Jacob."

Rachel's wails sent chills through his veins, but Leah was right. He would give Esau *all* his earthly wealth—if it meant saving lives of incalculable worth.

CHAPTER TWELVE

That night Jacob got up and took his two wives, his two female servants
and his eleven sons and crossed the ford of the Jabbok.
After he had sent them across the stream, he sent over all his possessions.
So Jacob was left alone, and a man wrestled with him till daybreak.
~ Genesis 32:22–24 (NIV) ~

Leah sat outside the opening of her tent with Dinah in her lap, grateful her six-year-old girl loved to cuddle.

"There's a nice breeze in the hill country." Zilpah fidgeted with a snagged thread on her robe. "The midsummer heat is worse than Harran during the day, but evenings are glorious."

Glorious? Zilpah never used pretentious words. Rachel did. Bilhah, when trying to impress Rachel. But never Zilpah.

Leah reached for her hand as Dinah yawned. "I know you're scared. So am I. But Jacob's God appeared to him on the road, Zilpah. He's with us."

She grunted. "I'd feel better if He was *with* us in a statue I could see."

The idea had occurred to Leah too. "I think I trust Yahweh more because He can't be formed by human hands. Rachel can't steal Him and hide Him in a saddlebag."

Zilpah chuckled and gazed into the starry sky. "You know the gods in our tents are simply representations of the gods in the sky, Leah. We heard in Damascus that even the Canaanites worship gods similar to ours from Harran."

Leah held Dinah a little tighter, wishing her daughter didn't have to hear the battle over the gods. She was awake far past her normal bedtime, but Leah wouldn't let her out of her sight with Esau's time of arrival still unknown. Rachel had been so angry that Leah kept the truth from her that she'd taken Bilhah and Joseph into her tent before the evening meal and hadn't been seen since.

"I'm tired of fighting about the gods." It was only a whisper, but she knew Zilpah heard. "I wish the four of us could make amends before Esau and his men come charging out of the darkness." She laid her chin on Dinah's head and reached for Zilpah's hand.

Dinah pointed at the sky. "Imma Zilpah, is that Inanna's star?"

"Yes, darling girl. The mother goddess shows herself especially bright just before dawn." Leah released Zilpah's hand. So much for making amends.

"The things Imma Zilpah told you about the star's beauty are true," Leah said, "but 'Inanna' is merely a legend. We know there's only one God, don't we, Love? Yahweh who created the heavens, the earth, and everything in them."

"Yes, Imma." Dinah brought her knees up and curled against Leah's chest, always sensitive to tension between her immas.

Leah shot a burning glare at her husband's fourth wife, the woman who had been Leah's handmaid and best friend. As close as a sister, Zilpah had been even dearer after Leah married. Dinah adored her and Bilhah, and the slave-wives doted on Leah's daughter. Must Dinah's education and affection become the next competition between Jacob's wives?

Zilpah rose slowly, eyes locked on Leah's. "I agreed to teach my sons as Jacob commanded, but it's different with a girl." Zilpah's eyes shimmered with emotion. In all their years together, Leah had never seen her cry. "I beg you to let Dinah honor the mother goddess. Without Inanna's blessing and protec—"

"That's enough." Leah stood, setting Dinah on her feet and stepping in front of her like a shield. "If you can't honor my wish to teach Dinah *only* of Yahweh, you'll teach her nothing at all."

Zilpah's obstinate stare drew out painfully like a blade. Finally, she inclined her head in grudging agreement and pressed a kiss atop Dinah's head. "I'll see you in the morning, little one."

Leah watched her friend disappear into the tent next door before looking down at Dinah's upturned face. "Let's get some rest. Abba wants us to wake early to meet your dohd Esau." Leah had hoped Jacob would call her to his tent as promised, which was part of the reason Zilpah had remained with them so long. With a last, longing look at her husband's darkened tent, she followed Dinah into their tent and lit two lamps.

Dinah went directly to her mat, and Leah lay down beside her. Her daughter snuggled close. "Joseph and I believe your Yahweh stories, Imma, but why can't the other stories also be true? Why can't all the gods live together?"

Leah stroked her hair, wishing Joseph could hear the explanation since he likely wondered too. "I had the same question when your abba Jacob first told me about Yahweh."

"You did?" Her head popped up, eyes round as melons. "You're not mad at me for asking?"

She pulled her girl into a ferocious hug. "Of course not. I won't ever be angry when you ask me a question." Praying silently for wisdom, Leah began, "Have your other immas told you the legend of how their gods made the earth and sky?" Dinah hesitated, no doubt fearful of causing more tension. "It's all right. I won't be angry."

"Yes," she said timidly, "but it sounded silly."

"Lots of legends sound silly." Leah hugged her tighter. "You asked if all the gods could live together. That would mean the legends are true, so let's see if they could be true, all right?" She felt Dinah's nod against her chest. "Have you seen one of Abba's sheep give birth to a lamb?"

"Oh, yes!" She sat up, eyes brighter than the lamps beside them. "He let me watch last spring."

"It's an amazing sight, isn't it? One living thing birthing another. Did the newborn lamb come out of many ewes or just one ewe's body?"

A slow grin curved her lips. "Are you saying only one God could give birth to Creation, Imma?"

Leah pulled her back down to lie beside her. "My smart girl. Yes, that's exactly what I'm saying." Dinah's giggles would likely delay her sleep, but the impromptu lesson was worth it.

"Leah." Jacob stood inside the tent, dim light casting shadows on his sober features.

"Good evening, Husband." Leah stood. "I'll send Dinah to Zilpah's tent—"

"No." Jacob lifted one hand. "No one will sleep this night, I'm afraid." Head bowed, he cleared his throat. "I must ask you to move the whole camp to the other side of the river." He looked up. "Immediately."

Mind spinning with questions, Leah chose one. "Now?"

His single, slow nod sped her heart rate. "I've awakened the older boys to tear down the tents. The servants will pack supplies and load the animals. You'll choose the campsite across the Jabbok."

"Me? Where will you be?" She scuttled to her feet, but he stepped back. "Jacob, tell me what's happening."

"The water level is low enough that the pack animals can move almost everything across the river safely. The shepherds may have to carry some of the smaller sheep and goats, but the dogs can help drive most of the flocks across." He shook his head and looked down. "I must remain on this side until morning—alone."

"What? No!" Leah hugged his waist, forcing him to look at her.

"Please, Leah. I can't explain." He seemed more sad than fearful. "Just do as I ask."

Her eyes caressed him with the love she dared not speak. Her strong yet tender shepherd seemed determined to keep his family safe, but from what? Had Yahweh warned him of new danger? Was Esau coming soon? Wouldn't the camp be closer to the danger if they crossed?

With a frustrated sigh, Leah silenced her questions. "Of course I'll do as you ask, Husband. But will you answer one question?" Only a short hesitation preceded the rising of his brows, an invitation of her query. "Who will be safer, Jacob—those who cross the river, or you, here?"

He forced a smile for Dinah, but it died when his eyes met Leah's. "Only Yahweh knows."

Leah woke when the first ray of light splashed across her face. She lay at the entrance, keeping watch as she'd promised. Rachel had been terrified by Jacob's late-night order to move everything and everyone in camp.

"I don't think Abba's gods hear me in this new land," she'd told Leah as the camp unpacked on Jabbok's northern shore. "I know you talk to Jacob's god. May Bilhah, Joseph, and I stay in your tent? We would feel safer with you." Joseph looked at her with those warm-bread brown eyes. Of course Leah would never deny him. Zilpah joined them too, so Dinah and Leah had squeezed four more bodies into their tent for the short night before Esau's arrival.

Leah sat up, stretched, and found Rachel sitting up beside her.

"Did you hear something?" The fragile skin beneath Rachel's lovely eyes was bruised with sleeplessness and terror.

"No. It's dawn." *Yahweh, give me patience.*

Rachel rummaged in the saddlebag she kept near her at all times and produced Abba's household gods. "I don't think they work outside of Harran."

"Why not trust Yahweh? You saw His light, and Jacob heard Him speak." *Jacob*. The memory of their husband waving goodbye on the other shore haunted her. Was he safe?

"How could you throw away all our traditions without a moment's regret?" Rachel sounded like a chastising imma.

Leah rolled up her mat, busying her hands to cool her temper. "Yahweh showed Himself to me personally. It's easy to follow when God proves Himself to you." She set aside the mat and met her sister's frustrated stare. "Was it Yahweh or His Angel who appeared to Jacob in the road?"

"I...well..." Rachel averted her eyes. "It could have been—"

"No maybes or could have beens." Leah bent low to capture her sister's gaze and then stood, lifting Rachel's focus. "Tell me. Yes or no. Do you believe Yahweh appeared to our husband?" Zilpah and Bilhah were awake now and seemed suddenly interested in the interchange.

"Yes," Rachel said without flinching. "I'm sure Yahweh appeared to Jacob, but that doesn't mean He wants anything to do with women from Harran. Yahweh is and always has been a man's god."

Leah shook her head, feeling more pity than anger. "Was it a 'man's god' that opened my womb seven times? Was it a 'man's god' that gave you Joseph?"

Rachel waved away her reply. "We don't have time for this. Esau could ride into our camp at any moment."

"Which is why you—more than anyone in camp—should cry out for protection from the God of Abraham, Isaac, and *Jacob*." Leah rushed from the tent before anger fueled unkindness. Why couldn't her sister-wives believe? They'd seen the same bright light she'd seen, the same scorched ground. Leah looked up into the eastern sky—streaked orange, yellow, and lavender. *Yahweh, evidence of Your presence is before all of us, every day.*

Her feet pounded the ground, walking toward their central fire. The camp was half its normal size—now considered Jacob's "second" camp after yesterday's gifting. Though later than their normal start, most still slept after the late-night relocation. Even the animals remained quiet. She stopped near the clay oven, where embers still glowed white. Closing her eyes, she blocked out every sound and soaked in the peace. But the rapid beating of her anxious heart disturbed the stillness. If only it raced from the brisk walk. Why couldn't she trust Yahweh's protection the way she challenged others to do? Why must she be so afraid of Esau and his men? Finding fault in others exposed the doubt in herself. *Yahweh, protect us all. We know not what lies ahead.*

"Good morning, Mistress." A shepherd's wife knelt at the bread oven. She added dried dung to stoke the fire.

Leah greeted her but felt suddenly suffocated by a waking camp. "Let the others know I've gone to meet Master Jacob." Without awaiting a response, Leah's feet took flight, churning as wildly as her thoughts.

What had become of the unarmed shepherds they'd sent with Esau's gift? Divided into five groups, the first shepherd was to offer two-hundred-and-twenty goats to Jacob's brother. If Esau received them peacefully, two-hundred-and-twenty sheep would follow. The third under-shepherd would offer thirty female camels with their young, forty cows and ten bulls, and—if Esau still remained peaceful—the final shepherd would give him twenty female donkeys and ten male donkeys. Each man was instructed to delay the offerings, allowing Jacob's second camp more time to prepare.

Prepare for what? Breathless, Leah halted her frantic pace to Jabbok's shore and braced both hands on her knees. "Yahweh, protect them," she gasped. The faces of those shepherds haunted her.

If Esau had shown any violence, surely one of the shepherds would have escaped to bring them word. What if they'd returned and found the Mahanaim camp deserted because of last night's relocation? She'd been awake most of the night. The shepherds would have passed their new camp to get to Mahanaim. And she'd placed their best fighting men at the corners of their new location. They'd raised no alarm. But what if Esau killed them all? What if—

No. She shook her head, as if dislodging fear.

She stood, stretched her arms toward heaven, and inhaled the morning air. "Yahweh is faithful." She whispered the reminder and took another calming breath. "You're no good to Jacob if you're as hysterical as Rachel." Grinning at the thought, Leah resumed her march toward the shore, feeling more peaceful somehow. Perhaps it was good that the shepherds hadn't returned. If Esau had killed them, he would have arrived more quickly and attacked at night. The longer Esau delayed, the greater chance he received Jacob's gifts with peace.

Emerging from a copse of trees, Leah saw a man walking toward her from the river. "Jacob?" she breathed. It couldn't be. The man had gray hair and walked with a limp, leaning heavily on a staff. But when his head tilted up, she saw his face. "Jacob ben Isaac!"

He fell to his knees at the sound of her voice. She ran through the tall grass, nearly tripping as it wrapped around her legs. She fell at his side then covered him like a blanket. He keened as if mourning, so she pulled him to her chest and rocked him as she did her children. "What's happened to you, my love?" The man she'd left last night was broad-shouldered and strong, his hair and beard sprinkled with gray, his face lined with wisdom. "Please, Jacob," she whispered, "help me understand."

When his wails turned to moans, he took several deep breaths and sat down with a groan. Silence stretched long until the morning's birdsong faded. Finally, Jacob lifted his chin and met Leah's gaze. She gasped at the light and wonder of his countenance.

"There are no words to explain the terrible majesty of our God." His face twisted with emotion again, and he covered his face to weep once more. Leah waited, fear abated. When her husband regained a measure of composure, he wiped his callused hands down his face. "I saw the face of Yahweh, Leah, and was somehow spared. He came as a Man—an Angel—I don't know. He wrestled with me all night long, but when He saw that He could not defeat me, He wrenched my hip."

Her heart skipped. "No! Are you—"

"It hurt terribly—and still hurts—but I wouldn't release Him until He blessed me." He was laughing and crying.

"What did He say to that?" Leah touched his face, amazed he was spared.

"He gave me a new name, Leah."

"What? Why?"

Jacob shook his head, refusing to answer. Was the new name so awful?

"Please, my love." Leah stilled his fidgeting hands. "Tell me the new name Yahweh gave you."

He looked up, brows pinched and lifted. "I am now *Israel*," he said sheepishly. "Yahweh said I'd struggled with God and men and I had overcome."

Overwhelmed with love and pride, Leah wrapped him in her tightest embrace. "It's perfect. You are *Israel,* indeed." His arms came around her, strong yet tender, and she felt a union with him beyond physical pleasure or emotional need. "Accept God's great gift to you, my husband."

"I'll name this crossing *Peniel.*"

"Yes, my love. Yes." The God they worshipped had strengthened her husband by making him weak to meet his brother. And He'd given her this moment to share with him alone. *Thank You, Yahweh.* "Esau will meet *Israel* today and all will be well."

Jacob's arms tensed. "My new name can't change my brother." He released her, and she looked into the fearful face of Jacob—not Israel.

"Surely the Man gave you some indication of Esau's intentions or how we might at least avoid him."

"Yahweh said nothing of Esau, so we proceed with my plan." He reached for her hands. "Help me stand."

Leah pulled him to his feet, dread crawling up her spine. "We've had no report of violence from Esau. Perhaps he comes peacefully."

"My brother doesn't know the meaning of peace." He winced with his first step toward camp. "When I fled Beersheba, he sent some from his clan to steal the bride price Abba had given me to take to Harran. I couldn't admit to Laban that I was both destitute *and* a weakling who was robbed on my journey." Jacob wrapped one arm over her shoulder, sniffing and lifting his chin the way he did when trying to impress Abba. "No matter what Esau says today, he'll always intend me harm."

Leah remained silent, measuring her husband's words. She could usually discern when Jacob told half truths to Abba, but was he lying to her now? Why had he never told her of the robbery on his way to Harran? If Esau came in peace, would Jacob accept it?

The camp ahead of them had come alive. The boys had already begun tearing down tents, and the women at the central fire packed the morning's food in separate bags to travel.

"You said you had a plan to meet your brother?" Leah focused on the camp ahead, her stomach churning with dread. "But how can you plan when you don't yet know—"

"I know Esau." His breath caught when the ground beneath them began to tremble. He looked to the west as an army of horses with riders spilled over a distant hill, riding fast toward them. Jacob grabbed her shoulders, eyes wild with fear. "Divide my children with their immas. The slave-wives will approach him first with their sons." Leah started shaking her head, but he continued. "Yes, Leah, yes. Just like the gifts I sent. Do you hear me? Zilpah and Bilhah with their sons must meet Esau first to test his intentions, and they must run if he shows violence."

"Not the children," she whispered in barely controlled panic.

"Yes. I must show him sons." He pulled her into his arms. "And then you and our sons must be next. You, our six sons, and Dinah. Then you must place Joseph behind you. And Rachel must be last, Leah. She must be the very last thing my brother sees." He kissed the top of her head and released her, staring into her eyes. "If he's shown no sign of attack by the time he gets to Rachel, we may have a chance of escaping with our family intact. I'll offer him all I have to keep my wives and children. Now, go!" He pushed her toward camp and turned toward the approaching army.

"What are you doing?" she screamed.

He wiped his face and turned with lifted brows. "I'm *Israel*. I'm going to contend with my brother."

Camp was in shambles, but it couldn't be helped. "Get the animals and go!" Leah told the shepherds. "You'll present first to Esau before the family." The servants and family finished packing, and by the time the animals were on their way, Leah made Jacob's will reality.

She had no time to soften the decision or offer assurances to the slave-wives, their children, or even her own sons that Jacob loved them. What did one say when a man had clearly ordered his family by the value he placed on their lives—or was it by how much he would mourn their deaths?

Leah placed Zilpah at the front, for Jacob hadn't spoken to her in years. Bilhah came next because she was at least helpful as Rachel's maid. Then came Gad and Asher, Zilpah's sons. Then Bilhah's boys, Dan and Naphtali. Leah's children traveled in more of a cluster, the older four boys huddling around their siblings as protectors, while Leah herself shielded Joseph behind her. Rachel stumbled behind them all, terror making her steps falter.

Jacob was far ahead of them, climbing a distant hill while his servants and shepherds drove the camp's remaining animals through a valley that separated two hills. The family reached the peak of the first hill when Esau and his army crested the one Jacob was climbing. Rachel released a low wail when Esau swung one leg off his mount and began running toward Jacob.

"Turn away!" Leah screamed at the children, yet she herself could not. Eyes fixed on the murdering bandit once meant to be hers, she searched for any weapon in his hand. What violence had he planned for the husband she adored?

Nothing. His hands dangled free as he drew nearer Jacob, the man feeble from his nocturnal fight. Jacob halted on the hill, bracing for the blow. The hairy red beast of a man grabbed him around the waist and flung him in a circle like a small boy.

From so far away, Leah couldn't make out their words, but Jacob kissed his brother's cheeks, and the two men appeared completely friendly—as if neither had ever wronged the other.

Leah looked over her shoulder and found Rachel's mouth agape. "Jacob wants us to meet him if Esau shows no signs of violence," Leah said. Rachel's tremors turned to shaking, yet she nodded silent consent. "Keep moving!" Leah raised her voice for the others. "It's time we all met Master Esau."

CHAPTER THIRTEEN

Then Esau said, "Let us be on our way; I'll accompany you."
But Jacob said to him, "My lord knows that the children are tender
and that I must care for the ewes and cows that are nursing their young....
So let my lord go on ahead of his servant, while I move along slowly
at the pace of the flocks and herds before me and the pace of the
children, until I come to my lord in Seir."...
So that day Esau started on his way back to Seir.
Jacob, however, went to Sukkoth,
where he built a place for himself and made shelters for his livestock.
~ Genesis 33:12–14, 16 (NIV) ~

Leah stood a hundred paces from the red-bearded man to whom she'd once been betrothed. Trembling as violently as the wedding night of her deception, she watched as the man she'd escaped assessed Zilpah, then Bilhah, and then their four sons. Still too far to hear conversations, she was amazed when the boys laughed and the big man offered a smile to Dan. Oldest of the four, Dan smiled back at the big man in friendly acknowledgment.

Jacob motioned Leah and her children forward next. She bent to whisper to Joseph, who still hid behind her. "You stay with your imma. If she tells you to run, you run like the wind and hide among the trees where we made camp last night."

"I won't leave Imma." His dark brows turned down. "I'll only run as fast as she can run, and we'll hide in a place she can fit too."

"Of course." Throat clogged with tenderness, Leah pulled her brave boy into a ferocious hug before herding her own children toward the man she'd feared most of her life.

Everything inside her screamed to hide her blue eyes. Turn them away. Cover the hideous feature that marked her as slave or pauper. The memory of Imma's lovely face surfaced—before the scars of Abba's rage. Before the sadness became too great. Leah stared at a face she'd imagined as Leviathan, holding Esau's gaze as she led her children toward him. A lopsided grin softened the warrior's countenance, and one eyebrow slightly raised made him seem almost friendly. *No matter what Esau says today, he'll always intend me harm.* Could she trust anything she saw or heard from this giant Jacob called a devil?

Now only ten paces away, Esau assessed her sons. His lips moved as if counting under his breath. He lingered momentarily on Dinah, making Leah's heart skip a beat. When his eyes returned to hers, she halted her brood before him. He grinned. So much like Jacob's smile. These twins of Isaac were so different yet similar.

"This is Leah," Jacob said, standing to his brother's right. "Imma to six sons and my only daughter." The children bowed as they'd been taught. Leah inclined her head, respectful yet controlled.

"Ah, yes." Esau's eyes roamed her head to toe. "I see the eyes that merchants speak of." Leah's cheeks burned, but she refused to look away. Esau took a step closer and placed his rough hand under her chin and drew too close. "My family shames those who are different. I don't."

Jacob nudged her aside, placing himself between them. "Next is my fourth wife, Rachel, and her only son, Joseph."

Still unnerved, Leah guided her children back. She looked up and found the man staring at her instead of watching Rachel's approach. He wasn't at all as she'd imagined him.

"Alas, my Rachel was barren until only a few years ago when Yahweh opened her womb, and she hasn't conceived again since." Jacob wasn't even subtle about dissuading his brother from Rachel.

Esau finally turned to greet Jacob's final wife and son. "So, this is the lovely Rachel, my brother's betrothed." He offered a respectful bow, but it was Joseph who drew his attention. "And what was your name, young man?"

"I'm Joseph." He straightened his shoulders, standing taller.

Esau knelt, meeting him eye to eye. "How many kills have you made while hunting, Joseph?"

The boy looked up at Jacob for permission to answer. Jacob gave a nod. "None, my lord. I'm only six and not yet allowed to handle weapons."

Leah's boys snickered, but her glare silenced them. Esau raised a brow, glanced at Leah's sons and back at her. "Let them laugh. Joseph should have had a bow in his hand at three and a dagger at five." He stood and clapped a meaty hand on

Jacob's shoulder. "Bring your sons to Seir—my red mountains—before you return to Beersheba so I can teach them to be men. Our parents aren't going anywhere. They're too stubborn to die." He laughed and squeezed Jacob's shoulder.

Rachel scurried over to Leah and slid Joseph behind them. "I don't want to go to Seir," she whispered. Leah didn't dare shush her for fear Esau would hear, so she grabbed her hand and squeezed to send the message.

"You go ahead of us," Jacob said. "My messengers will lead us at a slower pace for the women and children."

Esau scrubbed his bushy red beard. "I'll leave a few men to guide you."

"No, you're too generous." Jacob waved off his offer. "The kindness you've already shown is more than I expected or deserve. We'll see you in Seir as soon as we can." He sniffed and raised his chin.

Dread coiled in Leah's belly. Jacob was lying.

Esau's eyes lingered on his younger brother, a strange grin curving his lips. He knew it too. Silence fell between them until the air sparked with tension. "All right, Jacob. I'll see you in Seir." Without awaiting a response, he turned to his men. "Let's ride!" His mighty legs churned up the steep hill, taking him back to his stallion. The four hundred men with him never left their horses nor said a word. No weapons were drawn nor blood spilt. Esau ben Isaac had come in peace and gave every indication he was a man of his word. Unlike his brother Jacob.

When their horses disappeared on the opposite side of the hill, Jacob's shoulders sagged with relief. Rachel and Leah rushed toward him, and he wrapped an arm around each of them. "We're not going to Seir," he said. "That Leviathan will kill my sons, take my wives, and cut me up in his favorite red stew."

"Jacob, lower your voice!" Leah looked back at their children and spoke in a hush. "He seemed perfectly honorable. I thought I even heard him offer to give back your gifts when we first approached."

Rachel's eyes narrowed. "Don't be naive, Leah. Every haggler in the market knows that trick." She laid her head on Jacob's shoulder. "I agree with you, Husband. We dare not go to Seir and tempt the gods. They've saved us once. Let's be grateful and stay away from your brother."

Leah waited for Jacob to chastise her. Instead he removed his arm from Leah's shoulder and held Rachel tighter. "We'll travel a little farther today and see where Yahweh takes us." He kissed the top of her head and released her, shouting directions to the shepherds as he made his way up the hill to lead them.

Rachel hesitated after one step toward Joseph but turned back to Leah as if she'd forgotten to mention something. "Perhaps you'd have been better off marrying the brother you were betrothed to—instead of stealing mine." Zilpah, Bilhah, all the children—even the servants—heard Rachel's shameful rebuke. Now, all their eyes burned Leah with shame, leaving her more exposed than if she stood before them naked.

She bowed her head to hide her tears. *Yahweh, my wrongs are ever before me. Are my sins the reason Jacob's house will always be divided?*

In a silence that stretched to eternity, she felt a hand on her shoulder. "Come, Imma," Reuben said. "I'll set up your tent first." He bumped Rachel hard as he led his imma past her.

"You will feel your abba's strap if you touch me again," Rachel shouted at their backs.

Reuben's arm tightened around Leah's shoulder. "You married the right man, Imma." He spoke quietly, ignoring the threat. "You are Abba's Covenant wife, and he has eleven Covenant bearers only because *you* taught us well."

Leah covered a grateful sob and leaned into her firstborn's strength. He led her past the slave-wives and their sons to the safety of her children's waiting arms. Huddled around her, six boys and a daughter expressed their love and released their fears from the morning. Leah calmed them with the details of Jacob's new name, and soon his other sons joined the conversation. Dan, Naphtali, Gad, and Asher squeezed in beside their brothers. Even Joseph patted Dinah's shoulder as if seeking comfort from his heart-twin. Leah welcomed them all, hoping to strengthen their trust in Yahweh and salve their inner wounds.

Everyone had been wounded today. Jacob by Yahweh's Angel. Their family by the blatant display of succession. And Leah by the realization that though her husband had been given a new name, he was still Jacob, the deceiver. Though his fine words were perhaps what drew her to the one true God—for which she was grateful—his sons couldn't build a firm foundation of God's truth from the lips of a liar.

She glanced over the children's heads at Jacob and Rachel, who stood halfway up a hill, sharing a quiet moment. Jacob had commanded her to destroy the stolen gods, but she hadn't—and he'd likely never mention them again. Whether dealing with Abba, Rachel, or Esau, Jacob would rather deceive than confront. Rather charm than resolve. Had she married the right brother? She looked away, losing herself in the children's chatter.

Esau was a brute, and—if she believed the rumors—he didn't follow Yahweh. But she sensed sincerity. Esau had no intention of harming them. Here or in Seir. He would train Jacob's sons to be hunters like him, and that was worse than death to Jacob.

"Will you spend the whole day prattling with children?" Rachel carried a basket on her arm and wiped sweat from her brow. "It's nearly midday, and there's work to be done, Sister."

"I've been practicing with my sling." Reuben reached into his waist pouch. "I could hit her with a small stone from here."

Leah covered a laugh. "Your imma Rachel is right. Everyone, get your shoulder packs. Abba wants to travel a while before we make camp again." She shooed the children on their way and shared a conspiratorial wink with Reuben. Maybe she should learn to use his sling and deal differently with Rachel when they entered Canaan.

CHAPTER FOURTEEN

After Jacob came from Paddan Aram, he arrived safely
at the city of Shechem in Canaan
and camped within sight of the city. For a hundred pieces of silver,
he bought from the sons of Hamor, the father of Shechem,
the plot of ground where he pitched his tent.
There he set up an altar and called it El Elohe Israel.
~ Genesis 33:18–20 (NIV) ~

Three Years Later
Sukkoth, Jordan Valley

Three more caravans had arrived in Sukkoth the previous night. Once a clean and peaceful respite along the merchants' highway, Sukkoth had become a honeypot for the lowest creatures in Canaanite society seeking the sweetest of all evils. The travelers' temporary shelters crowded Jacob's conical clay homes. Though not as expansive as Abba's in Harran, they were safer than the tents where their servants' and shepherds' families slept. Drunken celebrations and lewd conversations filled the night air. Jacob had increased their shepherds afield, fearing the crowds would incite chaos and thievery. Leah watched the moon in all its courses across the sky. Were her impressionable sons safe in the fields? Or had they wandered into town to witness the debauchery?

"Why are we still in Sukkoth?" Leah slapped a spoonful of gruel into Jacob's wooden bowl, splattering some on her apron. "I thought Yahweh told you to return to the camp of your abba, Isaac, in Beersheba." She set the bowl in front of him and held out a spoon but gripped it tightly until he answered.

He gently worked the spoon from her grasp and kissed her palm, using the same charm that always wooed her. "I've found a plot of land for sale." He turned his attention to the gruel. "It's closer to the trade routes and offers plenty of grazing for our growing flocks and herds."

His eleven sons sat around him, watching, listening. The other three wives placed plates of cheese, fruit, and nuts on the leather mats in the center of the men's circle. None of them complained about Sukkoth. Why would they? There were plenty of pagan idols in the market. Had she become Jacob's only nagging wife? Rachel knelt beside the clay oven with Dinah, teaching her to bake bread. If they didn't leave Sukkoth, how could Leah protect her only daughter? Who else in Jacob's household would remind him that Yahweh called him to Beersheba?

Pressing down her frustration, she forced calm and knelt beside her husband. "I understand our need to trade and graze our growing flocks and herds, Jacob, but our speckled-and-spotted wool is valuable. The garments and rugs will sell anywhere. Why not return to Beersheba? Comfort your aging parents. Build for our future there?"

He turned slowly to face her, his features hardening into an impenetrable mask that had become too familiar. "I'm buying my first plot of land in Canaan, Leah. *My* land. *Israel's* land." He turned from her and announced to the boys, "We're moving to Shechem."

They offered no reaction. Why would they? The only time they saw Sukkoth was at dawn to break their fast, to hear Leah's stories of Yahweh, and to receive Jacob's work assignments. All but Joseph spent their days tending animals while they spent their nights in the fields. How would life be different in Shechem?

Leah returned to the pot of gruel Dinah was now stirring and noted a stolen glance between Jacob with Rachel. *She already knew.* Fury heated Leah's neck and rose to her cheeks. Had Shechem been her sister's idea? It was a larger city with more pregnant women on whom she could practice midwifery and incantations. In Sukkoth, she'd served as midwife for a few births, but the people here were transient, and she'd mentioned last month that she wished they lived near a gated city where she could gain the renown she deserved for the skills she'd been taught.

"Ow!" Leah's finger sizzled on the metal pot. She instinctively stuck it in her mouth to cool the burn.

"Let me see it, Imma." Dinah coaxed the hurting appendage into her hand. "That will blister," she said. "I'll fetch Imma Rachel's aloe." She was gone before Leah could refuse.

Rachel delivered a basket of warm bread for the men to share, and Leah served a bowl of gruel to each of Jacob's sons.

Zilpah and Bilhah retreated to their weaving chamber, having completed their family tasks of the morning.

"What will we do with our clay shelters?" Reuben asked, breaking the awkward silence.

"We sell them," Jacob said, spreading goat cheese on a piece of bread. "I've already had two men offer to buy the shelters we use for lambing, and another clan is interested in our family shelters. Bringing Harran's conical houses to Canaan could turn a handsome profit."

"That's how Yahweh blesses," Leah interjected. Still sucking on her smarting finger, she used the moment to teach their sons. "Because your abba was faithful in Harran, Yahweh can use even difficult circumstances to create a good future."

"That's right." Jacob offered his hand, and she grudgingly stood beside him to accept it. "Yahweh will bless us in Shechem, Leah. I'm sure of it."

Within a month's time, they'd sold all the conical shelters in Sukkoth and purchased tents to live on their new parcel of land within sight of Shechem's gates. During their last night in Sukkoth, Leah lay alone in her conical shelter. It was the second day of the week. Quiet. Only a few travelers, and Jacob had given several shepherds permission to combine the flocks and take shifts on watch. *Yahweh, help me to be content with the good decision to leave Sukkoth—even if our destination isn't where I'd like to go.*

When she snuffed out the lamp, the faint sound of laughter wafted on the night air. At first, she enjoyed it, thinking Jacob's boys were enjoying some good-natured fun. But when young men's laughter mingled with women's raucous voices, Leah shot out of bed like a rock from Reuben's sling.

Following the sounds through a hallway, she passed through Bilhah and Zilpah's weaving chamber. The women were still at their looms, Dinah spinning beside them.

"Imma!" Dinah dropped her spindle and stood, glancing nervously at her teachers.

"Are you deaf?" Leah ignored her daughter and aimed her ire at the women who should have stopped whatever their sons were doing.

"Leave them alone," Zilpah said, still focused on her weaving. "Let our sons meet the mother goddess tonight."

Dinah glanced up but looked away quickly.

"Get to my chamber, Dinah."

"But, Imma—"

"Now!" Her daughter stomped out of the chamber and into the connecting hallway.

Bilhah turned from her weaving to glare at Leah. "You can't control everyone. Our children must choose for themselves which gods they will serve."

"*Jacob's* children will serve the only true God." She stormed away, berating herself for allowing Dinah to spend so much time with her other immas. Leah should have known they wouldn't keep their promise to speak only of Yahweh. Had Rachel poisoned Joseph too? She was, of course, in Jacob's chamber and likely couldn't hear the ruckus their sons were making.

Following the sounds of celebration, Leah quickened her pace, passed through two hallways, and reached a third conical chamber with its door ajar. She stopped. Felt the sick rise of bile at the back of her throat. Did she want to peek inside? No, but if she didn't stop what was happening behind that door, her sons could ruin their lives. She inhaled a sustaining breath, pushed open the door, and watched as ten of Jacob's eleven sons made fools of themselves with women twice their age. Empty wineskins lay on the floor as did some of the boys. Reuben, now as well built as his abba once was, sat on a couch with a scantily clad woman draped across him.

"What are you thinking?" Leah's shout, like a clanging cymbal, silenced the revelry and brought Jacob's sons to their feet—at least those still conscious.

"Imma Leah!" Gad swayed, hiding a wineskin behind his back. "We were...we were just—"

"If your abba saw this atrocity," she said, "he'd be appalled at what Yahweh's Covenant bearers have done."

Simeon stepped forward, steadier than the others. "Abba gave us silver and said we should enjoy our last night in Sukkoth." Fixing his gaze on his imma, he took a defiant draw from his wineskin and wiped his mouth with the back of his hand.

Jacob should see what his silver purchased. "I doubt wine and women were his intention, Simeon. Your abba is an honorable man." At least she hoped he hadn't intended this for his sons. She glared at the woman who sat on Reuben with a wicked grin. "Get out." Leah kicked a discarded piece of clothing at her. "And take your friends with you."

She lifted one perfect eyebrow, stood, and kissed Reuben—thoroughly. The other women gathered articles of clothing and trailed behind their leader out the door. Jacob's sons glanced at each other sheepishly, shadows of guilt finally darkening the mood. Judah nudged Naphtali and Asher with his sandal. Passed out on the floor, the slave-wives' youngest boys groaned but scuttled to their feet when they saw Leah staring at them.

She turned her fury on Reuben. "Where's Joseph? He's your responsibility." He glanced at Simeon, and curiosity rose to concern. "What have you done?"

Every eye turned to the sound of muffled pounding at the back of the room. She pushed her way through her boys, but Levi blocked her path. "Abba said we had to take him, but he was ruining our fun."

Her hand rose, and Levi flinched—waiting for the blow. Leah caught herself before striking her third-born, but his wounded expression cut her.

"We wouldn't hurt him, Imma." Features hardening, he stepped back and pointed to a wooden chest. "Go. Save your precious Joseph."

"Levi—" More pounding cut her defense short, and she ran to the wooden box in the corner, lid jumping with every pounding. A sturdy stick had been poked through a metal clasp to hold the lid closed. She knelt, opened the lid, and gasped. "Oh, Joseph." She tried to untie the gag and blindfold, but she'd never be able to untie his hands and feet. "Get me a dagger! Hurry!" The poor boy lay on his side, weeping. Someone from behind her offered a knife, and she began cutting but was blinded by her tears and white-hot fury.

"Let me do it, Imma." Judah placed a hand on her shoulder.

She stood, trembling with rage, and waited until Judah freed his brother. He helped Joseph out of the wood box, and the two boys stood beside her. The others kept their distance while she stared into each face. Simeon belched loudly. Several snickered.

"You think this is funny?" Leah's whole body shook, churning up years of pain. "What kind of men pay women for pleasure? What kind of brothers prey on the youngest among them?" Their folly gave way to silence. Shifting uncomfortably, heads bowed, they were finally listening. "Your actions are like a pebble thrown into water, creating ripples that change lives. Joseph's life. Your lives. What you've done tonight will change how you experience the world. The choices you've made have also changed my respect for you."

Letting her eyes linger on each young face, she saw varying levels of regret. *Yahweh, let something I say reach their hearts.*

"Tonight's consequences will settle on you like a boulder in the morning. I want all of you to gather up the unfinished wineskins." When they didn't move, she raised her voice. "Now! Do it now!" Tentatively at first, they threw empty skins into a pile and gathered partially full wineskins into a single area. "You will pour the remaining wine into the slop buckets."

Reuben's eyes bulged. "But we paid a lot of silver—" She cut off his complaint with a stare that could have cut iron. "Yes, Imma," he said, quietly getting in line to obey.

"It would all end in a slop bucket anyway." She offered the insight while watching them complete the grudging task. When a few of them plopped onto couches, she hurried over to urge them back to their feet. "Oh no, my sons. Your night has just begun. I plan to stay, making sure your eyes barely blink all night. Then at dawn, you'll tell your abba what his silver purchased and receive your work assignments for our journey to Shechem."

"Why must Abba know?" Reuben's pleading eyes were as large as gold bangles.

Leah ached to bear the bitterness festering inside her. *Because your abba was drunk on our wedding night, and it's as much his sin as mine that this family is divided.* Instead, she veiled her heart as good parents do. "Because your abba needs to know what happens when he gives silver to eleven silly boys without providing wise guidance to spend it." Jacob's punishment would be tending his exhausted, vomiting sons tomorrow on their way to Shechem. Leah would pay for her lax parenting during the long night ahead.

Jacob stood with his eleven sons at the gates of Shechem and counted out one hundred pieces of silver to King Hamor. "Shechem is honored to acquire a neighbor of such trade renown, Jacob ben Isaac. Your raw wool and garments will bring many merchants to our city market."

"These fine grazing lands mean healthy flocks and quality wool." Jacob bowed to the Canaanite king. "May Yahweh bless both our households."

"And let us seal our new partnership." King Hamor extended his hand toward the covenant field he'd prepared, where a heifer, goat, and ram had been cut in half and the halves placed opposite each other. Jacob followed Shechem's king, where the two men would covenant together by walking between the pieces.

Leah watched with interest, remembering the story Jacob had taught her about Yahweh's Covenant with Abraham in which the Lord provided the animals and only He passed between their halves—assuring Abraham only Elohim could accomplish all that was promised. For today's covenant, Hamor had provided the heifer and Jacob the goat and ram. Hamor's family stood on one side of the butchered animals to observe the ceremony and Jacob's family stood on the other.

Hamor lifted his hands and addressed them. "Let us now cut this covenant and be of one heart and mind even as these animals have given their lives to unite us." Both families raised their voices, the women's tongues ululating as Jacob and King Hamor walked side by side with bare feet on the blood-soaked ground. Jacob's sons raised their arms and bellowed like victors after battle. Zilpah banged her timbrel, leading the women in dance.

Hamor's family joined the celebration—all except his queen and crown prince. The queen was exotic and foreboding, eyes rimmed with black lines and bright green powder. Leah tried not to stare. Her son, Shechem, stood beside her. Tall and dark-skinned, his black hair and eyes made him equally mysterious, but a wide smile gave him a warmth that Hamor's other sons lacked. He raised a brow and nodded at Leah's perusal. Her cheeks warmed. She'd successfully avoided staring at the queen but woefully failed with the handsome prince.

Purposefully, she scanned the others enjoying the day. Rachel and Dinah danced together, twirling in a circle. Without permission, Leah's focus wandered back to the crown prince, who studied Dinah intently. Not a sinister gaze but too intrigued for Leah's liking. She took a few steps to block his view and issued a silent warning. No need to ruin a celebration, but neither would she allow her nine-year-old daughter to be ogled. Shechem pressed repentant hands together and bowed. Then he flashed a brilliant smile before rejoining the celebration. Yes, Leah would watch that one.

Breaking into Rachel and Dinah's circle, she joined the dance, abandoning concerns she'd carried too long. Why not let joy fill her? Jacob owned his first plot of land in Canaan— another of Yahweh's promises fulfilled. The ground southwest of Shechem would belong to Abraham's descendants forever— to her sons and their sons and generations after them. Overwhelmed at the thought and winded from the dance, she found respite under a nearby tree and watched Jacob and Rachel mingle with Shechem's royalty.

The slave-wives danced and entertained Jacob's household, moving away from the king and his family. Leah felt a stab of loneliness. *Where do I fit?* Jacob ben Isaac had earned the title of Prince while in Sukkoth, and she had helped him achieve it. Every day, she went out to the animal shelters with him to record the numbers, the grain, the hired help's wages, and the cost of supplies. She was even training Joseph in record-keeping—a firstborn's right—instead of Reuben. At Jacob's command.

She watched Dinah, now dancing with Zilpah and Bilhah. For three years Leah had trained Joseph to be Jacob's firstborn, leaving her daughter in the care of the pagan women in camp. Dinah had grown enamored with Rachel's midwifery tricks. What else had Rachel taught her? She sniffed back stubborn emotions, afraid to open the floodgates on this happy occasion. Prince Shechem caught her eye and walked toward her. "I don't want to deal with you right now," she murmured.

"Shalom," he said. "Isn't that how your people greet each other?"

"It is." Leah offered a cool smile and looked away, hoping he'd leave.

"May I sit with you?"

Dare she say no? "Of course." She offered another half smile.

He sat across from her, not beside her, and looked unapologetically at her eyes. "Do you mind if I ask your heritage? The color of your eyes is different than any I've seen. Beautiful!" he added quickly. "But different."

Leah turned to the young man and found him intensely searching her gaze. Perhaps he was truly curious. "My imma was Mitanni. Some have dark eyes. Others light, like mine."

"Your daughter, I noticed, has your eyes."

Silent warnings blared. "Dinah is nine." Leah smiled, softening her tone at the tightening of his jaw. "Too young for a prince's attention."

He looked over his shoulder. "My mother is Egyptian."

Leah nodded but didn't respond.

When he returned his attention to Leah, his gaze was more intense. "My mother has taught me many things, Mistress Leah, but two will most interest you. First, because my mother is unique, I appreciate distinctive women." He paused as if waiting for her to reply.

"And the second thing she taught you?"

"She taught me to wait patiently for the things I want most." He rose to leave but looked down before he took his first step. "It's been very nice to meet you—and your light-eyed daughter."

CHAPTER FIFTEEN

Now Dinah, the daughter Leah had borne to Jacob,
went out to visit the women of the land.
When Shechem son of Hamor the Hivite, the ruler of that area,
saw her, he took her and raped her.
~ Genesis 34:1–2 (NIV) ~

Seven Years Later

Spring had come to Shechem. Leah's wet feet slipped inside her dew-soaked sandals as she climbed the limestone terraces on her way to the fields. Calling her sons with the ram's horn to break their fast would be easier, but Shechem's citizens had complained years ago about the shepherd prince's early mornings. So Leah's early-morning trek through their growing fruit trees and vineyard had become her sacrifice of praise. Inhaling the fresh scent of almond blossoms, she communed with her God, recounting yesterday's victories and presenting today's challenges. Glimpsing the high stone walls of Shechem, she tamped down frustrations that threatened her peace. Close neighbors had been both blessing and curse.

"Come!" She stood at the corner of a pasture and waved her dishcloth, gaining Reuben's attention. His shrill whistle alerted his brothers. The undershepherds would keep watch until Jacob's sons returned, and then the hired men ate with their families. The system had worked for nearly seven years, and Jacob's livestock had almost doubled, getting fat on lush green pastures.

Leah waited for her boys, who buzzed around her like bees near a hive. Men now, they'd always be her boys—*all* of them— laughing and poking, joking and shoving.

"Gad thought he saw a lion and wet himself." Simeon, always stirring the pot, taunted Zilpah's oldest.

"I did not!"

"Didn't see a lion?" Naphtali shoved him. "Or didn't wet yourself?"

Leah grabbed Gad's waist and pulled him close. "Enough teasing. Gaddy is braver than all of you. He was the first to try my hyssop bread yesterday." All of them groaned and made vile noises. Even Gad nudged her away, and Leah laughed with them. "So I should leave the cooking to Zilpah and Bilhah?"

With their taunts now aimed at her, Gad mouthed a silent *thank you* as they neared camp.

Rachel and Dinah knelt together at the bread oven as usual. Gone was the day Dinah ever helped Leah make and serve the gruel. Dinah chose Rachel now—in everything. At sixteen, Leah's grown-up girl was beautiful, opinionated, and as unpredictable as waves on a sea. When Dinah leaned over and whispered something in Rachel's ear, Rachel covered a gasp and giggled like a friend hearing a secret. Leah hadn't the luxury of friendship with her only daughter.

Reuben's strong arm slid around her shoulder. "Someday, she'll realize you're better than Imma Rachel." While the other boys sat in their circle around Jacob, her firstborn lingered a moment longer to whisper, "Remember how awful your sons were at sixteen?"

She kissed his cheek and winked. "You're still awful."

"What?" He twirled her in a circle, nearly knocking the bread basket from Rachel's hands.

"Enough nonsense!" Jacob growled.

Reuben set her down gently and returned her wink. He'd grown accustomed to his abba's grumbling. Leah returned to the gruel pot to begin serving her men. Rachel and Dinah brought over two baskets of bread, but the moment Rachel caught a whiff of gruel, her pallor turned a sickly gray. She shoved her basket at Dinah and ran toward the waste pile. She was pregnant again. Leah knew, but Rachel hadn't told their husband. Dinah looked at Leah like a male lamb on castration day. Did she think Leah would tell Jacob? Had Rachel so successfully turned the girl against her true imma?

She should have insisted Dinah stay with Zilpah and Bilhah to work the wool, but Rachel had mentioned to Jacob that she needed an assistant. Leah allowed Dinah to become her apprentice. Shechem's women spoke highly of Rachel's midwifery, and word traveled fast. When Leah heard she incorporated Inanna in her practice, Leah forbade Dinah to continue.

"But I'm teaching her about the Canaanite goddess Asherah too," Rachel said. "She shares many traits with Harran's mother goddess. Isn't it important that we come to know the gods in whose land we live?"

Jacob heard them shouting and stepped in. "Our Dinah knows Yahweh's truth," he said, brushing Leah's cheek. "She's like you, too smart to be taken in by false gods." Dinah had hugged him and shot invisible daggers at Leah with her bright blue eyes.

Rachel returned from behind the tents, Deborah's arm around her waist. The old nursemaid was more faithful than the finest herd dog. No matter how weary she was, she always found the strength to tend the woman she'd helped bring into the world.

One more reason Leah envied her sister.

"Any trouble overnight?" Jacob's daily question to his sons received the same one-word answers. "We'll need to move the lambing ewes closer to the tents," he said to Reuben. "Divide your brothers into groups of three for lambing and rotate watch in the lambing tent with the undershepherds."

"Will all eleven of your sons take their turn at the watch?" Reuben's tone dripped with challenge. Jacob's sons kept heads bowed, shoveling in bread and cheese to fill the silence.

Jacob, however, set aside his meal and leaned closer to the firstborn, seated at his right. "Joseph will continue to learn the merchant and trade skills of our camp." He paused. "Do you have a problem with that?"

Leah had seen bitterness against Joseph taking root in all Jacob's sons, but Reuben had reached his limit. He raised his head slowly, and when he drew breath to speak,

Leah intervened. "I think Dinah should learn my job as Joseph is learning yours, Jacob." Leah's abrupt declaration drew every eye. "Bilhah and Zilpah trained her to work the wool. Rachel taught her midwifery. I think it's time I taught her my skills."

Jacob, caught off guard by the request, set his focus on Rachel. But before he could answer, Dinah fell to her knees beside him. "Please, Abba, I don't want to keep records. I like midwifery, and Imma Rachel says I'm good at it."

Rachel stepped to her side. "She's a great help to me now that she's learned most of the herb combinations, and—" Placing a hand on her belly, she added, "When our second child arrives, Dinah will be able to continue until I've recovered enough to return to my duties."

Jacob leaped to his feet and engulfed his dear wife in a heartrending hug. Leah bowed her head, knowing her arguments were mute. But the determination of an imma's love still forced words from her lips. "Dinah is *my* daughter, Jacob, not Rachel's."

It sounded petty and pathetic, causing Jacob to release Rachel. "She is *our* daughter, and you have raised her well." Turning then to Dinah, he cupped her chin and spoke to her. "You are capable, intelligent, and compassionate, Dinah, but you must also show yourself wise as you are given more responsibility. You may continue your work with your imma Rachel."

"Thank you, Abba!" She hugged him and then Rachel.

Leah turned toward the empty pot of gruel to hide. Jacob stood too close behind her, placed his chin on her shoulder, and whispered, "It's been too long since you've visited my tent. Perhaps Rachel wouldn't mind if you came tonight—"

Leah spun and faced her startled husband. "Have I ever refused you, Jacob?"

"Uh…no. I…don't—"

"Then take heed to this moment, Husband. You should have Rachel tonight." She shoved him aside and marched to her tent before saying something she'd regret.

Leah lay on her sleeping mat, alone in a tent too big for one person. As expected, Jacob refused to sleep with Rachel now that she was with child again. But since both he and Dinah were angry with Leah, Joseph would share his abba's tent and Dinah chose to sleep with Rachel. Leah would sleep alone. *Yahweh, will I be alone forever?*

Perhaps it would be better if Jacob never called her to his tent again. Remembering the closeness they shared during Rachel's first pregnancy, she couldn't imagine opening her heart to him again. *It hurts more, Yahweh, every time he tosses me aside.*

Dawn's light already cast its glow through the splits in her dark tent. She'd slept later than usual after watching the moon move through its courses. With a languid stretch, she stood and slipped on her robe with a woolen covering, hoping there was no frost on the fruit trees. Most mornings, she was grateful for her walk to the fields to call their sons. This morning, she would need the sacrifice of praise to remind her Yahweh's power extended even to immas and their daughters.

Yahweh, give me words to make peace with Dinah.

Leah slipped out of her tent and found the camp blooming like spring flowers. Some of the servants' children were playing near a large oak tree, and Jacob had gathered some of his shepherds around him in lively conversation. Perhaps today would be a good day after all.

When she arrived at the central fire, the gruel had already been started, but Rachel sat at the bread oven alone. "Where's Dinah this morning?" Leah tried to sound casual, asking on her way to the fields.

"I sent her on an errand." She answered without looking up.

Leah halted and turned toward her evasive sister. "An errand so early?"

"Mm-hmm." Rachel turned the small circles on the clay dome, still refusing to meet her gaze.

"Rachel." No answer. "Rachel!"

Leah reached for her arm, but her sister stood and stepped away. "Leave me alone, Leah!"

"What's going on?" Jacob called out, taking long strides toward them.

"Nothing," Leah said, eyes fixed on Rachel's. "I simply asked Rachel where she sent *our* daughter so early this morning."

Jacob arrived and stood between his two wives, hands extended, as if any moment they might begin clawing at each other.

"I thought she was going to hit me, Jacob." Rachel bowed her head, dabbing at her eyes.

Leah hadn't considered hitting her until that moment. She rolled her eyes at their husband. "Have I ever hit anyone?"

He pulled Leah close and whispered, "You know how emotional—"

"I can hear you." Rachel folded her arms and glared at them both.

"Why not just tell me where you sent Dinah?" Leah folded her arms, matching her sister's stubbornness. Jacob turned to Rachel and lifted his brows. Leah would have danced at the victory if Zilpah played her timbrel.

"I sent her into the city to collect silver from a merchant." Rachel lifted her chin, daring Leah to object.

As the avalanche of *what ifs* battered Leah's heart, she began to tremble. "You. Sent. *My* daughter. Alone. Into Shechem."

"Stop." Jacob lifted his hand. His face was the shade of ripe grapes. "Call the boys to eat, Leah. I'll deal with this."

"No, Jacob. She can't just—"

"I agree." He turned and drew her face close, speaking in a barely controlled whisper. "She's put Dinah in danger. It won't happen again. Do you hear me? I'll go get our daughter myself." He stared into her eyes, waiting to release her until she nodded. Then, kissing her gently, he said, "Go. Call our sons to break their fast."

When he released her, Leah didn't dare look at anyone. Or speak. Or even think. She obeyed her husband and placed one foot in front of the other, trudging the path up the terraces to the fields where her sons were waiting. Her heart held no praise, but the birds still sang. Her mind raced with fear, but her face turned toward the sky. *Yahweh, how can I praise You when I have nothing but fear and torment to offer? Protect my Dinah in a city that holds too many dangers to count for one as young and lovely as she.*

The boys realized something was amiss the moment they saw her. "Abba said he'd find her," she said, hoping he'd be gone when they returned to camp.

He wasn't.

Seated on his cushion at the central fire, Jacob had already started his bowl of gruel when his sons arrived. Rachel was nowhere in sight, which meant Bilhah baked the bread—and burned it.

Leah ran the last twenty paces. "Why haven't you gone already?" Her tone sounded more accusatory than she intended.

Jacob didn't turn to answer but continued spooning gruel into his mouth. Joseph sat on his left—as usual—but his head was bowed. Gruel untouched. Rachel emerged from her tent, dressed in her finest robe, a shoulder bag slung across her body.

Jacob looked up slowly from his gruel. "I'll accompany Rachel to the city and escort them home."

Rachel stood ten paces away, eyes swollen and weeping. "I've told you, Jacob. You need not accompany me. I sent Dinah to collect silver from Nebal the merchant, whose wife delivered last week. It's a simple matter—"

"If it's a simple matter," Leah shouted, "where's my daughter?"

Jacob shot to his feet, eyes sparking with warning. "Enough, Leah." He walked to Rachel, tenderly supporting her elbow. "Please don't upset yourself, my love. I merely want to see you and Dinah safely home."

"But it's humiliating." She pulled away, hysterical. "If Prince *Jacob* marches into Shechem to demand his daughter *and* his silver—don't you see?" Looking up then, her doe eyes filled with more tears. "One morning of silly panic can ruin seven years of my hard-won respect among the Shechemites."

Jacob sighed and kneaded the back of his neck—and Leah knew. Rachel had won. Leah hurried to the pot of gruel to hide her tears.

"All right," she heard Jacob say. "But if you haven't returned by midmorning, I'm coming to Shechem to find you both."

Rachel stuffed some burnt bread into her bag and hurried on her way. Leah looked over her shoulder and saw Jacob walking toward the pastures. Their sons ate in silence, and Reuben kissed her cheek before returning to the fields.

Joseph waited beside her. "I'm worried too."

Leah pulled him into a fierce embrace and felt his shaking. "We'll keep busy until your imma returns with your sister." When she released him, he quickly turned away, but not before she glimpsed his tears.

After gathering her writing utensils, she and Joseph began their morning routine without Jacob. While checking her records with the previous month's livestock counts, they noted significant discrepancies. Jacob would blame her. Skewed numbers. Faulty sums. Of course, he'd never believe Joseph could make a mistake. Not Rachel's perfect son. *Stop it, Leah.* It wasn't Joseph's fault Jacob treated him like a fragile Persian vase.

She laid her arm over his shoulder. "Let's go to the fields and recount the animals—flock by flock and herd by herd. It will keep us busy while we wait." They met Jacob on their way to the fields, and he joined their morning inspection. As they chatted with the shepherds, whether in camp or afield, all three kept watch on the path to Shechem. By midday, they returned to camp, put numbers to parchment, and determined the discrepancies were valid. Had the animals been lost or stolen? Was one or more of their shepherds cheating them?

When Leah glanced at the city path and saw only one silhouette approaching, the livestock shortages seemed inconsequential. She covered a gasp. Jacob and Joseph followed her gaze and raced to Rachel before she reached camp. The edges of Leah's vision blurred, listening so hard it hurt. But she couldn't hear anything. Blinking away tears, she tried to look away—but couldn't. She watched the grave news unfold in Rachel's tears, and it crescendoed in Jacob's soul-splitting wail. When her husband fell to his knees, Leah knew. Dinah was dead.

Joseph knelt to comfort his abba, but Rachel stood over them both, scanning the fields until she found Leah. Locking eyes, she began a determined march toward her older sister. With every step, Leah hated her more. She would never forgive her for Dinah's death. Never.

Five paces away, Rachel stopped, eyes burrowing into Leah's soul. "Dinah is safe. Married to Prince Shechem. She'll be queen someday, Leah." Looking over her shoulder, she leaned closer and lowered her voice so Jacob and Joseph wouldn't hear. "What's so terrible about that?"

Anger and hate roiled inside, and Leah lunged at her sister. Rachel dodged the attack and ran, leaving Leah on her knees. She emptied her stomach. "Noooo!" She rolled to her side and shrieked, "Noooo!" Squeezing her eyes shut, she fought the images playing on her mind of her daughter's defilement, while she and Jacob and Joseph did nothing—nothing—to save her. *Yahweh, how could You let my only daughter fall into the hands of a pagan?*

Gentle hands slipped beneath her, lifting her, cradling her. "Shhh, Imma." *Joseph's voice.* "I'm with you."

She let him carry her, burying her face against his shoulder as they entered camp. She didn't want to see anyone. Didn't want to admit the tragedy. The reality of their loss. He bowed to enter a tent and set her on a mat. She turned toward the wall and curled into a tight ball, silent.

"May I stay with you?" he whispered. "Abba ran to the pastures, and I don't want to be with Imma Rachel right now."

"Of course," she said, rolling over to look at him. The pain on his young face shattered her heart into smaller pieces. She sat up and opened her arms. "You are my son, Joseph, and you may stay as long as you wish."

He shook with heaving sobs, and their tears fell until late that night. Neither of them was hungry, so Zilpah left two full water skins inside the tent flap and left. They shared fond memories of the twins' childhood, of Dinah's strong will, of their broken hearts. And they slept. Neither of them sure how they'd live another day without Dinah in their world.

CHAPTER SIXTEEN

When Jacob heard that his daughter Dinah had been defiled,
his sons were in the fields with his livestock;
so he did nothing about it until they came home.
Then Shechem's father Hamor went out to talk with Jacob.
Meanwhile, Jacob's sons had come in from the fields
as soon as they heard what had happened.
~ Genesis 34:5–7 (NIV) ~

Jacob lay beneath a sprawling oak, having watched the moon move across the sky. It had been years since he'd spent a night in the fields. The effort to breathe overwhelmed him. Everything inside him felt numb—except regret. Why hadn't he gone with Rachel to retrieve Dinah? Why hadn't he gone looking for them both at midmorning instead of counting livestock?

Perhaps one more emotion lingered. Dread. The thought of telling his sons that he'd failed to protect their sister was worse than death. *Rape.* That was the crime Hamor's son committed against Jacob's only daughter. Rachel said Dinah went willingly to the prince's chamber, but what does a sixteen-year-old girl know? Prince Shechem was twice her size and had a silver tongue. What pagan rites were performed at a Shechemite marriage?

How could Hamor allow his son to steal Jacob's daughter—no contract or betrothal or bride price? Had Shechemites turned into Hittites, shunning courtesy and custom?

More emotions surfaced. Rage warred with sorrow as he imagined his little girl pleading for help—with no one there to save her. Burying his face in his hands, Jacob released decades of fury, letting sobs rack his body. Falling on his side, he groaned at the pain. *Why, Yahweh? Why my beautiful Dinah? Is this judgment for my sins? Punishment? Then why not punish me?*

No angel came to wrestle. No answer came at all.

"Answer me!" Jacob struggled to his knees and shook his fist at the sky. "Tell me what You want!" His fist fell to his side in the silence. He already knew. Pressing his face into the dirt, he pictured Leah's face and the disappointment he saw in her eyes every day. When he'd met Esau, she'd challenged him to obey Yahweh and go to Abba's camp in Beersheba. Jacob refused. Too enamored with his importance and growing wealth, *Prince Jacob* made a life in Sukkoth. He'd earned the respect of a king with the land purchase in Shechem—or so he thought. But at what cost?

Now my only daughter is a pagan princess, and I have failed You so thoroughly, Yahweh.

He sat down heavily, scanning his rolling pastureland and the livestock roaming it in the growing light. Worthless—all of it—unless his sons grasped the wealth of Yahweh's Covenant. Leah knew it. She'd carried the privilege more reverently than Jacob. Pounding his fists against his forehead, he cursed himself for a lifetime of mistakes. *Yahweh, forgive. Yahweh, save.*

He would tell his sons about Dinah this morning when they returned from the fields. He pushed himself to his feet with the staff he'd made in Mahanaim. His hip was stiffer than usual this morning, another reminder of his failure to become *Israel* instead of Jacob. He started toward the path leading to camp, wondering if Leah would tell his sons before he had the chance. Did she hate him for letting this happen to their daughter? He owed her more than a simple apology. How could he ever make up for all the failures?

His sandal slipped on a rock, twisting his hip, and he winced. Somehow the pain was more tolerable today—maybe because the ache in his heart was unbearable.

With his next step, he looked toward the east and saw his shepherd sons running toward him. Jacob felt the blood drain from his face. *They know.*

Levi, the quickest, arrived first. "Abba, have you heard?"

"Heard what?" Maybe they meant something else.

"Dinah." Reuben panted when he and the others caught up. "Prince Shechem defiled her."

"How did you hear if you were in the fields—as you should have been?"

His firstborn's jaw tightened, but Simeon shoved him aside. "One of the undershepherds came back from a night in the city and heard the rumor."

"It's not a rumor," Jacob said, watching the truth do its harm. "Shechem took your sister into his chamber, raped her, and called her his wife."

The range of emotions he'd felt appeared on their faces, but it was impulsive Simeon who voiced his intentions. "We'll kill him."

"Don't be foolish," Jacob said, a chill raising gooseflesh on his arms. Of all his sons, Simeon was the one who might do it. "You'd bring down Hamor's wrath, and possibly more Canaanite towns, on our camp. We must deal shrewdly—"

"How can *Israel* not be outraged?" Reuben's tone was accusing. "Shechem has shamed Dinah—shamed *us*. The time for dealing shrewdly is over."

The other boys murmured their approval, each word like a blade cutting Jacob deeper. "What good will violence bring? Can it make your sister pure again? Can it turn back time?" He stared into the faces as different as his speckled and spotted flocks, but the condemnation in their eyes was the same—and he would endure it no longer. "You believe you can lead this family better? Fine. *You* will decide how we proceed with Hamor and Shechem." He pushed through their circle and didn't even acknowledge their shock. Let them feel the weight of leadership. Perhaps they'd be slower to attack.

Anger propelled him to Leah's tent. He must tell her the boys knew. He slapped the tent flap aside and nearly bumped noses with Joseph. "What... Why are you—"

"Is there more news on Dinah?" Leah stood beside Rachel's son.

"No... I..." He reached for Joseph. "I'll find a way to make this right—"

"How, Abba?" He recoiled. "Will my sister ever be the same?"

"Joseph, we'll—" But Joseph pushed Jacob away and ran out of the tent.

He started to follow, but Leah caught his arm. "Leave him alone. Joseph needs time to wrestle with his faith. We all do."

Jacob searched her weary features, his throat constricting. "I envy your wisdom."

She bowed her head. "I speak only from my heart."

It was then that he noticed the dust in her hair and her torn neckline—signs of mourning the dead. He grabbed her arms. "Our daughter isn't dead, Leah."

"She might as well be." As she lifted her blue eyes, the sparkle of life he'd at first hated—and then admired—was gone. "If she must live as a pagan in Shechem's palace, the Dinah that Joseph and I know will wither and die."

Her strength awed him. Her faith inspired him. And in that moment, Jacob faced the most terrifying possibility of his life. "Leah, I can't…" She turned away, and with a sob, he reached for her hand. "Please don't hate me. I need you."

She pulled him into her arms. "I could never hate you, Jacob ben Isaac. You are the husband I love and the one who taught me of Yahweh. You are my life.…" Her words trailed into tears, and they wept together, shutting out the rest of the world. How could she still love him? *Yahweh, my Leah is among Your greatest gifts.*

When they'd both calmed, Jacob took her hand. "Come, Wife. I've left our sons in charge of the camp. You and I need time alone." He led her toward his tent. She submitted to his guidance, plodding like a blind woman with no strength. He held open his tent flap, and she entered ahead of him. He bent to enter, but before he stood to full height, Leah screeched.

"You!" She flew into a rage at Rachel, who had been waiting in the corner.

They slapped, kicked, and screamed. "Stop! Both of you! Stop this!" Jacob tried to separate them but received blows from them both. Desperate, he grabbed their robes and shoved them apart. "I said *enough!*" They leveled stares at each other, seething at best, murderous at worst. All three dripped blood, Rachel from her nose, Leah from a deep scratch on her cheek, and Jacob wiped it from his lip.

"*You* stole my daughter." Leah spat at her sister.

"It's not my fault." Rachel wiped her nose and looked at Jacob. "How could I have known Prince Shechem would—"

"I've told you for years he couldn't be trusted!" Leah shouted.

"Abba!" Reuben slapped the tent flap aside. "King Hamor approaches. What should we do?"

He wanted to say, *You decide, since you and your brothers seemed so sure of yourselves.* But he was the patriarch. Hamor would only speak with Jacob.

"He's broken covenant." Leah slapped Jacob's hand off her robe. "Hamor said his people would be of one heart and mind with us, but his son broke that promise."

"He's the king," Rachel said, caressing Jacob's hand. "Dinah will have wealth and honor, my love. Why stir the anger of an influential Canaanite king?"

Glaring at his wives, he felt like a mouse caught between a lion and a bear. Of course he was furious with Hamor's son, but Shechem had weapons that his clan didn't have. Dare he begin a war with a king of Canaan?

"Jacob." Leah gently turned his chin to face her. "Get Dinah back and take us away from here. Please. You are the Covenant bearer. Consider Yahweh and our daughter, not trade or livestock, and God will protect us."

Her words were like salt in his wounds. Even in the darkest moment, she was more righteous than he. More proof that he should let someone else make decisions today. "Go, Reuben." He gestured toward the coming king. "I'll speak with Hamor, but you and your brothers will decide our family's response to Prince Shechem's actions."

"But you're the patriarch!" Leah caught his arm with his first step.

He pulled her close, breathing out the words. "I will show hospitality to King Hamor, and my wives will serve us while our sons and I negotiate."

The soft sadness in her expression turned hard as stone. "As you wish, Husband." She shoved him away and turned to Rachel. "*You* will work as hard as the rest of us—no matter how sick you are with his child."

She marched out like a soldier to battle, and Jacob realized then—he should have let Leah negotiate with King Hamor.

CHAPTER SEVENTEEN

Because their sister Dinah had been defiled, Jacob's sons replied deceitfully
as they spoke to Shechem and his father Hamor.
~ Genesis 34:13 (NIV) ~

Hamor had come with enough men to discourage retaliation and a wagon full of treasure. Leah fumed silently
while she and the other women began grinding grain and preparing platters of food to feed them. Rachel took her place at
the bread oven, her nurse Deborah beside her, while Leah
directed the others to their tasks.

Jacob and his sons met the king's contingent on the north
side of camp. Six royal guards surrounded Hamor after he dismounted his black stallion. "Jacob, my brother, have you heard
the happy news?" He approached, arms open wide, pretending
his son hadn't treated Dinah like a prostitute.

"This is not our way, Hamor." Jacob stood at the edge of
camp, arms at his sides, with eleven sons as his guard.

Hamor's gait slowed, his soldiers tightening in formation.
His smile remained. "Please, my friend. Sit and talk with me."
Placing an arm over Jacob's shoulder, he motioned to the cen-
tral fire. "I think you'll feel differently after I've explained."

With a single nod, Jacob fell in step beside the king. Jacob's eleven sons trailed behind him and the king's guards followed their regent. The processional passed the three-sided cooking tent, where Leah and the others prepared the morning meal.

Leah opened a wineskin and spit in their best wine. She'd save it for the king and his escort.

Watching the men settle around the fire, she glimpsed Rachel at the oven—staring at her with a wry grin. *She saw me spit in the wine!* Mortified, Leah considered dumping it out, but then Rachel sneezed into the bowl of dough while hiding behind her head covering. Leah turned away to hide her shock. They'd planned to serve the fresh bread to Hamor and his escort while giving the leftovers to Jacob and his sons. Why had Rachel added her vile ingredient to the king's bread when she seemed fine with the marriage?

After filling glasses with the tainted wine, Leah placed them on a tray and stole another glance at her sister. Rachel was waiting with a broad smile and covered a chuckle—as if they were children playing tricks in Abba's courtyard. Leah found nothing worthy of a smile this morning. Leah's impulse to spit in the wine was childish but pure in its hatred. Rachel's antics were just shadows of life in Laban's house, trying to rekindle a friendship by hating the same enemy.

"The yogurt, fruit, nuts, and cheese are ready," Zilpah said, standing with Bilhah beside Leah. "Should we begin serving?" The women held platters and bowls in both hands.

Leah picked up her tray of wine and grabbed a pitcher of water with the other hand. "We'll serve our guests first, of course. Rachel's bread will be ready any moment, and they'll receive our best wine. This morning's decisions determine Dinah's future. King Hamor and his men deserve everything we place before them."

"My son is quite taken with your daughter," Hamor was saying as Leah set aside the pitcher to begin placing the wine before her guests. "He considers Dinah his wife already, and the queen and I believe it's a good match, Jacob. Your tribe can intermarry with my family and Shechem's nobles. Buy more land. Trade among us."

Leah stood over her husband, staring. Would he glance her way to see the warning? Esau married Canaanite women and was considered a murderer by Isaac and Rebekah because of his wives' pagan worship. How could the Covenant bearer even consider allowing his sons to marry pagans?

"Let me introduce my sons," he said instead. "On my right is Reuben, my firstborn and lead shepherd." He continued in order of their birth, as they were seated around the fire, refusing to look at her—or to rescue Dinah. Rage surged through Leah, so she set a cup of her specially prepared wine before her husband as well as their guests.

Before Jacob reached Joseph with his introductions, a commotion near Hamor's horses drew everyone's attention. Raised voices and the animals' unrest drew Jacob and the king to their feet, trying to see over those seated around the fire. Suddenly, Prince Shechem emerged from the north side of camp.

At the sight of him, dreadful images played in Leah's mind of her daughter's forced wedding. Last night's defilement of the girl she'd trained in Yahweh's laws. Leah picked up the pitcher of water, wishing she'd had a weapon instead. She would have used it.

"Excuse me." Alarm shadowed Hamor's face as he raced toward his son. Royal guards surrounded both regents as they converged on one another fifty paces from the fire. Hamor's strangled whisper could still be heard despite his attempt to quell it. "I told you I'd take care of this. Go back to the city right now."

"I'll not hide behind walls." Shechem pushed past his father's attempts to stop him, continuing toward the fire. "I'm not ashamed of marrying the woman I love." Halting barely a single pace from Jacob, Shechem bowed to one knee. "I come to beg favor in your eyes. I'll pay whatever bride price you name because your daughter is a treasure beyond the wealth of any kingdom. I love her and must have her as my wife."

Leah trembled, barely able to hold back her cries of injustice. Shrieks of accusation riddled her tongue, but she bit her lip so hard she tasted blood.

Jacob's sons stood, several clenching their fists. Hamor flanked his son now, features strained, but Prince Shechem seemed oblivious to the danger. Looking up when the silence stretched long, he reached for Jacob's hand and pressed it against his forehead. "Please, sir. Your daughter has captured my heart. I am yours to command." He bowed his head again and waited like a servant for Jacob's verdict.

Leah held her breath. *Please, Jacob. Tell him Yahweh won't allow it. Please.*

Removing his hand from Shechem's grasp, Jacob turned to King Hamor. "I'm an old man, King Hamor. Your son speaks of a future for the next generation of my family, so I believe it wise that the next generation answer him." He motioned toward the sons he'd begun introducing. "I think it best for you, Prince Shechem, to sit beside your abba and negotiate directly with my sons."

Shechem fairly leaped to his feet and took the place of honor at his father's right hand, whispering something indecipherable to Hamor. When the two sat down with their guards again, they waited quietly for Jacob to resume introductions.

Jacob began the negotiations. "As my firstborn, Reuben will speak for his brothers."

He nodded to Reuben, who nodded respectfully to Shechem, as if he'd spoken to a thousand kings. "Though we're pleased you realize Dinah's priceless worth as our only sister, Prince Shechem, we can't in good conscience give her to you as a wife. It would be shameful for any of our women to marry a man who isn't circumcised." Leah felt a surge of pride. Her son had spoken with the courage that had escaped her husband. Dinah would be home before midday. *Thank You, Yahweh!*

"However," Reuben continued, and Leah's heart seized, "if you become like us by circumcising *all* the males in Shechem, we will not only agree to let Dinah remain in your palace as your wife, but our clan will also intermarry with other Shechemites and settle among you." Leah dropped the clay pitcher, and it shattered. Water splashed all over Jacob, Reuben, and the prince.

"I believe Leah is feeling unwell," Jacob said, motioning for Zilpah to assist. "She should rest in her tent."

"No!" Leah said, shoving Zilpah away.

"Mistress Leah." Shechem stood. His eyes bored into hers, and it seemed the whole camp stilled. "I didn't force myself on your daughter. She came willingly into the city, willingly to my chamber, and has willingly agreed to be my wife."

Before Leah could call him a liar, Reuben stood between them. "If you—and all the men of Shechem—refuse to be circumcised, we'll take our sister and leave Shechem. The land we've purchased will, of course, remain our possession, but we'll use it only for summer grazing. We'll do the bulk of our trading farther south."

The pride Leah had felt drained away like the water from the broken pitcher seeping into the ground. The men in her family would sell Dinah's life—no, Yahweh's Covenant—for the price of a few foreskins.

Prince Shechem glanced down at his father, lifting both brows in silent question. Hamor hesitated for less than a heartbeat before an almost imperceptible nod gave assent.

"It is agreed!" Shechem stretched out his right arm, and Reuben locked wrists to seal their agreement. "I'll speak with the elders at the gate today," the prince promised.

Leah stumbled back, and this time she let Zilpah steady her. Feeling nauseous, she left the sordid world of men behind her.

Three days had passed since the men of her household betrayed Dinah. Leah hadn't left her tent. She couldn't face her sons or Jacob. She could barely breathe or lift her head off the lamb's wool square on her sleeping mat. Zilpah had tended her, bringing food twice a day and emptying her waste pot. It was all she needed to survive—but did she want to?

Yahweh, are You there? Are You real? No answer. Had she believed a lie all these years? Had she taught Jacob's children of a God who didn't exist? Was Yahweh no different than the stone statues Rachel and the slave-wives trusted?

She shook her head, dislodging the blasphemous thoughts. *Forgive me, El-Roi—the God Who Sees. I know You're real.* She'd felt His presence. Experienced His approval each time He gave her a son—and then her daughter. She'd seen His light scorch the road and believed Jacob wrestled with His Angel. *But where were You when Dinah needed a protector?* Wasn't Yahweh in Shechem's chamber? Or had the prince told the truth—and Dinah went willingly to his chamber? Did she love him?

"Leah?" Rachel's voice outside her tent brought Leah to her feet.

"Stay out."

The flap opened, revealing a moonlit night and her sister's red-rimmed eyes. "You'll want to hear what I have to say."

"I want nothing—"

"Simeon and Levi plan to rescue Dinah."

"What?" Leah covered a gasp. "Just the two of them?"

She nodded. "Joseph overheard them talking. They took swords."

"No!" Leah pressed fists against her eyes. "How many children must I lose before Jacob leaves this place?"

"Leah."

"What!" she shouted, glaring at the sister she hated.

Rachel's face twisted with emotion. "I'm so sorry."

She covered her sobs, but Leah refused to console her. How many times had she begged forgiveness only to repeat the same hurtful actions? Leah turned her back. She didn't have the energy to comfort her sister when three of her children could die in Shechem tonight.

"It's all my fault," Rachel whined. "I should never have let Dinah go into the city alone. You warned me about the prince, but I didn't think he would..." Her words died without Leah's acknowledgment. "I'm sorry."

Tears stung Leah's eyes too, but only the sounds of Rachel's sniffling and Leah's silent blame filled the tent. Why did Leah feel guilty for Rachel's grieving? Everything she'd said was true. It was her fault. She shouldn't have let Dinah go to the city alone. But Jacob hadn't spoken to Rachel or called her to his tent since the morning they discovered Dinah was gone. Was he angry about Dinah or continuing his caution with Rachel's long-awaited pregnancy? Would Leah ever reach the point where she didn't care?

Leah whirled on her sister. "I don't want to hear your apologies. I want to know more about Simeon and Levi."

Rachel wiped her face and gestured to Leah's mat. "May I?" Leah nodded permission, and they sat across from each other. "Joseph told me the brothers never expected Shechem to agree to circumcision. It was only a ploy to get Dinah back, but after he agreed, the boys were certain the city elders would stop it. When the whole town was circumcised three days ago, Simeon and Levi began talking about sneaking in to rescue Dinah."

Leah shook her head, disgusted. "Why didn't Joseph tell you sooner so we could stop them?"

"Simeon and Levi are always blustering about something." A defensive spark hardened her tone. "How was Joseph to know they'd actually *do* it?"

"You're right." Plus, Joseph wanted to win his big brothers' approval. Tattling on them would have betrayed their trust. "Simeon and Levi are grown men now. I probably couldn't have stopped them anyway." Leah rolled her eyes and pulled her sister into a hug.

Rachel squeezed her so hard Leah thought her head might pop off, but for the first time in ages, it felt real. "I am sorry, you know," Rachel whispered. "I'd never do anything to hurt our Dinah."

"I know." They held each other in the silence until the night air carried a strange dissonance. "Do you hear that?" Leah released her sister and tilted her head, concentrating harder.

"What?" Rachel's brows furrowed. The sound rose to something familiar, and their eyes met in a moment of panic. Both leaped to their feet, ran outside, and met Jacob coming from his tent. Looking toward the city, they heard rising wails and saw the sickening glow of their sons' wrath.

Shechem was burning.

CHAPTER EIGHTEEN

The sons of Jacob came upon the dead bodies and looted the city
where their sister had been defiled.
They seized their flocks and herds and donkeys
and everything else of theirs in the city and out in the fields.
They carried off all their wealth and all their women and children,
taking as plunder everything in the houses.
~ Genesis 34:27–29 (NIV) ~

Jacob's whole camp stood watch as the moon moved across the sky. Leah and Rachel flanked their husband with Bilhah and Zilpah beside their mistresses. The remaining nine sons of Jacob pounded the ground with their swords, demanding to rush into the city to defend Simeon and Levi. Thankfully, regaining his authority, Jacob refused them and silenced all dissent.

"They're only two men against a whole city!" Judah pleaded.

Reuben spoke before Jacob. "Let their blood be on their own heads." Leah covered a sob, not sure which hurt worse—the thought of losing three children in Shechem or the irreparable damage these days had caused. *Yahweh, forgive. Yahweh, save.*

Just before dawn, something stirred in the tall grass north of their camp. Leah pointed in silent terror, but the men of their camp had already started toward the disturbance. Swords drawn. Crouched. Ready for the fight. As the sky changed from amethyst to amber, the noisy approach of two ox-drawn carts grew nearer. Curiosity and hope drove Leah into the fray, passing armed servants and shepherds until she reached her husband in the lead.

"Get back!" he hissed, but by then she'd seen the drivers.

"Simeon! Levi!" She ran to her boys, tall grass tangling around her legs. Laughing and crying, she could hardly believe her eyes. "I should take you over my knee, you two—" But she gasped when she was close enough to see them clearly. They were soaked in blood. There wasn't a space larger than her fingertip without its stain. Their eyes, empty and cold, stood out like white beacons in a red sea.

Somber and silent, her sons didn't acknowledge her as they approached or even glance at her when they drove past. Both carts jostled and jingled, full of gold and silver, rugs and tapestries and—

"Dinah!" Leah's heart leaped into her throat. "Stop, Levi! Stop this instant!"

He obeyed without acknowledging her. Leah climbed over the bounty to the immeasurable treasure of her daughter. "She's bleeding! Rachel! Rachel, hurry!"

"It's not her blood." Simeon had halted his cart too. "It's Shechem's."

Leah looked into Dinah's eyes—distant and unseeing— and pressed her ear against the girl's chest. Her heartbeat was rapid and strong. "Dinah?" She shook her. No response. "Dinah, can you hear me? Say something. Dinah? Dinah!"

Clutching at her daughter, Leah fought those pulling her from the cart. Focused on Dinah, she tried to grip the wooden sideboards, but strong arms restrained her. "Imma, you must let us move her to your tent. Imma, look at me!" Reuben's wide eyes peered at her with concern. "You and Imma Rachel can tend Dinah while we decide what to do."

"What to do?" As if waking from a stupor, she relaxed in Reuben's arms. He released her to stand alone and then lifted his little sister from the cart as if she were a newborn. Rachel circled Leah's waist, and Bilhah and Zilpah fell in step.

"Your violence in Shechem will make us a stench to the Canaanites and Perizzites in this land," Jacob shouted at Simeon and Levi. The tremor in his voice betrayed fear as much as fury. "We're too few in number to defend ourselves if they band together against us."

Leah stopped and turned, praying her husband's prediction wasn't true. Surely, Simeon and Levi had considered such retaliation before placing their whole camp at the mercy of surrounding nations.

Levi and Simeon had climbed down from their carts and stood side by side, facing their abba. "Would you rather we do nothing?" Levi shouted.

"He treated our sister like a prostitute." Simeon's voice broke. Leah resumed her walk to the tents but heard her son's rant. "The whole city is like a ripe apple waiting for harvest, Abba. Must we remain simple farmers, or will we take what Yahweh has given us and seize the plunder of Shechem? We can take the virgins and children, who haven't spoken vows to their gods, as slaves, and adding the city's livestock will more than double..."

Leah pressed her hands over her ears to avoid hearing Jacob agree with the plan. He should teach their sons to be men of honor, Yahweh's righteous Covenant bearers. But she no longer lived with that delusion. Why hope and be disappointed? *He is less* Israel *now than when You named him, Yahweh!*

"Shechem! Shechem!" Dinah's sudden shrieks broke through Leah's frustration and replaced it with fear. Leah ran the final twenty paces, bursting into her tent. Dinah, wide-eyed, was flailing and kicking Reuben and Judah. Judah grabbed her waist and swung her to the floor. Reuben knelt over her, pinning her arms to a mat.

"What's happening?" Leah stood at the entrance with her sister-wives.

"She wants to go back to Shechem," Reuben said, using considerable strength to hold her. "She thinks the prince still lives."

Rachel grabbed Leah's hand and squeezed. "Please, Leah." She turned to face her, and Leah saw only compassion. "Though we called her defiled, I think Dinah truly loved him. We must treat her as a widow in mourning."

Dinah's fury suddenly ebbed to a stillness worse than death, and Reuben's horrified whisper drew Leah's attention. "Dinah?" He released her arms and listened for breath. When he looked at his imma, his cheeks were the color of the pearls around Dinah's neck. "She's still breathing, but—" He bolted to his feet, pressing thumb and finger against his eyes, while his face twisted with emotion.

"Go," Leah said to Judah. "Both of you."

Both her boys ran from the tent, grief unleashed in deep, bass sobs that faded in the distance.

Dinah's four immas surrounded her, kneeling close at her side. The girl stared at the ceiling now, unblinking. Dried tears stained her cheeks. Leah touched her hair, and she flinched. "Dinah, can you hear me?"

No answer.

"You're home, my love, where you belong."

Nothing.

Zilpah removed a small, stone image of the Canaanite goddess Asherah from her pocket. "Please, Leah," she whispered, "let me plead with the goddess of this land to forgive our neglect and bring healing—"

"Zilpah, if I see that atrocity again," Leah said, "I'll draw up your divorce papers and have Jacob sign them." Her lifelong friend slipped the stone idol back into her pocket.

"Leah." Rachel's voice quaked. "I have no herb or potion to help Dinah."

"She'll be fine after we leave Shechem. Once she's surrounded by her family and remembers what it's like to be home—"

"Shechem was my family," Dinah whispered. Then she turned her pale blue eyes on Leah. "This is not my home."

Rachel coaxed Dinah to drink a cup of poppy tea, and at last she slept—albeit fitfully. "Go tend to camp," Rachel said, when she caught Leah peeking outside. "Dinah has four capable immas, but our camp has only one Leah to organize it for departure."

Guilt had ridden her shoulders all morning. After Jacob's angry explosion, he'd retreated to the pastures, leaving his sons drunk on their newfound authority. Following Simeon's advice, they'd gathered every able man and sturdy cart to pillage Shechem. Now past midday, Jacob still hadn't returned from the fields, but their camp was bulging with wagonloads of treasure and even more frightened young women and children. She hurried to her supply chest to get a wax tablet and begin recording. Had anyone considered how they'd feed the extra people? Or how much food, tents, and supplies were needed to provide for a camp that had doubled in size—in a single day?

She noticed Joseph, with his wax tablet in hand, approaching Reuben who had just returned to camp with another wagonload of plunder. Of course, Joseph had thought of all those things. He began tabulating the contents as he walked toward Reuben's cart, and a measure of pride eased her worry. Joseph had seamlessly taken over her duties and was pointing at a gold chest. Reuben shouted, "No!" Rachel's son was a gifted administrator, but he held little sway with his brothers. Leah was too far away to hear their conversation, but it was evident Joseph lost the battle. Leah would meet with him before the evening meal and compare her records to get an accurate accounting of Jacob's growing wealth.

"But I found her!" Gad's voice, loud and angry, came from behind one of the tents.

Leah rushed toward the sound and arrived at the moment Levi's fist connected with his half brother's chin. Gad was on the ground, unconscious, before Leah could call out a warning.

"You may have found her," Levi said, standing over him, "but she'll be my wife."

"Levi ben Jacob!" Leah stabbed her fists at her hips.

Guilt shadowed his features. "He started it," Levi said, pointing at Gaddy. "Everyone agreed. The oldest brothers get first pick."

She glared. Silent. Hoping his conscience would do the work. Or did he still have a conscience after last night? "Is violence your answer to everything now?"

He stared back, belligerent, for little more than a heartbeat before his chin began to quiver. "I didn't know, Imma." Pressing the heels of his palms against his eyes, he bowed his head. "Simeon said we would kill Shechem. Only Shechem. But he went wild when the guards came in." Her man-child fell on her shoulders, releasing pent-up emotions from his horrific night.

Leah held him tightly, consoling but whispering the truth. "We all make mistakes, Levi, but only those who take responsibility for their actions are forgiven."

A sudden blast of the ram's horn interrupted the moment. Levi pulled away like he'd been stung and wiped his face. Gad stirred, shaking his head. He jumped to his feet when he saw Leah standing by Levi. "Imma Leah! I...uh...we, um."

"I know," she said. "You and Levi want the same girl, but are you sure she didn't refuse her gods just to save her life?"

Neither offered an answer. "Get to the fire, and we'll talk about how to choose a wife—calmly—after we hear what your abba has to say."

The boys exchanged a scornful look, and Leah followed them to the center of camp, where Jacob waited. Though he looked exhausted, his shoulders were lifted and his eyes brighter. He reminded Leah of the Jacob she'd known in Harran. His lips moved without a sound as he scanned those gathering. Like a good shepherd, he was counting his flock.

When at least one member from each family was present, he began his announcement. "Yahweh appeared to me in the field today, making it clear we're to leave here and settle in the city of Luz—the place I called *Beth-El*, House of God. It's the place Yahweh first appeared to me on my way to Harran. My God has been with me from that moment, wherever I've traveled, even though I haven't always been faithful to Him. But from this moment forward, every person in my household—slave or free—will worship Yahweh alone." A wave of whispers worked through the gathering, and Jacob lifted his hand for silence. "We will spend the rest of this day purging *all* foreign gods from this camp and purifying ourselves before we begin tomorrow's journey."

A subtle mutiny erupted where Deborah, Bilhah, and Zilpah stood with Rachel. "Husband," Rachel ventured, "may I speak with you privately?"

"Of course, in a moment."

She looked as if he'd thrown cold water in her face.

"We'll meet at the spreading oak at dusk," Jacob continued. "We'll bury every foreign god in this camp as well as anything of value that signifies your allegiance to them. If I find any pagan gods among you, the person owning them will be put out of the camp permanently." He turned to Rachel. "No matter your role or station. Any questions?" When no one spoke above a whisper, Jacob clapped his hands. "You're dismissed until we meet at dusk by the spreading oak."

No one lingered. Excited chatter escorted both those in support of Jacob's changes as well as those opposed. He covered the distance between himself and Rachel in three long strides. "Now, what is it you want to say?"

She turned a panicked plea toward Leah but found no sympathy. Neither the other wives nor Deborah dared defend her. Down on one knee, she pressed his hand to her forehead. "Jacob, please." Her tears were instantaneous.

Why not? They've always worked before. Leah watched, cynical but praying Jacob would finally stand firm.

"I know Yahweh gave me Joseph," Rachel admitted. "But as real and powerful as you believe He is, I know my gods are equally real and powerful. If you force us to betray them—and force all the Shechemite captives to betray their gods—you're essentially declaring a war of gods." She looked up then, cheeks streaked with tears. "Please, Jacob. The evil that's come upon us under your God's so-called protection is like an anthill compared to the mountains that will fall on us if we reject the ancient gods of Harran *and* Canaan."

Jacob pulled his hand away and stepped out of her reach. "You would be wise to worry more about disposing of your idols and less about superstitions. I assure you, Yahweh will keep us safe when we're obedient."

Rachel stood, wiped her cheeks, and aimed her eyes at him like weapons. "You may force my obedience, Jacob ben Isaac, but by all the gods I worship, you *will* be sorry."

CHAPTER NINETEEN

Now Deborah, Rebekah's nurse, died and was buried under
the oak outside Bethel.
~ Genesis 35:8 (NIV) ~

A fter every idol had been buried under the largest oak on Jacob's property, a pall settled over the camp. Wailing began shortly after and lasted long into the night. Rachel wept quietly by Dinah's mat. Even with a stronger dose of poppy tea, Dinah slept very little. Leah dabbed her daughter's forehead with a cold, wet cloth, but by the moon's zenith, Leah could endure Rachel's weeping no longer.

"Even if you don't believe in Yahweh, why can't you trust our husband's decision? I would think, of all people, *you* owe him loyalty and respect."

"Owe him?" Eyes wide in the lamplight, she scoffed. "I think we've both paid enough to our husband." She winced and pressed on her belly.

"Are you having contractions?" Leah didn't want to be concerned, but the sweat on Rachel's upper lip worried her.

"It's false labor."

"How far along are you?"

She narrowed her eyes. "Don't pretend to care."

"I've tried not to care for almost thirty years, and I still can't stop." Leah rolled her head around to stretch tired muscles and let her gaze rest on her sister's surprised expression. "Now, tell me how far along you are."

Rachel looked away. "By my calculations, five months."

"Why are you still so nauseous? Shouldn't that be done by now?"

"Every pregnancy is different, Leah. Perhaps a trained midwife knows more about birthing than you."

Leah stared at the familiar pinch of her sister's lips and laughed. "You still look twelve when you're angry."

Rachel tried to hide her grin. "You're ridiculous." With a sideways glance, she surrendered to a smile. But not for long. Brushing Dinah's hair from her forehead, she gazed at her with an imma's pure love. "I'm worried about our girl. I believe she and Shechem truly loved each other."

The declaration was like a dagger. "It doesn't matter, Rachel."

"It doesn't matter?" She stared in disbelief.

"He was a pagan." Leah's cheeks flamed. She wasn't ashamed of her faith in Yahweh but embarrassed that she couldn't express the reasons for her passion. How could she ever make Rachel understand?

"The heart chooses who it will love, Leah. Love is not ruled by a god."

"But only one God loves perfectly, Rachel, and can empower pure love."

She fell silent at Leah's words, seeming to chew them like sinewy meat in a stew. "When I began training Dinah as my apprentice, I insisted she pray to Inanna during the births. She refused and said she would return to weaving if she must invoke the aid of any god but Yahweh." Her words held both regret and respect as she lifted Dinah's hand to her lips and kissed it. "I can't imagine the horror she witnessed or how she'll ever recover, Leah, but I'm certain she called on *your* God alone while it happened."

Leah's breath caught. Closing her eyes, she placed herself in a palace chamber, lying beside Jacob, and tried to imagine how she would feel if two wild men rushed in and killed him while she lay beside him. She covered a sob and looked down at her daughter.

The innocent girl that left camp five days ago was gone. They'd washed off Shechem's blood, and her outer shell was still lovely, but she was so broken inside. Her breathing unsteady, she jerked while sleeping and occasionally cried out, as if reliving her night of horror in dreams. She hadn't spoken since declaring Jacob's camp no longer her home.

"Will any of us recover?" Leah whispered.

"We can try." Rachel reached across Dinah's sleeping form to squeeze her hand. "I'm willing if you are."

Could it really happen? Would Jacob's strict adherence to Yahweh's command finally unite Leah with her sister? She kissed her sister's hand. "We'll work together to bring Dinah home."

Despite their fear of Canaanite reprisals, the illnesses—body and soul—of several women turned a one-day journey to Luz into a week of painstaking travel. Dinah still hadn't spoken or moved from her mat. Rachel experienced periodic contractions, and her nurse, Deborah, simply wasn't herself. All three women traveled in a blanket-lined cart while everyone else was armed with weapons collected from Shechem's plunder—except, of course, the captive maidens and children.

Understandably grieving, those new to Jacob's clan couldn't be trusted with weaponry or food preparation, though they seemed more frightened than vindictive. Thankfully, Jacob had quelled his sons' claims on prospective wives, convincing them Shechem's virgins would be more inclined to forgive Yahweh's Covenant bearers if given time to mourn their dead and learn about their God.

"How can we be sure the girls of Shechem won't lead our sons into idolatry?" Leah lay in Jacob's arms during their first night in Luz. It was the first time he'd called for her—for any of his wives—since Dinah's ordeal began.

"You've given them a strong foundation," he assured her. "Our years in Shechem proved that possessing Yahweh's Promised Land entails more than owning it. We must *dispossess* idolatry in order to protect His Covenant and truly bless all nations."

His comment birthed a niggling unease. "What do you mean, *dispossess*?"

Rising on one elbow, he hovered over her, brow furrowed. "Well, I *don't* mean tricking them into circumcision and slaughtering every male among them. Do you think I condone Simeon and Levi's violence?"

She framed his face between her hands, regretting her offense. "You're only this volatile and defensive when you're frightened. What's bothering you most?"

He rolled to his back, resting a forearm on his head. "Has Dinah spoken?"

"Not yet." She hadn't eaten either. "But she will." *Please, Yahweh, let it be so.*

"I haven't visited her because I'm afraid she hates me." Jacob slipped a hand into hers, showing unusual tenderness. "It's my job to protect her and I fail—"

An eerie howl raised the hair on Leah's arms. Both Jacob and Leah bolted to their feet and ran toward the sound. Jacob was first to enter Rachel's tent, but Leah nudged him aside when he halted at Deborah's mat.

Rachel knelt beside her maid's crumpled body, rocking and keening. "No, Inanna! I beg you, don't take her!"

Leah approached slowly, cautiously. "Rachel?" Her sister continued rocking but fell silent. Kneeling beside her, Leah forced herself to look more closely at her sister's lifelong nurse. The woman's distant stare and ashen pallor proved she was gone. "What happened?"

Rachel fell into her arms, sobbing. "She asked to gather water from the stream. She felt better today, so I allowed her to take the smallest pitcher." It appeared the old woman had fallen. Leah noticed the broken pitcher beside Jacob's sandals, a muddy spot telling the rest of the story. "I should have refused to let her do anything."

"She loved serving you." Leah rocked her sister. "You couldn't have known her time was coming. Dying is a part of living."

Pulling away, Rachel glared at Jacob. "She was fine before we left Shechem. The war of the gods has begun, Jacob ben Isaac. Your blasphemy will destroy this family." She buried her face against Leah's shoulder and didn't see how her words cut him.

Leah shook her head at Jacob, hoping to contradict the ridiculous accusation. But he slipped from the tent, shoulders slumped with another heavy mantle of guilt.

"How many more will die before he bends the knee—" Rachel's head popped up and Leah turned when they heard shuffling behind them.

Bilhah and Zilpah entered with several shepherds' wives, heads bowed in respect. "We've come to honor Deborah for her lifetime of loyalty."

Offering a nod of thanks, Leah nudged Rachel to sit up. As if she herself were walking dead, Rachel moved stiffly, obeying instructions on which herbs, spices, and oils to gather from her midwifery supplies. The other women worked together like loom and shuttle to wash, anoint, and wrap Deborah's body. By dawn, her earthly shell was ready for the grave Jacob and their sons dug under a large oak they'd admired while entering Luz.

Jacob stood between Rachel and Leah while the boys lowered Deborah's body into the ground. "Since from dust we were made, to dust we all return," he said, while those in attendance filed past the grave to sprinkle a handful of earth as a symbolic offering and then returned to camp. When everyone had gone, except Jacob, Leah, and Rachel, Jacob turned to his second wife with tears. "I'm truly sorry about Deborah, my love, but you must trust me—trust Yahweh. There is no war of the gods. There is only one God, and my family is His Covenant bearer."

Without waiting for her reply, Jacob walked away—but not toward camp. About fifty paces from the oak stood a large rock. He picked up a fallen tree limb, wedged it against the rock's base, and pushed down to dislodge the stone. Leah and Rachel watched in silence as he placed it on its side like a pillar. Then, using the flask of oil at his belt—normally used to treat animals' wounds—Jacob poured the entire contents over the rock and knelt by the impromptu altar.

Rachel sneered. "He commands me to be rid of my stone gods, yet he worships a rock in a field?"

Leah slipped her arm around Rachel's waist, hoping a gentle explanation would help. "It's not the rock he worships. He did the same thing when we bought land in Shechem and named the altar there *El Elohe Israel*—the God of Israel is mighty. Think of all that these rocks have seen, Rachel, and if they could talk—oh, the tales they could tell. This stone will stand for generations, and our sons will tell their sons about all we've experienced in Luz."

Rachel pulled away, red-rimmed eyes accusing. "Will they tell how Jacob's God killed Deborah? Or did Inanna's wrath kill her? Which god is tormenting us, Leah?" Her questions devolved into hysteria, and Leah pulled her into a tight embrace.

Rachel didn't want answers, and she was mourning more than Deborah's loss. Jacob seemed truly angry with her and she with him. Had their love died as well? Since leaving Shechem, she'd also lost the renown of a midwife. It would take years to rebuild her reputation wherever they settled. But perhaps the greatest loss for them all was Dinah. Rachel felt responsible for their daughter's trauma. *Yahweh, forgive me, but I still blame her. Soften my heart.*

Still holding her sister in her arms, she felt the first step to forgiveness was truth. "Yahweh doesn't torment, Rachel. He teaches. When lessons are hard, we can still trust they're good."

"Good?" She tried to pull away, but Leah held her tighter.

"Yes, good," she whispered, desperate to be heard. "You have a child in your belly. That's good. Yahweh struck fear into the Canaanites so we reached Luz safely. Good. Our descendants will inherit this land. Good. Good. Good." She released her sister and pointed to their husband, still on his knees. "Can we live in Luz with reverence for the God our husband *knows* is real?"

But the crease between Rachel's brows screamed refusal. When she drew breath to answer, an otherworldly rumble stole her voice. The ground shook so hard they had to hold each other to keep from falling.

"What's happening?" Rachel cried.

Without answering, Leah started toward Jacob, but a cloud of light enveloped him at the rock where he worshipped. Leah fell to her knees and pulled Rachel down with her. "Yahweh!" Leah cheered over the thunder—and an abrupt silence made Rachel's whimpering as loud as her shout.

Wide-eyed, the sisters glanced at each other and then at Jacob. Still enveloped by the bright cloud, his lips moved but they couldn't hear a sound. "Has he gone mad?" Rachel asked. "Or is there a god truly speaking from that cloud?"

"Yahweh is real," Leah whispered, still staring at their husband. "How much more proof do you need?" Silence answered, drawing Leah's gaze from the cloud to find Rachel sitting on the ground, ignoring the miraculous. "Why aren't you watching? Don't you want to see—"

"If I believe in Yahweh now, there's too much I must change." She looked up, her stony expression replaced with sadness. "I can't, Leah."

"I don't understand." Sitting down hard, Leah felt her anguish war with confusion. "You're saying you would believe—but you won't *change*?"

She hugged her knees to her chest and turned away. "You've known me my whole life. Why ask?"

CHAPTER TWENTY

And God said to him, "I am God Almighty; be fruitful and increase
in number.
A nation and a community of nations will come from you,
and kings will be among your descendants.
The land I gave to Abraham and Isaac I also give to you,
and I will give this land to your descendants after you."
~ Genesis 35:11–12 (NIV) ~

Three Months Later

A rooster's distant crow announced the dawn, and Leah
turned over on her mat. A thin slice of new day fell across
Dinah's sleeping face. She studied her daughter in the stillness. The reawakening had happened slowly during the past
months. She locked eyes with Joseph first—her almost-twin.
He'd coaxed her to eat a bowl of broth that day, and he'd visited every day since. Rachel received her first smile a few days
later, a gift that lightened her guilt. But it was Leah's hand
Dinah refused to let go. Leah she wanted beside her each night
when the nightmares tortured.

Leah tucked a golden tendril behind Dinah's ear, and her
daughter's lips curved into a lazy smile. "No nightmares."

"Your first peaceful night." Leah brushed her cheek.

Though still lovely, Dinah's haunting past permanently creased her brow. "I've kept you from Abba's tent long enough." She opened her eyes. They were already misty. "I can't imagine the misery of sharing the husband you love with another woman—let alone three."

The realization that her daughter now understood a wife's love startled Leah. "I don't suppose he'll call for Zilpah again." She grinned, teasing rather than admit her daughter's love for a pagan.

Dinah grinned with her, a worthy memory. The night after Dinah's awakening, Leah requested to stay with her instead of going to Jacob's tent. Rachel was unavailable because of pregnancy dangers, so Jacob summoned Zilpah for the first time in years. Not long after the camp grew quiet, Jacob's painful cry split the night air—and then his angry, "Get out!" Jacob growled at Zilpah beside the central fire the next morning, "If you weren't so good at weaving, I'd divorce you." Bilhah's raised brow warned away his approach, so only Joseph had endured his abba's snoring after that.

"It's good to see you smile." Leah laced her fingers with her daughter's.

Dinah studied their hands. "Do you think Imma Bilhah and Imma Zilpah will ever worship Yahweh?"

"I don't know, Love, but at least they gave up their idols."

She nodded, still thoughtful. "I haven't heard Imma Rachel speak of any god since..." Letting her words trail off, she pondered a while. "When Deborah died, something inside Imma Rachel died with her."

Leah tipped up her chin, forcing her to look into her eyes. "Our camp is more unified than it's ever been because your abba calls us to worship every Sabbath at *Beth-El,* the altar by the oak. So far, Rachel goes only to worship her grief, but I pray a day will come when she can see beyond Deborah's Oak of Weeping to worship the God who loves her."

"Does Abba still love her?"

The question stole Leah's breath. "I don't...I..." Her cheeks warmed like a maiden, and she sat up to escape Dinah's intense gaze. "That's between your abba and Rachel." But the night he had called Rachel to his tent had caused a ruckus no one could ignore.

Tensions between them had grown unbearable, and after Jacob slept two weeks alone, he was moodier than a bridled old mule. Rachel had started shouting the moment she crossed his threshold, and a surprising sadness gripped Leah when she heard the hatred passing between them. Could they ever regain the love they'd once known? She'd begrudged their relationship from the beginning, but receiving Jacob's favor while he was so angry with Rachel felt heavy and cumbersome. She loved him and was grateful for his attention, but she felt no pleasure in her sister's pain.

"You love your God more than me!" Rachel had shouted that night.

"Yes, and you should be grateful." The silence that followed was excruciating. Both Leah and Dinah pressed their ears against the tent wall to hear the whispers in the next tent. "Don't you see, Rachel? The more faithful I am to Yahweh, the better husband and abba I can be." Their voices had grown quieter, the silences longer, and Leah's hope for their love was rekindled.

Dinah seemed to still want more of an answer, and the memory gave Leah a measure of confidence. "I believe your abba will always love Rachel, but I think the day she believes in Yahweh will be the happiest day of his life."

Dinah's chin quivered. "Love is hard to kill." She turned quickly on her back and stretched, seeming to avoid the grief that still held her captive.

Her obvious pain raked like razors over Leah's heart. Still not ready to confront Dinah's love for Prince Shechem, Leah changed the subject. "Will you work with Joseph again today?" He'd been teaching Dinah what he'd learned about record-keeping since Rachel was too distraught to begin midwifery in Luz.

"I think we'll inventory food stores today," she said, returning to her side to face Leah. "What will you do?"

"I'm weaving with Bilhah and Zilpah. I started a new blanket yesterday."

"Hmm." Dinah closed her eyes and lay on her back, the subtle warning that her emotions were rising and their conversation was over. Still quite fragile, Dinah could seem almost normal one moment and completely disconnected the next.

"I love you." Leah kissed her cheek before she stood.

"I love you too, Imma." A single tear slipped from one eye and made its way down her cheek.

Rachel slipped into the tent, looking over her shoulder like a spy. "I need a favor," she whispered. Her face and ankles were already puffy. She'd grown large with this pregnancy, swollen like an old wineskin full of new wine.

Dinah stood and kissed her cheeks. "What favor?" Leah was less anxious to help, since the only one her sister would likely deceive would be Jacob.

"My delivery is close—I can sense it—and it's going to be a difficult one. I need Inanna's help." She lifted her hand to quell Leah's objections before she could speak. "I need one of you to visit the Luz market and purchase her for me. I've already asked Bilhah and Zilpah, but they refused."

"Of course they refused," Leah said. "Jacob made it clear that *anyone* found with an idol will be removed from the household—permanently."

"But he wouldn't remove you, Leah," she pleaded. "And he would never say anything to Dinah. Please!"

Leah grasped Rachel's hands. "Rock and wood statues can't help you, Rachel, but we'll pray to Yahweh, and you'll have a beautiful baby."

Dinah nudged her aside. "Lie down, and let me examine you again." She'd been caring for Rachel throughout the pregnancy, using the skills she'd taught her. Dinah pressed on her belly and carefully checked her inner parts.

"Well?" Rachel stared up at her.

Helping her second imma sit up to face her, Dinah sighed. "You're right. The baby will come soon. But Imma is also right. Yahweh is the only *living* God who can help you on the birthing bricks. Trust Him, Imma Rachel. He proved faithful to give you Joseph. Why can't you trust Him to safely deliver this baby?"

Leah's heart swelled with pride. She'd never heard her daughter speak of Yahweh so plainly or profoundly. But Rachel refused to look at either of them. "I should have known neither of you would help me." She rolled to her hands and knees and refused when they tried to help her stand. Finally on her feet, she glared at them. "When my labor goes wrong, you remember that Inanna is the only god that helps pregnant women." Then she marched—more like waddled—from the tent.

Dinah laid her head on Leah's shoulder. "Please don't be angry with her."

"I feel more pity than anger, Love."

"Do you think she'll ever believe in Yahweh?"

Leah hesitated. Her daughter was mature enough to know the truth. "She believes. She just refuses to surrender."

Two days later, Leah was weaving with Bilhah and Zilpah under the shade of a giant oak when Jacob's shrill whistle wrested her attention. Coming from the fields on the outskirts of town, Jacob waved his arms wildly. Rachel walked beside him.

Leah dropped the shuttle and ran. *Yahweh, protect her.* How could a midwife be so stupid? If she knew labor was close, why would she risk walking all the way to the pastures in the heat of the day?

"Is she all right?" she shouted, still a hundred paces away.

"Fine." Jacob hurried toward her with his step-hop-stick method, protecting his God-wrenched hip. Rachel now lagged behind, cheeks like round red apples.

Leah stopped and pressed against the pain in her side. She was too old to run these hills. Unable to wait longer, she raised her voice for Jacob to hear her. "Why did you whistle and why did Rachel meet you in the fields?"

"We're leaving Beth-El," he said flatly as he halted in front of her.

A chill raced through her veins. "No, Jacob." Her boldness startled even her. "Yahweh told us to settle in Beth-El."

"Yahweh told *me*," he corrected. "In Harran, He said to return to the land of my abba. We leave for Beersheba at dawn—if you can prepare the camp in time."

Looking beyond him, Rachel grabbed her belly and winced in pain. Her ankles were the size of young tree trunks. "Forgive me, Jacob." Leah would try a gentler approach. "Of course, you are the Covenant bearer and you determine where your household settles. But can you see how dangerous travel would be for Rachel right now?" She pointed at her sister. "Though I'm sure Rachel wouldn't admit it, both she and Dinah agreed your child could come any day."

Rachel joined them in time to hear Leah's objection. "I'm capable of travel," she said. "It's why I walked to the fields today. If I can walk that far, I can certainly ride a donkey or in a cart for two days."

Jacob studied his pregnant wife. "You've wanted to leave Luz since the moment we arrived." He cupped her fiery cheeks.

"You must tell me the truth, Rachel. Are you well enough for the journey? A merchant's caravan can make it in less than two days, but if we break it into three days' travel, can you make it to my parents' camp?"

"I promise, Jacob." Her voice broke. "Please. I can't have this child in the city where Deborah died."

His expression softened, and he wrapped her in a fierce hug. His closed eyes, creased forehead, and frown were external proof that an inner battle raged. Yet as Jacob ached with indecision, Leah knew with certainty that if they left Luz, Rachel would deliver her child on the road to Beersheba. With deep foreboding, she would beg him once more to think with his head, not his heart. She knelt before him and waited for him to notice her posture.

"Leah, what—"

"She's trying to manipulate you, Jacob." Rachel's sharp tone was no longer pleading.

"Not manipulate," Leah said, head still bowed. "I'll only recount Yahweh's calling as I remember it, so you can correct my errors. Did Yahweh say, 'Go up to *Beth-El*, settle there, and build a second altar'? When you obeyed Yahweh and built that altar after Deborah's death, didn't Yahweh appear to you again and reaffirm His Covenant? Didn't he say, 'I am *El Shaddai*. Be fruitful and increase in number'? Shouldn't we protect the child Rachel carries as part of Yahweh's command to be fruitful and multiply?"

She looked up then, tears streaming down her face. "I love you, Jacob ben Isaac, and I will follow you wherever you lead.

I'm simply asking you to follow Yahweh first and foremost—not the raw emotions of my grieving sister."

Shifting Rachel gently to shelter her against his right side, Jacob offered his left hand to help Leah stand and drew her to his chest. "I thank Yahweh for you," he whispered, barely audible against her ear. "Rachel has vowed to die by her own hand if I don't take her away from Luz." Horrified, Leah tried to pull away, but he held her too tightly. "You can't fix this, Leah. We must leave."

CHAPTER TWENTY-ONE

Then they moved on from Bethel. While they were
still some distance from Ephrath, Rachel began
to give birth and had great difficulty.
~ Genesis 35:16 (NIV) ~

Joseph and Dinah rode on matching white donkeys as Jacob's household began the second day of their journey to Beersheba. Rachel lay on the blanket-lined bed of an ox-drawn cart, Leah jostling beside her. She'd started contracting yesterday at midday, so the caravan stopped atop a mount across from the famed city of Salem. Jacob and his sons entered the city to replenish supplies but returned empty-handed with few positive words for the city once ruled by Melchizedek, the God-honoring king to whom Saba Abraham paid his tithe.

"We should reach Ephrath by midday." Leah leaned back, stretching her arms out on the cart's sidewalls and breathing in the autumn air. "Isn't it beautiful, Rachel?"

"It's desert." She turned on her side, pulling her knees to her chest.

Leaning over her, Leah placed a hand on Rachel's hard belly. "How strong is the contraction?"

"Uuuuuuuh." Rachel squeezed her hand for a count of seventy and then pushed her away. "Stop coddling me. The whole caravan need not stop for a few contractions. Let's travel quickly so we can get to Beersheba. If I give Isaac another grandson, maybe he'll consider me a *real* wife to Jacob after all."

Ignoring the possibility of Isaac's hostile welcome, Leah tried some teasing. "Midwifery has made you brave, Sister. What happened to the girl who needed a midwife in Abba's guesthouse for a week after delivery?" She chuckled, but Rachel buried her face in the blankets. When Leah realized her shoulders were shaking, she knew she'd said something terribly wrong. "I'm sorry, Rachel. I was only playing. Please forgive—"

"It's me!" she shouted, pushing herself up on one elbow. "I'm the one who should apologize because *you* were treated like a servant in Abba's household, and I did nothing to stop it." Her features twisted with pain again, and Leah offered her hand to squeeze for another contraction. Instead, Rachel took it and kissed her palm, eyes glistening. "Was it the hardship that made you strong, Leah? I've always envied you."

Dumbstruck, Leah could only shake her head. Rachel envied her? "If I were strong, little sister, I never would have agreed when Abba asked me to trick Jacob into marrying me. He convinced me that Esau was Leviathan, and because you and I were always close, he was sure we could share a husband."

In that moment of naked truth, they pondered the profound blunder—and then laughed. "I guess we've both proved Abba wrong." Rachel sobered and picked at a loose thread on the blanket beneath her. "Even agreeing to trick Jacob required strength. Pretending on the wedding night and then spending a whole week with him when he was so angry…" She shook her head and looked at Leah again. "And you've won more than his love. You've won his respect. Something I've never had."

"You could have it." Leah pressed the words into the windows of Rachel's soul. "There's a level of intimacy you can only reach when you serve the same God."

Brow furrowed, Rachel appeared surprised—or perhaps perplexed. With a gasp, she looked down as a sudden gush between her legs soaked the blanket beneath her.

Leah pounded the side of the cart. "Stop the caravan!"

"No!" Rachel shushed her. "I'm fine!" She shouted at those looking back and then leveled a threatening glare at her sister. "We keep going until the pain worsens. I want to travel as far as possible before telling Jacob I've broken my promise."

"Broken your promise?"

"Remember?" Rachel's expression softened. "I promised to have this baby in Beersheba."

Two Days Later

Leah removed the damp cloth from Rachel's burning forehead and rinsed it in cool water to reapply it.

"Another push now, Mistress." Ephrath's midwife was a stranger and far too polite, but they'd sent for her at dawn— when it was clear Rachel wouldn't survive. Leah had sent Dinah from the tent, fearing she'd blame herself for Rachel's death. "I know you're tired," the woman coaxed, "but you'll want to name the baby before you—" She glanced at Leah, seeming startled at the truth she'd almost uttered.

"Why isn't the baby coming?" Leah's patience had run out with the last blood-soaked cloth.

The woman pushed on Rachel's abdomen. "I think the baby's stuck on something."

Brilliant. Ephrath's midwife was worthless. Leah called for one of the camp's maids. "Send a messenger to Jacob in the fields. Tell him to come now—hurry. Joseph and Dinah too."

Bilhah, who sat behind Rachel to support her back, laid her forehead on the laboring imma's shoulder and wept. Zilpah knelt at Rachel's right knee, opposite the midwife, and exchanged a forlorn glance with Leah. How could their family exist without Laban's youngest daughter bringing life and beauty to camp?

Leah crouched at Rachel's side, soothing her with a cool cloth and sweet words. "Listen to me, Sister, and remember what Dinah said about Yahweh and this moment on the birthing bricks. Do you remember? Rachel. Listen to me. Do you remember what our daughter said about Yahweh?"

Rachel licked her chapped lips, gray now from loss of blood. "I remember," she whispered.

"He's the only *living God* who hears you on these bricks," she said, urgency raising her voice. "He'll hear you, Rachel. Yahweh will hear you if you ask for His help."

She tried to shake her head no. "He won't."

"He will. Don't you dare be stubborn now. He *will* hear you, my love, but you must ask. I know you believe, but you must trust Him as Jacob's Covenant God and embrace your place in it. He's more of a gentleman than any of Abba's gods. Yahweh has invited us into His family, and He'll welcome you home— no matter how far you've strayed."

A tear seeped from the corner of Rachel's eye, but she said no more.

"We need to get the baby out," the midwife said. "Or we'll lose them both. We might have lost the baby already. I don't really know."

"Find out!" Leah shouted. Eyes wide, the woman reached into the womb.

Rachel arched her back, spending all remaining strength on a push and pained cry. "Yahweh, help me!" Bearing down until the whites of her eyes turned red, Jacob's beloved gave him a twelfth son.

"Yahweh, save!" Jacob ran across the tent, falling at her side. "Rachel!"

"His name... *Ben-Oni*...son of trouble." Eyes unfocused, Rachel slipped into delirium. "Yahweh, help... Son of trouble."

"No, no, no." Jacob held her hand against his chest and wept as her blood drained to the ground. Dinah and Joseph stood behind their abba, holding hands, weeping quietly.

Leah turned her attention to Zilpah and the maids. "You may go."

The midwife rubbed the baby with salt and wine but looked up at Leah's command. "I'm so sorry. I need to finish the—"

"Finish what?" Leah rose and snatched away the baby. "You did nothing, and there's nothing for you to finish."

"Imma..." Dinah nudged her aside. "Thank you," she said to the woman.

The midwife glared at Leah. "No one could have saved her."

Leah stared at Rachel's baby, already smacking his lips, searching for nourishment. She looked up and found the midwife leaving. "Wait!" she called out. "Is there a woman in Ephrath we could hire as a wet nurse? We'll leave at dawn and settle in Beersheba."

The woman looked as if she might flee rather than answer. With one hand on the tent flap, she said, "A woman lost her child yesterday and has no husband. I'll send her." She rushed out before Leah could thank her.

"I said go!" Jacob's harsh tone drew Leah's attention. He stared at Bilhah, teeth clenched, jaw muscle flexing.

Leah reached over Rachel's body to calm him. "Jacob, Bilhah loved Rachel as much as we—"

He turned a fiery stare on her. "You'll leave with her if you test me on this."

The baby started fussing, and she couldn't risk being sent out before Jacob held his son. She bowed in submission, watching Bilhah relinquish support of Rachel's body to Joseph and hurry from the tent. Dinah shot a questioning glance at Leah and Joseph, but neither had an explanation for Jacob's severity—and none dared ask.

"Jacob," Leah ventured. "Husband, look at your son."

"I can't." His face remained buried against Rachel's body.

"Jacob, did you hear her call on Yahweh with her last breath?"

The question lifted his head, and a hopeful glint brightened his eyes. "She believed?"

"The name of no other god passed her lips, Jacob. Just as Abraham believed and it was credited to him as righteousness, our Rachel cried out only to Yahweh. She finally surrendered to the one true God. We will grieve her death, to be sure, but we can also rejoice that this son she gave you led her to Yahweh."

Jacob's face twisted with a riot of emotion. Sobs ushered forth with praise as he reached for the babe in Leah's arms. "He is not *Ben-Oni*—son of trouble—but rather *Ben-jamin*—son of my right hand—for he was born through Yahweh's strength and my Rachel's courage."

"Yes, Benjamin." Leah pulled Dinah close and stood beside Joseph. "It's a good name."

"May I help you and the other women prepare Imma Rachel's body?" Dinah's blue eyes swam in tears.

Drawing breath to forbid it, Leah was halted by something in her daughter's expression.

"Please, Imma," she said. "I didn't get to say goodbye to Shechem. Let me say goodbye to Imma Rachel."

"She needs to do this." Joseph kissed Leah's cheek. "I'll help Abba with Baby Benjamin until the wet nurse arrives. You must let others help you now that—" He cleared his throat and swiped at his eyes. "Now that my imma is gone."

Joseph carried his imma's body to a clean mat and then spoke a few quiet words to Jacob. Then Jacob looked at Leah, suddenly stricken. "Where *will* we bury her?"

Leah kept silent. She'd already considered the question, but the decision needed to be Jacob's.

Shaking his head, he looked down at Benjamin as if discussing it with Rachel's newborn. "We're a day's journey from my family cave at Machpelah. Should we try to—" But he fell silent and lifted his gaze to Rachel's firstborn. His expression no longer panicked, he spoke with tender confidence. "Your imma must be buried here in Ephrath, Joseph. We'll mark her grave such that every generation will realize she fought her last battle bravely." With a longing look at the wife he'd loved from first glance, Jacob walked into the afternoon sun with a part of Rachel in his arms—and Joseph at his side.

Leah took Dinah's hand and led her to the mat where Joseph had laid his imma. "Yahweh has given us a few moments alone while Zilpah gathers supplies for the anointing. Are you sure you want to be a part of this?"

Dinah looked down at Rachel's body and gently cradled her hand. "What difference does it make that Imma Rachel believed in Yahweh after a lifetime of pagan worship?" She stared at the ravaged flesh left behind. "Where is she now, Imma? What happens when someone dies?"

Such weighty questions for one so young, and Leah knew she wasn't only asking about Rachel. "I don't know exactly." She started with the truth and sat down opposite her daughter, the lifeless remains of her beloved sister and unintended rival between them. "Your abba shared with me some teachings from the House of Shem, which said everyone is destined for

Sheol—the pagans to wander forever, but the faithful will rise again and see Yahweh with new eyes."

"Do you think *anyone* can believe?" Head bowed, she sniffed back emotions. "Would Yahweh forgive a pagan who turned to Him before their last breath?"

Hesitating, Leah considered carefully before answering. Had Dinah spoken to Shechem of Yahweh before her brothers killed him? What if the prince had believed? Hadn't the ancient King Melchizedek of Salem worshipped the Most High? Who was Leah to set limits on the infinite Creator of all things?

Finally, she looked again at her daughter, whose head remained bowed as she continued wiping tears. "I believe Yahweh displays His greatest power," Leah said, "*not* in thunder or fire or even death. Rather, I think He demonstrates His power most profoundly through forgiveness—and I believe He forgave Rachel the moment she called out His name."

Dinah's head shot up, and her face bloomed with a smile. "I believe it too, Imma."

Zilpah and Bilhah entered the tent, carrying fresh burial spices, oil, and new cloth from Ephrath's market. "We've told the other women not to come," Zilpah said. Dinah helped Leah to her feet, and they took a basket from each of Jacob's slave-wives. "We wanted to honor Rachel with family alone." Leah and Dinah hugged them both, and the four women began the private task, shared by those who knew Rachel best and loved her still.

By nightfall, they'd buried Jacob's beloved and gathered at the central fire for the evening meal. Joseph stayed at Jacob's side, while the other boys remained at a distance, unsure of how to comfort their wounded abba. Bilhah hadn't been the only recipient of an undeserved tongue-lashing. Reuben also had been upbraided for returning from the fields early when he'd heard of Rachel's death.

Leah served Benjamin's wet nurse a plate of dried fish, bread, and figs. The girl seemed kind and well mannered. Best of all, she held no allegiance toward the gods of Canaan, who demanded children's blood and innocence. She even seemed intrigued by a God who could follow her to Beersheba.

When the meal was done, Jacob disappeared into Rachel's tent, and Leah encouraged Joseph to attend him. She and Dinah had invited the wet nurse to share their tent to keep a watchful eye on Baby Benjamin. Three women and a babe in a tent made for two was trying, especially with the newborn. At the first shades of pink in the eastern sky, Leah felt as if she hadn't slept at all.

"You should be with Abba," Dinah said quietly. Leah turned over to face her daughter. "You can't fix me, Imma. Abba needs you, now more than ever, and I'm a grown woman. I must find my place in this camp. Alone. Without a husband. Without Imma Rachel. Without you." Her voice broke. "And someday without Joseph. He'll marry and love another more than me."

Tears blinding her, Leah stroked her daughter's cheek. "Love doesn't divide, Dinah. It multiplies. Joseph will always love you in a way he loves no other. But yes. I must give you space to walk the path Yahweh has prepared for you."

"Thank you." She curled into the bend of Leah's arm as she'd done when they watched the stars. "But I'll always need you, Imma."

Leah's eyes slid shut, the words a balm to her soul. "And I'll always need you, Daughter." She lifted her head. "To help with the cooking." Both giggled like children and grudgingly donned robes and sandals to begin preparations for the morning meal. Leah was first to exit and noticed Jacob lurking in the shadows at the entrance of Rachel's tent. "What are you—"

Pressing one finger against his lips, he pointed at Bilhah's tent, two structures down from Leah's. What did he want her to see? Was he angry that Zilpah and Bilhah weren't the first ones awake to help with the morning meal? He'd been so ill-tempered with Bilhah for the past two days—more like a month. She could understand if it was Zilpah, after she'd rejected him in his tent, but—

"Reuben?" she said, as her firstborn emerged from Bilhah's tent. His head snapped her direction, eyes wide. He opened his mouth but then closed it without a word. Hair and beard askew, what could he say? Prickly dread crawled up her neck as Jacob stepped out of the shadows and stood beside her. She glanced at him and back at their son. "Reuben, why were you in Bilhah's tent?"

"Will you force him to say it?" Jacob stood close enough that she felt his trembling rage. "He's been ogling her for months. Last night he slipped into her tent."

"I comforted her because you treat her worse than a slave!"

"Reuben!" Leah's shock matched her shame.

But Jacob's fury changed to a dangerous smile. "Comforted her? You've spent your last night in comfort, boy. From this night forward, you sleep in the fields—since you can't control your animal instincts."

"Jacob, please," Leah pleaded, "don't make a decision while you're angry."

Reuben was suddenly beside her, too close to his abba's fury. "Bilhah lost Deborah and Rachel, yet you showed her nothing but contempt. I don't think you even know how to love!"

Jacob slapped him with an open hand, and Leah found herself trapped between two angry men. Reuben drew back his fist, and Leah screamed. "Stop! Stop it, both of you!" Holding up her hands in defense, she ducked, hoping to avoid the blow. When silence followed, she looked up and saw both men glaring. Panting. Furious still, but quiet.

A flutter beyond Reuben's shoulder drew her attention. Bilhah stood at her tent's opening. Hand over her mouth, she was weeping, horrified. As she should be.

Leah tilted her head to look up at her compassionate son. His greatest strength had become his weakness. "Have you forgotten everything I taught you about Yahweh and His Covenant? You're the firstborn, Reuben. The one to inherit—"

"He gets nothing," Jacob said. "And Bilhah's tent will be moved outside of camp." He turned and strode into his tent.

Head bowed, Leah stood in the screaming silence. *Yahweh, have mercy on us all.*

CHAPTER TWENTY-TWO

Jacob came home to his father Isaac in Mamre, near Kiriath Arba
(that is, Hebron), where Abraham and Isaac had stayed.
~ Genesis 35:27 (NIV) ~

One Week Later

In the dim lamplight of his tent, Jacob lay facing the woman whose deception had changed everything he thought his life would become. The fine lines around Leah's blue eyes bespoke years of pain—and the wisdom that came with it. He traced the slight curve of her lips. She was holding back a smile. A week ago, he didn't think they'd ever smile again. Her healing presence had done its work. "Do you know how much I need you?"

"I know." A shadow of sadness crossed her features, but just as quickly her pleasantness returned. "You've never been able to love me, but I think being needed is better."

"What?" Confused, and a little annoyed, he sat up. "Of course I love you. I was angry the morning after our wedding, but who wouldn't—"

She sat up and pressed two fingers against his lips. Smiling. Peaceful. "You need me, but Yahweh *loves* me." She offered a gentle kiss, still tempting after thirty years. "I have all I desire."

He pulled her into his arms and rolled to hover over her. "Leah bat Laban, I *do* love you." Pausing, he raked his memory for a single time he'd said it. "I'm sorry it's taken me this long to speak the words."

Her eyes filled with moisture. "Thank you," she whispered. "I pray our sons can be as good to their new wives as you've been with me."

"Your suggestion that they marry before we arrived in Beersheba was a good one. When my parents see their grandsons have wives, it will be one less thing for them to criticize." He rolled to his back again, thinking of all the ways he'd failed his abba since he left over thirty years ago.

Leah snuggled against his chest. "Please tell me we won't become our parents—conniving and critical."

Jacob's thoughts wandered to Reuben's betrayal. He'd exiled Bilhah permanently outside of camp but hadn't divorced her. Still, her sons, Dan and Naphtali, were furious with him— and with Reuben. "How will we keep this household from scattering to the four winds?"

She pulled his chin down to capture his gaze. "You've already started by giving our sons wives. Women are the glue, Jacob. We're a jumble of emotions and ideas and questions, but Yahweh gave us to men so we can add color and beauty and life to your world." She kissed him thoroughly, then drew back and grinned. "That was a reminder."

He pulled her closer and breathed in her scent—saffron and cloves. "I hope our sons chose well." They'd released Shechem's virgins to stay in Ephrath or become betrothal candidates for Jacob's sons. All but four stayed, hoping to be chosen. Jacob forbade Joseph a wife, believing him still too young to take on the responsibility. He'd planned to forbid Reuben a choice, but Leah cautioned him to hear from Yahweh before removing Reuben from the inheritance. Jacob heard nothing, so Reuben chose a wife. Joseph and baby Benjamin were the only sons of Jacob waiting to be married.

"It was kind of you to give them a wedding week," Leah said, drawing circles on his chest. "Camp has certainly been quiet." The teasing in her voice made him smile. "But I think everyone will be ready to begin the journey to Beersheba tomorrow."

Tomorrow. Jacob had been anxious to appease Rachel when they left Luz, but the idea of seeing his parents again made his stomach twist with dread.

"Jacob?"

"What?"

"Are you anxious to see Isaac and Rebekah?"

"Yes," he said. "*Anxious* is a good word."

The morning after his sons' wedding week was complete, Jacob and Leah also emerged from a refreshing week sequestered together. However, Rachel's absence pierced him like an arrow when he spied Benjamin with his wet nurse.

A mix of grief and terror stopped him abruptly. "I don't want to see anyone," he whispered to Leah.

Wrapping her arms around his middle, she looked up with intoxicating eyes. "Benjamin is a part of you and a part of Rachel. He and Joseph are brothers. And we're all your family, Jacob. Do what you must, and we'll be right here when you're ready."

She waited, without pushing, not judging.

Jacob inhaled a sustaining breath. Reaching for Leah's hand, he proceeded to his place at the head of the central fire. His sons stood respectfully until he was settled. Leah sat behind his left shoulder, as he'd requested, while both new and familiar faces served the morning meal. Jacob ate slowly, watching and listening as this new household searched for routine. Stolen glances between his sons and their wives added a welcome playfulness, and the easy banter of youth almost made Jacob forget Bilhah sat at the oven where Rachel used to bake bread.

By midmorning, Joseph and Dinah had organized the camp under Leah's supervision, and Jacob had readied the shepherds to drive the flocks and herds. He climbed onto his camel's saddle, wincing at the pain in his hip and thanking Yahweh for the reminder. If he'd contended with the Angel of God and prevailed, surely he could face Abba again—and likely gain more lasting scars. Leah caught up to him before Ephrath was out of view, riding her ancient camel.

"If that beast dies on the way," he teased, "we're leaving her for the jackals, and you'll ride a donkey."

"Jacob, she can hear you!" Leah leaned over to stroke the creature's neck. "He didn't mean it, Willow."

"I certainly did," he mumbled, and sudden grief stole his breath. Rachel wasn't vying for the place beside him. He tried swallowing the emotions, but they came in waves, too fast.

"Jacob, it's all right," Leah said quietly. "It's all right to miss her. I miss her too."

Eyes forward, Jacob responded with a nod and let his tears flow into his beard. He was thankful he led the caravan so no one else could see.

With fewer people in camp and everyone healthy, Jacob's household travelled quickly. In less than a day's travel, the landscape looked more like home, and Jacob recognized Ephron's field in Machpelah. He began searching for the terebinth trees that marked his family's burial spot. "There, Leah! Do you see the cave?" He pointed west and circled his arm to the south. "Saba Abraham purchased this whole section from Ephron the Hittite when *Savta* Sarah died. It was the first land Yahweh provided to His Covenant bearer."

"And you purchased the second."

Leah's eyes shone with pride, but Jacob still felt the ache of guilt. "Not that anyone will possess it again in my lifetime."

"It's ours, Jacob, and your abba will be proud." She sounded like she was chastising one of their sons. "You must be confident when you meet Isaac. You've proven yourself a prince among men."

Esau was Abba's prince, and Jacob had been Imma's. "At least we can spend the night in Hebron. It's where Saba Abraham lived after Savta Sarah died. I'll stir up more courage before we see my parents in Beersheba tomorrow." The lowlands of the *Shephelah*, with its gently rolling hills, made travel easy for the carts, but its grassy rug made munching animals difficult to push forward. Moving south-by-southwest, Jacob noticed his family's flocks. Would his business-minded wife notice? He watched her study them as they led their camp farther into Abba's territory.

"Jacob, these flocks have no notch to distinguish their owner."

He chuckled. *Of course she noticed.* "They're Abba's flocks, and none of his livestock are given any mark or blemish so all can be considered for sacrifice."

With a creased brow, she studied the animals while their camels plodded across an entire field. Returning her attention to Jacob, she asked, "Doesn't it make your animals more susceptible to theft? Isn't it easier for others to cut their notch into an unmarked ear?"

He lifted his hand, halting his shepherds, and watched his own speckled and spotted flocks mingle with Abba's black goats and white sheep. "Our livestock is easily distinguished by color, but when we move to Hebron—the place Saba Abraham taught me of Yahweh—I will also leave their ears unmarked. There, Yahweh Himself will protect them."

Leah's face lit with approval, and he felt its warmth like the sun's rays. "Were you close with your Saba Abraham?"

He hadn't considered the deeper memories he'd face when they reached Hebron. "I suppose. He died when I was fifteen, but I remember him as a mountain of faith and determination."

They rode in silence. Jacob breathed in the scents of home, and Leah shaded her eyes from the midafternoon sun. "Is this a winter camp for your family?" she asked. "It's larger than I expected for a second site."

And it was larger than Jacob remembered it. "I'm sure this was Saba's Hebron camp." He coaxed his mount with the leather crop, rushing into his rising angst. Leah followed, Willow keeping pace despite her spitting protests.

When they reached the camp's perimeter guards, Jacob obeyed their command to halt but gave them no time for demands. "I'm Jacob ben Isaac, returning from a long absence in Harran with my wiv—"

"Welcome, my lord." The guards bowed on one knee. "Master Isaac will be most pleased you've come home."

Startled at the welcome, Jacob cleared his throat and continued. "My wives and I, our children, servants, and livestock will make camp on the edge of Hebron and continue to Abba's camp in Beersheba at dawn."

The guards looked up, equally startled. "Your abba's camp is here, my lord. Your imma lives in Beersheba."

Suddenly unable to speak or swallow, Jacob's mouth was as dry as Harran's summers. He turned slowly to Leah, screamed at her in the silence. *Abba is here? Now?*

Straightening her spine, she addressed the guards. "Is Master Isaac well?" Her voice was calmer than Jacob could have managed.

"He's not well, Mistress." The guards exchanged a wary look, and the spokesman added, "He's dying."

Jacob scoffed but covered the rude noise with a forced cough. "We've had a dusty ride." It was a pathetic excuse, and the guards' disapproval showed in their narrowed eyes. But how could they believe Abba was dying? Isaac ben Abraham said he was dying thirty years ago when Jacob stole the blessing from Esau.

"Please take a message to Master Isaac," Leah said. "Tell him that his son Jacob has returned with his whole household and looks forward to sharing a meal in his tent this evening."

"Leah!" Jacob protested.

"And you may also tell him that Jacob's wife—Laban's *elder* daughter—will help serve the meal."

Her words had the desired effect when both guards bowed deeply. "Our master's son has married a woman as capable as Mistress Rebekah. We'll deliver the news and prepare Master Isaac for your arrival." The spokesman hurried away, leaving his comrade with a ridiculous smile that he didn't even try to hide.

Jacob reined his camel to return to camp, muttering at his wife. "If the guards are any indication, Abba will adore you and send me into the desert without water."

CHAPTER TWENTY-THREE

[After Jehovah-Jireh provided a sacrifice on Mount Moriah,]
Abraham returned to his servants, and they set off together for Beersheba.
And Abraham stayed in Beersheba.
~ Genesis 22:19 (NIV) ~

Sarah lived to be a hundred and twenty-seven years old.
She died at Kiriath Arba (that is, Hebron) in the land of Canaan,
and Abraham went to mourn for Sarah and to weep over her."
~ Genesis 23:1–2 (NIV) ~

Leah consulted with Zilpah and Bilhah about the menu for the evening meal, while Jacob instructed his shepherds on how to introduce themselves to Abba's men. Grazing land was plentiful, but herders were notoriously territorial. The last thing her husband needed was an argument between his men and Isaac's on the day they arrived.

At dusk, Jacob led a small contingent of his household to his abba's camp with Leah riding beside him. Three ox-drawn carts followed, carrying both servants and supplies for their reunion meal. The same guards welcomed them, escorting the master's son and his wife. The camp was arranged with tents in circular rows, and paths like spokes of a wheel led to central ovens and Isaac's large tent.

Both Leah and Jacob stopped with a gasp when they saw his tent. Leah reached for Jacob's hand, squeezing it as emotion tightened her throat. Isaac's tent was made of Jacob's speckled-and-spotted goat's hair.

"I've never seen anything like it." Jacob's mouth hung open at the display of his abba's pride.

"He paid handsomely for the skins." The guard gave him a sideways glance and resumed their march.

Jacob blew out a nervous breath and continued, tightening his grip on Leah's hand. "Calm down," she whispered. "Our women prepared a lovely meal, and you're the chieftain of a great household."

"Not to Abba." He kept his voice low to be sure the guards couldn't hear. "To Isaac ben Abraham, I'm the son too busy studying to hunt. I'm the son Yahweh favored before birth rather than the firstborn. And I'm the son who evidently caused the rift between my parents."

"We don't know why your parents live in separate camps."

"They didn't live apart until after I left for Harran." He shook his head, shame written on his features. "Imma's part in my deceit was probably too much for Abba to forgive. Something similar happened to Saba Abraham and Savta Sarah when he obeyed God and nearly sacrificed Abba on Mount Moriah. Though Saba didn't go through with it, the fact that he almost did—and hadn't told Savta Sarah before he left that morning—it was something she never forgave. From that day on, Saba Abraham lived in Beersheba and Savta in Hebron. After Savta died, Saba Abraham moved to Hebron to be closer to her burial cave."

Leah finally understood so much about Jacob's family. "Did you say Isaac was always closer with his imma, Sarah?" Jacob nodded. "And you were always closer with your imma, Rebekah—like Isaac with Sarah?"

Jacob stopped walking. "What are you saying?"

The guard stopped, frustration drawn into a single bushy brow. "Master Isaac is waiting."

"Keep moving, and tell him we'll be there in a moment." Jacob's terse reply got another nasty glare.

Leah framed Jacob's face, demanding his full attention. "Consider that the displeasure you felt from your abba may have been because he was displeased with *himself*—and he saw too much of himself in you." Her husband's brow furrowed, so she continued the thought. "Perhaps he favored Esau over you because Esau was the man Isaac wished he had been. Esau was a hunter. A warrior. But you, like your abba, enjoyed learning and studying the stories of Yahweh."

Jacob's expression dawned with wonder, mirroring what Leah felt. "Do you realize how long I've wrestled with what more I could have done to win Abba's approval? When all the time, it's been Abba's battle, not mine. What a gift you are to me, Leah bat Laban." He pulled her close and kissed her forehead then grabbed her hand as they finished their approach to Isaac's tent.

The guards and carts waited outside, and Jacob released her to make final preparations with the meal and servers. In the time it took to assign her daughters-in-law their duties and prepare the food trays, Leah lost sight of her dear husband. "Jacob?" One of the guards pointed toward the back of his abba's tent, and she found him standing alone like a stone pillar, looking as if he might vomit.

"Jacob?" From inside the tent came barely a whisper. "Is that you, my son?"

Jacob's eyes widened, but he didn't move.

Leah grasped his strong right arm and rose on her tiptoes to whisper, "Remember *Beth-El*. Remember the Jabbok. You are the Covenant bearer as surely as is the man in that tent—as surely as your twelve sons are."

He nodded and whispered, "Yahweh, forgive. Yahweh, save." And he started toward the entrance, Leah two steps behind. He slowed the moment he crossed the threshold, and Leah halted beside him. On a straw-stuffed mattress lay the shrunken form of a man. Frailer than a child, Isaac ben Abraham looked as if death might claim him any moment.

"Jacob, is it really you?" He stared without seeing, a white film over rheumy eyes.

"Yes, Abba. It's Jacob, come home to stay."

Gaunt cheeks, sunken eyes, and lips stretched over protruding teeth, the skeletal face somehow brightened with joy. "Praise be to El-Shaddai, who has brought you safely home before I die."

Leah watched her tortured shepherd fall at his abba's side and weep. Covering a sob, she halted the servers at the entrance with their trays of food and wine and let the long-overdue reunion nourish the souls of abba and son.

When the aroma of roasted lamb and freshly parched grain filled the tent, Isaac's bony hand patted Jacob's back. "Let's reminisce while we eat." He laughed, seeming somewhat refreshed. "I smell food!"

Jacob released him, and Leah stepped aside, allowing their sons' wives to serve the meal they'd prepared for the patriarch they'd heard so much about. Jacob coaxed his wife closer to Isaac's bed. "Abba, I'd like to introduce my wife Leah, Laban's elder daughter."

Isaac's brow furrowed. "I heard what Rebekah's brother did to you, and this one helped with the deception."

Her cheeks burned at the unexpected censure, and red splotches began appearing on Jacob's neck.

"Esau visited me after meeting you near Sukkoth," Isaac continued. "Tried to use Laban's trickery to condone his marriages to those Canaanite, Hivite, and even Ishmaelite women." Isaac dipped his bread in the lentil stew. "Mmm, this is quite good, Jacob. Did you help the women make this?"

Had he just insulted Jacob? Was his welcome feigned? Jacob's face was as red as the beets in Isaac's salad. Refusing to let careless words cause another rift between them, Leah drew closer to the patriarch's bed and knelt beside him.

Setting aside his bread, Isaac looked up, sensing someone's presence. He sniffed the air and said, "Laban's daughter smells like my Rebekah." A mischievous grin curved his lips. "Are you lurking so you can strangle me while I eat this fine meal?"

For a dying man, he certainly had maintained his humor. "If I were bold enough to strangle you, I'd at least be merciful enough to wait until after the honey cakes."

He raised his brows and then turned blind eyes toward Jacob. "I understand why you've kept her." He held out one hand toward Leah, and she pressed it against her face. He drew her closer to kiss her cheek. "You'll do just fine. Where's the other one, Jacob?"

Leah's head snapped toward her husband.

Jacob inhaled a quick breath, blowing out calmly before answering. "Rachel died giving me a twelfth son."

Isaac pulled his hand from Leah's. "Would you mind taking the food away, dear, and asking the servants to wait outside? But I'd like you to stay so I can speak with you and Jacob together." She checked for Jacob's approval and, with his nod, did as Isaac asked.

After their daughters-in-law stepped outside, Leah knelt with Jacob beside his abba's mattress. Jacob reached for her hand, seeming as nervous as she. "What is it, Abba?"

"Your brother still hates you," he said without honey. "I suspect since it's been more than ten years since you promised to visit him in Seir—and you haven't—you still hold ill will toward him as well."

Eyes focused on her knees, Leah wished she wasn't included in this conversation.

"It's true," Jacob said finally. "I'm not sure Esau and I will ever trust each other."

"He's your brother," Isaac said. "He's reconciled to the truth that you will have Yahweh's blessing and eventually possess the Promised Land of Canaan. But he's earned his own fortune in the land of Seir. Can't you accept his success?"

Jacob's face reddened again, and she prayed he would remain silent about the bride price Esau stole from him on the way to Harran. *That* was the fortune he'd traded for the land in Seir and then bartered and betrayed the Hivites for more and more land. Squeezing her husband's hand, Leah silently pleaded for gentleness with the abba they'd returned to honor. Jacob pulled his hand from her grasp and rubbed his forehead, thinking.

Yahweh, give him a wise and humble heart, quick to listen, slow to speak, and abounding in grace and forgiveness.

"Jacob, why can't you simply draw a boundary line between you and your brother?" Isaac asked, exasperated. "Then the two of you agree not to cross it."

Letting his hand fall to his lap, Jacob sighed. "Abba, may I ask you a question?"

"Of course. Anything."

"Is that what you and Imma have done—drawn a boundary line and agreed not to cross it?"

Isaac's gaunt face lost the little color it had gained. "I won't speak about your imma."

"You exiled her because of her part in *my* deception," Jacob said—a statement, not a question.

"No." Isaac sounded like a petulant child.

Jacob glanced at Leah, unconvinced. "No?"

"I said, I won't speak of it—"

"I deserve to know why—"

"She hates me!" His reedy shout was barely a croak, but he trembled with the effort and turned his face away. A few heartbeats of silence and he confessed, "She grew tired of my dying."

Pity surged through Leah at the rejection this man suffered. Rehearsing Isaac's life, she saw the repeated theme and felt kindred understanding. How must he have felt—at barely sixteen—when Abraham, obeying Yahweh's command, took him to be sacrificed on Mount Moriah? No wonder Jacob called Yahweh the *Fear of Isaac.* Isaac lived with Sarah after the incident and was inconsolable after her death. Only his marriage to Rebekah comforted him, yet she helped Jacob deceive him—and now had rejected him completely.

"Abba Isaac, I know the pain of feeling unloved." Leah placed her hand gently on his arm. "But we're here now, and we want you to live. We have a renowned healer in our household, and I'm sure she could find something to help ease your pain—no matter how many days Yahweh gives you."

Jacob lifted both palms, begging the question, *What healer?*

"Where does she come from?" Isaac pulled his arm from her touch. "I'll have no sorcery in my camp."

Leah almost chuckled at his tenacity. "She worships only Yahweh, I assure you. Her name is Dinah—your granddaughter."

CHAPTER TWENTY-FOUR

Isaac lived a hundred and eighty years. Then he breathed his last
and died and was gathered to his people, old and full of years.
And his sons Esau and Jacob buried him.
~ Genesis 35:28–29 (NIV) ~

Dinah stood in Leah's small tent, looking as incredulous as
Jacob had when she mentioned their daughter's herbal
skills to Isaac. "I'm trained to deliver babies, not treat old men's
brittle bones."

"You know the *herbs*," Leah said. "Rachel taught you how each
plant affects the body—any body. Women, men, old, young."

"It's not that simple, Imma."

"It is that simple." Leah gripped her shoulders, forcing her
to face her. "You said you must find your place in camp. On
your own. Separate from me. Separate from Joseph. This is it,
Dinah. Something you can do to help the whole family and
honor our patriarch."

"No." Jacob's single word turned both women toward him.
He stood at the tent flap, head bowed, squeezing the back of
his neck.

Leah could fight one of them but not both. "Jacob, we
started this day thinking we had time to build our courage

before meeting your parents, but the time for courage is *now*. Yours and Dinah's. Unless you have another plan for our daughter's future—"

"I meant *no,* I don't want Dinah to care for Abba simply to help the family." He dropped his hand and lifted his eyes to meet his wife's. "I believe I've found my courage, Leah, and you can wait in my tent. I'll speak with my daughter alone."

"But I—"

"I'll join you shortly." He took two steps toward her, put his hands at her waist. "I love you, Leah. Now, leave."

Both flustered and elated, she stole a quick kiss from Dinah before hurrying outside. She'd walked three steps toward the neighboring tent when she realized she *must* hear what they were saying. Removing her sandals, she shifted to the shadows and crouched at the side of Dinah's tent to listen.

"...can be harsh, but he will love and protect you like no other if you are loyal to him."

"But, Abba, what if I fail?"

Leah couldn't hear the whispers between them, but Jacob's commanding presence and tender concern for their daughter had borne Leah's weary heart up to the clouds.

"I think that will be best for you, for Abba's camp, and for my household," Jacob said.

"I'll try, Abba. Thank you for believing in me even...even when..." Dinah's words were garbled by her emotions, and Leah suddenly felt as if she was trespassing on sacred ground. These were moments only Jacob should share with their daughter.

Quietly, she hurried to Jacob's tent, exhausted but grateful. She poured two cups of watered wine, took a small sip, and lay down on the large double mat that she and Jacob now shared.

Leah was next aware of Jacob's snoring. She saw the brightening eastern sky outside and realized she'd slept soundly through the very short night. Trying to rise without waking her husband, she rolled to her knees but was tackled by the man she adored. Rolling over each other several times, they laughed and were nearly exhausted by the time Leah rested on her husband's belly.

"We're too old for that silliness," she said, pillowing her hands under her chin.

"Agreed." He was fairly beaming. "Dinah will stay and care for Abba while we set up our permanent camp at Beersheba."

"What?" Had she slept through a whole day of discussions? "When did you decide to move camp to Beersheba?"

"It's not even a decision, Leah. It's the way we must live." His mood darkened. "Esau visits Abba regularly. I refuse to subject my family to his mocking and violence."

"Perhaps now that you're both older and wiser, you'll be able to overcome the differences that drove you apart. You could spend more time—"

"You heard how Abba still favored Esau."

"How did he favor your brother?"

Jacob looked as pained as if she'd stabbed him. Tipping to one side, he toppled her to the ground, reached for his robe and sandals, and walked to the tent flap.

"Jacob, wait," Leah said. "Talk to me."

He stopped but didn't face her. "We leave midmorning. You should introduce Dinah to Abba when you say goodbye to him. I think you'll like Imma, and she'll be pleased to finally have a daughter."

One Year Later

Beersheba Camp

After the morning meal dishes were cleaned and put away, Leah stole a few moments alone in the kitchen while Zilpah and Bilhah retired to the courtyard to continue their weaving. Leah uncovered the prepared chickpeas she'd been saving for a special surprise and put them in a medium-sized bowl. She began crushing them into a smooth paste, adding enough olive oil, garlic, cumin, and water to make it smooth and tasty. After lifting the dish towel from her shoulder to wipe sweat from her brow, she grabbed a leftover crust of bread to sample her special treat. "Mmmm, perfect."

The familiar *swish-thud-step* came from the hallway, and Leah fought the urge to hide. Jacob's imma appeared at the kitchen doorway, stooped and leaning on her cane. "Why are you in my kitchen?" Rebekah hadn't cooked anything since she sent Isaac to Hebron thirty years ago, but it was still *her* kitchen.

"Would you like a taste?" Leah asked as politely as possible and held out the basket of this morning's bread.

Rebekah took a fist-sized piece of bread, scooped up a generous portion of the spread, and shoved the whole thing into her mouth. Lolling it between her gums, since she'd lost all but four teeth, she suddenly spit it into her hand. "Uuhh! Are you trying to kill us all?"

Leah turned to get a pitcher of fresh water, thankful she could hide her rolling eyes. "Why don't you go lie down, Imma? It's too hot for you to be up and around." Living in Rebekah's mud-brick home instead of their household tents had been… difficult. With less breeze, less space, and fewer friendly faces, Leah felt like a prisoner in the southwest lowlands of Canaan.

The sound of a camel's gallop drew her attention—Rebekah's too. Horses were more common in Canaan's Shephelah, so a camel meant a messenger needed quick travel for a longer distance. Rebekah was out the door, arriving in the courtyard with that cane faster than Leah could follow. The enclosed garden was a lovely space in spring and autumn but hot and dry as a baked mud-brick in summer's heat.

The messenger reined his camel to a halt. "It's urgent, Mistress. Master Isaac summons you to Hebron camp."

"Humph," Rebekah snorted. "I'm not—"

"I meant Mistress Leah," the messenger said, brows pinched. "Your daughter says you and Master Jacob should hurry."

Rebekah raised her cane in the air, causing the camel to bellow and spit. "It's always urgent with Isaac, and he's always dying." She started back toward the house. "Take that awful chickpea spread with you, Leah. That should finish him off."

Leah cast an apologetic glance at the messenger. "I'll pack a shoulder bag in the house. Would you go to the shelter and ask the herdsman to prepare my camel and Jacob's for the journey? We'll lead Jacob's camel out to his flock and collect him on our way." The messenger nodded and went immediately to the task, while Leah returned to the house to collect a few of Isaac's favorites. Candied dates. Nut cakes. Surely Isaac wasn't really dying. But Dinah had never urged them to hurry before.

Leah was adjusting to her new camel. Willow died soon after their arrival in Beersheba, and her new dromedary was faster but had much less personality. "Jacob, we must go!" Leah shouted as she and the messenger approached. The three riders were soon on their way north, their dromedaries' long legs and smooth strides carrying them to the Hebron camp before dusk. After they dismounted near the lean-to stables, Jacob and Leah rushed toward Isaac's tent, dusty and tired. She longed to splash her face with water and drain a cup of sweet wine, but concern helped her match Jacob's quick pace.

Almost to the row of tents nearest center, they about ran headlong into Esau. He and four members of his clan blocked their path. "Thank you for coming so quickly." His tone dripped satisfaction. "I knew you wouldn't come if I invited you, so I sent one of Abba's men with that extra little message from your lovely daughter."

"If you've touched her—" Jacob's hands and teeth clenched, ready for a fight.

Leah stepped between them. "Stop it, both of you." She turned to Esau. "Your games are ridiculous. We're here now. What do you want?"

His smug expression dimmed. "So he's convinced you to hate me now too?" She saw something vulnerable beneath the hairy red monster who lived to torture Jacob.

"I don't hate you, Esau. I don't even know you. But I certainly don't appreciate being frightened into thinking Isaac or Dinah could be ill and arriving to find you've played us for fools." He listened so intently, she felt a little vulnerable herself and nestled closer to Jacob.

"Please," he said, gesturing toward a large black tent to their right. "Join me in my tent for the evening meal. We can discuss the reason for my invitation."

"I'd rather see that Abba is safe." Jacob started to walk away, but Leah snagged his hand.

She offered a tentative grin. "I'm hungry. Let's hear what he has to say."

He brushed her cheek, harshness softening, and then pulled her under the shelter of his arm before addressing Esau. "We'll join you for the meal *after* we check on Abba and Dinah. It won't take long."

Esau inclined his head. "They'll no doubt be happy to see you. They're feasting on the bounty of my hunting, but I'm sure they won't mind the interruption."

Jacob forced a polite bow and fairly dragged Leah toward Isaac's tent. "Won't mind our interruption," he mumbled.

"Please try to be civil, Jacob." Weary from the journey and tired of Jacob's family, Leah longed for kindness. Somewhere. Somehow. She was starved for it like a beggar yearning for bread.

She and Jacob slipped into Isaac's tent and found Dinah feeding him small bites of wild game. The old man groaned with pleasure after each morsel, and their daughter's delighted laughter proved her service more than compulsory. Jacob and Leah stood unnoticed at the entrance, and Leah realized Esau had been right. They were indeed interrupting.

"Shalom, Abba." Jacob stepped closer, and Isaac sobered. "Esau?"

Jacob blanched. "No, Abba, it's Jacob. I've come with Leah for a short visit. Esau wanted to speak with us."

Dinah ran to hug Leah, and she drank in her daughter's welcome. "I've missed you, my sweet girl." Nearly six months had passed since she'd visited Hebron. Jacob had come once when Esau was there, and he hadn't returned since—nor allowed Leah to go even with an escort.

"Are you all right?" Dinah peered into Leah's eyes when she released her. "You seem tired."

Leah waved away the concern. "Of course I'm tired. I just rode a galloping camel all day." She avoided more questions and the emotion roiling in her belly by hurrying over to greet Isaac with a kiss on his cheek. "It's good to see you looking so well. I told you our girl was a great healer."

"Imma..." Dinah ducked her head shyly.

"Why did you gallop all day?" Isaac's body was failing, but his mind was as sharp as a blade.

The tent went suddenly still, and Leah regretted her words. "My young camel loves to gallop."

"Hmm." He nodded, obviously unconvinced. "And you say Esau summoned you?"

"He didn't *summon* us." Jacob's tone spoke more than Leah's words.

"Jacob will stay and talk with me." Isaac waved the women out. "Leah and Dinah can eat their meal with Esau."

"What?" Leah shot a panicked gaze at Jacob.

"Leah stays with me." Jacob placed a possessive arm around her shoulder. "I'll talk with you as long as you'd like, Abba, but my wife will not enter Esau's tent without me."

"Sit down, Jacob." Isaac patted the ground beside his mattress. Jacob looked first at Leah and then at Dinah, indecision etched on his features. Leah nodded and gestured toward Isaac. What could be the harm? Isaac certainly couldn't overpower his strong shepherd son.

Jacob settled on the packed dirt beside his abba, and Isaac placed a hand on his arm. "Your wife and daughter are going to walk out of this tent and speak with your brother now—"

"No, Abba, they're n—"

"And I'm going to explain how I've forgiven you for deceiving me."

Color drained from Jacob's face just before he bowed his head. "Can you promise me Leah and Dinah will be safe in Esau's tent?"

"If your wife and daughter don't feel safe, they need not enter his tent." Isaac lifted his sightless eyes in their direction. "Well, are you going or not?"

Dinah immediately nodded, coaxing Leah with silent assurance that she felt safe. Leah nodded her assent and then remembered Isaac couldn't see her. "Yes, we'll go," she said.

Isaac's hand tightened on Jacob's arm. "Now, it seems you're the only one who still fears your brother, and we're going to see if we can remedy that while they're gone."

CHAPTER TWENTY-FIVE

Esau took his wives from the women of Canaan:
Adah daughter of Elon the Hittite, and Oholibamah
daughter of Anah and granddaughter of Zibeon the Hivite—
also Basemath daughter of Ishmael and sister of Nebaioth.
~ Genesis 36:2–3 (NIV) ~

The moment Leah and Dinah left Isaac's tent, Leah clutched her daughter's arm and whispered, "Did you know about Esau calling us to Hebron tonight?"

"No! I didn't know anything until I saw you and Abba standing in Saba Isaac's tent."

"But you trust Esau?" Even as she said it, Leah knew the answer. From the moment she'd encountered him at the Jabbok, she knew Jacob's brother was rough but transparent.

"I do, Imma. He's not...polite. He says what he's thinking without regard for who hears or their opinion of him." She shrugged. "It's intriguing."

Intriguing. A good description of Jacob's red twin.

"What's this?" Esau waited outside his tent and flung his arms open when he saw them. "I ask for my ugly brother and his lovely wife, and I get two beauties instead? The gods have smiled on me tonight! Come, come, and we will eat and talk."

Leah flinched at the mention of pagan gods in Isaac's camp. "There is only one God, Esau. Have you forgotten your abba's teachings?"

His bawdy laughter ushered them into the tent. "You're grown from the same seed as my imma. Rebekah's fire lives in Laban's daughter." He directed them to a low-lying table and spoke to an older woman holding a pitcher. "Pour our guests some wine." Though she offered no acknowledgment, she filled Dinah's cup—and then sat down beside Esau, ignoring Leah entirely.

"Thank you," Dinah said, giving her imma a sidelong glance.

"I am Basemath, daughter of Ishmael, mother of Esau's second-born son."

Leah took a sip of Dinah's wine, parched from her journey. "It's nice to meet you, Basemath." The woman glanced at her—focusing a moment on her eyes—and then returned her gaze to Dinah.

"Your eyes…," she breathed, barely a whisper. "Esau said they were unique."

Dinah blushed and lowered her head, avoiding the strange woman and reaching for Leah's hand under the table.

"We're leaving now." Leah started to stand, but Esau's next words stopped her.

"Dinah will need a husband."

Dinah gasped and looked up. "No. I can't…I mean…" She turned to Leah, her eyes filling with panic and tears.

Leah wrapped her shoulders and pulled her close. "Dinah was married before and—"

"We know." Basemath finally addressed Leah, her expression and tone softening. "Merchants brought news of Prince Shechem's marriage to the daughter of a Bedouin prince—a blue-eyed girl—and his sons who slaughtered the city."

"It was a foolish and brutal act that neither Jacob nor I condoned."

"I loved him." Dinah lifted her head, peering at the woman so intrigued by her.

"A woman's heart matters little in a man's world." Basemath tilted her head, showing surprising compassion. "I'm sorry."

Leah wondered at first if she was mocking, but Basemath seemed truly grieved for Dinah. Regardless, Dinah was trembling from head to toe, and Leah saw no reason to continue the conversation. "Thank you for inviting us, but Dinah has no desire to marry again right now."

"Wait." Esau reached across the table, trapping Leah's free hand. His strength was startling, but his eyes held no threat. "I see your daughter is upset, but surely you could stay and continue the conversation with Basemath and me. Let Dinah return to Abba's tent, and I'm sure Jacob will soon join us." He released her hand and sat back. "Please, Leah bat Laban. I wouldn't have asked you both to come if it wasn't important."

Leah felt as if she were sitting at a crossroads and had no idea what waited for her in either direction. If she stayed to hear Esau's proposal, would Jacob feel betrayed? If she left, would she be refusing a viable solution for her daughter's future happiness?

She leaned close to Dinah, whispering her decision. "Return to Isaac's tent and tell your abba to join me here as soon as he can. Make sure he understands that Esau's wife, Basemath, is with us, and I'm not afraid."

"I'll tell him." Dinah stood and offered a quick bow before hurrying outside.

When Leah returned her attention to Jacob's brother, he appeared almost as surprised as he was pleased. "You are a courageous one, Leah bat Laban."

"And much more beautiful than my husband reported." Basemath aimed her accusation at Esau, but he ignored her.

Esau clasped his hands together and laid them on the table between them. "I believe I've found a way to retrieve at least a part of the Covenant blessing Jacob stole from me. Your older sons are married. I suspect Jacob will choose a princess for his favorite son, Joseph. And the baby who killed pretty Rachel won't be grown for many years." It was as if he was reading a bill of sale. "I've come to respect your daughter. She's kind to Abba, and I think Basemath's great-great-grandson would be a good match."

Leah studied the woman beside Esau, confused. "Basemath has a great-great-grandson? Is he of your seed, or someone else's?"

Esau's guffaw burned Leah's cheeks. "Of course he's mine."

"How can you have great-great-grandchildren, and Jacob has a newborn?"

He slammed his fist on the table, all humor gone. "Because I married at forty and started my family—like real men should."

Fury overcame blushing, and Leah met his reproach, unafraid. "Yahweh's men don't marry pagans."

Eyes narrowing, he sat back and studied her. "I'm no fool, Leah. To bring Yahweh's blessing to my clan, the man I've chosen serves only Yahweh. Have you heard the merchants speak of Job of Uz? He's honest, good, fears Yahweh, and fights evil with goodness. He's considered the wealthiest man in the East, and I want Dinah to marry one of his seven sons."

Leah sneered, wondering if she'd misread Jacob's brother. "If this is another game, I like it even less than this evening's trickery."

His eyes held hers. "It's no game. I want the blessing that was stolen from me. Your daughter's womb can bring offspring of the Covenant bearer's lineage into my clan."

There it was. No honey. No spices. The bitter truth. Intriguing indeed. "Jacob must consent," Leah said.

"No." Esau rolled his eyes and snorted. "You know he won't."

"He will if Isaac commands it."

Esau held her gaze, a slow grin curving his lips. "You know my abba will agree to anything I ask of him."

Leah leaned forward, refusing to play his game. "Isaac will do as Yahweh commands, and I believe he'll do what's best for Dinah."

Sobering, he turned to his wife, who nodded her agreement. He clapped his hands, rubbing them together, and said, "Let's enjoy my wild meat!" Basemath retrieved trays full of food and began serving while Esau made conversation. "When you leave Hebron tomorrow, your beautiful daughter will continue to care for Abba. Jacob can believe I brought him here to create boundary lines for our clans, and I'll return to Edom to protect my clan."

"Absolutely not," Leah said, trying not to enjoy the most tender game she'd ever tasted. "Jacob must know the truth."

He set aside the bread he was using to scoop his stew. "You're not at all the way I imagined." His penetrating gaze made her uncomfortable, so she stared into her bowl. Where was Basemath? If Jacob arrived now, he'd see her alone with his brother and explode.

"We've all made decisions based on misperceptions." Heat rose in her cheeks. Did he know she'd tricked Jacob into marriage because she feared their betrothal?

"Perhaps we can avoid more mistakes by getting to know each other better." Panic snapped her head up, but she found Esau staring absently into his cup of wine. "Has Jacob ever told you about our first hunt with Abba?" He laughed and began the story, talking about his twin and their childhood adventures, days when they were young and kinder. Leah told him of Joseph and Dinah, their twins from two immas, and was thoroughly astonished by the man's wit and charm.

When they had finished their meal, Jacob still hadn't come. "I'm sure you're anxious to rejoin your husband." Esau rose from the table, and she was more than a little sad that Jacob had missed the evening.

"Thank you," she said, moving toward the exit.

"I'll escort you to Abba's tent." He opened the flap for her, another surprisingly polite gesture. The moon had risen high in a cloudless summer sky. Only a few guards patrolled the camp, and for some reason Esau seemed almost nervous, hands clasped behind his back as he raked his sandal across the dusty earth.

"I've waited many years to say this since that day we met near the Jabbok." He spoke barely above a whisper, halting her with a gentle touch on her arm. "I always believed Jacob stole the two most important things in my life. My birthright as first-born, which he swindled for a bowl of stew. And you know how he deceived Abba to get Yahweh's Covenant blessing."

Leah looked away. "Yes, but he thought—"

"What I'm trying to say is…" He turned her chin back toward him so he could look into her eyes. "When I saw you eleven years ago, that's when I really hated Jacob—because that's when I realized he'd stolen the greatest treasure of all."

Her stomach rolled at his declaration. What was she to say? She loved her husband desperately. "Esau, I—"

Bowing on one knee, he lifted her hand to his forehead in pledge. "If you ever need help, Leah bat Laban, I will come at your command." He looked up then, mischief sparkling in his eyes. "And you don't even have to trick me."

She inclined her head in a respectful bow. "I'm honored by your kindness," she said. "And it's my earnest prayer that Yahweh will find His way into your heart, Esau, and not just your clan."

They shared an understanding smile, neither willing to give up the life they had for the life proposed. As they approached Isaac's tent, Jacob was just leaving. His countenance darkened the moment he saw his brother, but Leah rushed into his arms, nestling into his embrace.

"I love you, Jacob ben Isaac, and tonight more than ever, I know Yahweh chose the right brother to be his Covenant bearer."

EPILOGUE

Then [Jacob] gave [his sons] these instructions:
"I am about to be gathered to my people.
Bury me with my fathers in...the cave in the field of Machpelah...
which Abraham bought along with the field as a burial place
from Ephron the Hittite.
There Abraham and his wife Sarah were buried,
there Isaac and his wife Rebekah were buried,
and there I buried Leah."
~ Genesis 49:29–31 (NIV) ~

AUTHOR'S NOTE

So many unknowns make Leah's story a mystery. Did she deceive Jacob willingly on what was supposed to be Rachel's wedding night? Which of Jacob's wives worshipped Laban's household gods? Was Leah's only role to make babies, or did she have other responsibilities in Jacob's household? Because of spotty historical information, Leah could have been a hero or a villain. But there was one *biblical* clue that led me to believe this ordinary woman of the Bible was truly faithful to Yahweh.

Leah was the only wife interred with Jacob in Abraham's family burial cave. In the Old Testament, the place of burial oftentimes reflected a person's life of faith. For instance, evil kings like Ahaz and Manasseh were *not* buried in King David's tomb (2 Chronicles 28:27; 33:20), but the faithful high priest Jehoiada was buried with kings (2 Chronicles 24:15–16). Did Rachel, Bilhah, and/or Zilpah worship pagan gods? We don't know, but since Rachel was Jacob's favored wife—yet buried outside the family's tomb—I've portrayed her as an idolater in the story.

Another unknown is how the afterlife was viewed during the patriarchal period. The concept of heaven and hell is more a New Testament concept, and Jewish scholars are divided on what their ancestors—before the kings and prophets—believed about life after death. Rather than borrowing one scholar's opinion over another, I used Job's words (Job 14:11–13; 19:25–27) as a guide. He, like many other Old Testament writers, mentions Sheol as the general destination after death; however, Job also speaks of a bodily resurrection in which he will see God with new eyes. Since the Book of Job is dated to the Patriarchal era, I adopted his theology for this story.

I hope you found Leah to be a strong yet believable character. I've known several Leahs in my lifetime—women whose husbands cherish something or someone more than they do their wives. I suppose there are male Leahs out there too—husbands whose wives place children or career before them. Regardless of gender, the Leahs I've known who thrive regardless of their circumstances have done so as the Leah in my story did. They find worth and strength through an intimate relationship with the only One whose love never fails.

Someone precious to me was a Leah all her life. Her husband experienced a debilitating health crisis, and he suddenly cherished her. It was a miraculous change and startling at first. But rather than let bitterness rob her of the loving days she had left with him, she asked Jesus to help her receive *His love* through her husband's changed heart. It's truly been a beautiful thing to watch—and part of the reason I needed to write Leah's story.

Thank you for reading an experience so very close to my heart.

FACTS BEHIND
the Fiction

✦

RACHEL STEALS THE HOUSEHOLD IDOLS

The Bible tells us, "Rachel stole her father's household idols and took them with her" and that she hid them "in her camel saddle" (Genesis 31:19, 34 NLT). But what would those idols have been?

They were probably small figurines, doll-sized, possibly chiseled from stone or carved from wood and dipped in silver or gold.

Hittites lived in Turkey, where Rachel and Leah grew up. Hittites bragged about having a thousand gods. That was about 4,000 years ago. Back then, Middle Eastern—or as scholars would call it, Ancient Near Eastern—gods came in many forms. Rachel may have packed a god figurine of a lion-headed man or of a man with the legs of a bull, or simply a figurine that looked like a person.

THE ANCIENT WORLD WAS FULL OF VARIOUS IDOLS. SHOWN HERE IS A BAAL FIGURINE SIMILAR TO ONE THAT RACHEL MIGHT HAVE TAKEN FROM HER FATHER'S HOUSE.

Canaanites to the south, where Jacob's family was headed, worshipped Baal as their top god. He was a god in charge of fertility in family, flocks, and fields—three of the most important aspects of life at the time. If they needed rain in the dry Middle East, he was the one the Canaanites would pray to. His image often shows up in artifacts, holding what looks like a lightning bolt.

Rachel stole what amounts to her father's portable church. Many people had no worship center. They expressed their faith with rituals in front of their idols. And many worshippers said they believed these gods were living inside the figurines.

When Rachel stole Laban's idols, she thought she was looking out for her family. She didn't know Jacob's God. Apparently, until they left Harran, his wives worshipped the family idols. In ancient Turkey, believers could name a need and find a corresponding god.

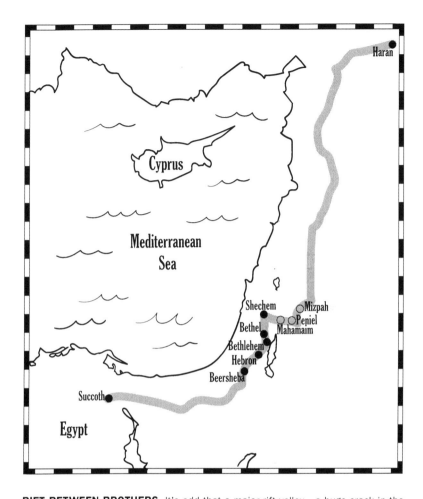

RIFT BETWEEN BROTHERS. It's odd that a major rift valley—a huge crack in the earth's crust beneath the Jordan River and Dead Sea—separated twin brothers Jacob and Esau. Their relationship shattered when Jacob stole the blessing their father, Isaac, intended to give Esau, as the oldest son. Decades later, the brothers met and reconciled. But Esau settled east of the Jordan River Valley, in the rocky territory of Edom, in what is now the Arab country of Jordan. Jacob returned to Canaan, now called Israel and Palestinian Territories. He settled first in the hills of Shechem, today the city of Nablus, about a two-day walk north of Jerusalem. He moved after his sons killed all the men in Shechem in retaliation for the local prince raping their sister, Dinah. Jacob moved the family farther south, to Bethel, which was about a day's walk north of Jerusalem, and eventually they settled in the hills of Hebron. His travels covered around 500 miles.

JACOB'S PATH TO MARRIAGE

When Leah's father, Laban, tricked Jacob into marrying her, Laban invoked a surprise tradition he didn't tell Jacob about: the oldest sister had to get married first.

Laban had seven years to tell Jacob. That's how long Jacob worked for the right to marry Rachel. During this betrothal, Jacob was already calling Rachel his wife: "Give me my wife so I can sleep with her" (Genesis 29:21 NLT). Until Jacob woke up in the light of a new morning, he didn't realize he had been tricked.

But he was willing to work another seven years for Rachel. Laban's "tradition" reads like a con. It's a one-of-a-kind story among the ancient wedding traditions.

Here are some of the wedding practices in Leah's day that would have accompanied a traditional marriage:

Negotiations. Leah's father, Laban, would have negotiated the marriage with Jacob's father, Isaac. It was uncommon for the groom to negotiate for his own bride.

Money for Father-in-Law. Jacob didn't have the traditional "bride price" money to reimburse Laban for the loss of his daughter, so Jacob agreed to work seven years. That's a very high number that Jacob's father, Isaac, likely would have rejected in the negotiation. The maximum payment later preserved in Jewish law was 50 shekels (Deuteronomy 22:29). A worker at the time of Leah got one shekel or less a day. At that price, Jacob would have paid for his bride in two months.

Weeklong Celebration. On the wedding day, a procession of the groom's friends would go get the bride and escort her to the groom's house. Typically, the bride was veiled—certainly Leah was. Relatives traveled from near and far for what must have felt like a family reunion. The celebration often lasted a week or longer, partly because of the distance guests had to travel.

238

Hugs and Blessings. At the end of the first day, in some traditions, the groom wrapped a cloak around his veiled wife and received blessings for prosperity and many children. If there was a wedding contract, that's when it would have been read. Wedding contracts did exist, though there's no mention of them in the Old Testament.

Wedding Night. After the blessing, the couple went to their tent to consummate the marriage. There is much speculation about why Jacob failed to recognize which woman he was with until the next morning. Some scholars say he was too drunk from the feast. Others say that during those seven years he worked for Laban, he worked out in the fields and not around the family, so he didn't get to know Rachel very well at all. These scholars wonder if Laban might have even lied to his daughters and told them that Jacob was working to marry Leah.

Wedding traditions varied, and Leah's wedding varied more than any other reported in the Bible because her father was a crafty and deceptive negotiator.

JACOB, THE WILY TRICKSTER

Jacob didn't just trick his brother out of the family inheritance, he stole his father's dying wish: a blessing elderly Isaac intended for his oldest son, Esau.

The blessing was something intangible, but perhaps even more cherished than the inheritance, which was the family estate: sheep, goats, and anything else Isaac owned. A man's son could hold the assets of an inheritance in his hands. But the blessing was something he held in his heart.

When a Hebrew father thought he was on the verge of dying, he would call in his sons and give them a blessing. These blessings were part prayer, part wish, and part prediction. Yet they were more. People seemed to believe there was power in a blessing to make things happen.

Years later, Jacob would bless his sons. To his son Judah, he said, "All your relatives will bow before you" (Genesis 49:8 NLT). Sure enough, Judah's family grew to become the dominant Israelite tribe and home of the nation's capital, Jerusalem. In time, the Jewish nation took the name of Judah.

Sadly, some fatherly blessings read more like curses. Jacob called his sons Simeon and Levi violent men who "crippled oxen just for sport. A curse on their anger…. I will scatter them among the descendants of Jacob" (Genesis 49:6–7 NLT). Levites didn't get any tribal land. Simeon's tribe got swallowed up into Judah.

A curse was just about all that Isaac had for Esau after Jacob stole these good words: "May many nations become your servants…. May you be the master over your brothers…. All who curse you will be cursed" (Genesis 27:29 NLT).

The words of leftover "blessings" is why Esau vowed to kill his thieving little brother: "You will live away from the richness of the earth, and away from the dew of the heaven above. You will live by your sword, and you will serve your brother" (Genesis 27:39–40 NLT).

The Bible doesn't say what became of the inheritance. By the time Isaac died many years later, Jacob and Esau were already rich with livestock and big families.

JACOB TRICKS ESAU INTO GIVING UP HIS INHERITANCE FOR A "BOWL OF POTTAGE" (GENESIS 25:29-34 KJV)—RED STEW. BASED ON A PAINTING FROM C. 1896-1902 BY JAMES TISSOT.

ONE WIFE IS ENOUGH

Some of the best-loved men in the Bible apparently loved more than one woman. So they married them. In some cases, a man and wife simply wanted a baby that the wife couldn't provide, so they used a surrogate—an enslaved woman often known as a concubine. Abraham had children with Sarah and her slave, Hagar.

Concubines like Hagar often lived the life of a second-class wife. They were part wife and part slave. The husband got all the privileges of a wife, but the woman remained a slave, or at best a marital associate with meager rights under ancient law. But whatever her rights—such as the right not to be sold after giving birth—they were less than the rights of a wife.

King David had at least seven wives before he had an affair with Bathsheba. He added many more wives and concubines in the years that followed.

Wise King Solomon married 700 wives and gathered 300 concubines. In time, some of his wives from other cultures led him into idolatry—this man who was "wiser than anyone else in the world" (1 Kings 4:30–31 CEV). His reign and his life ended on this tragic note.

The fact that many Bible heroes married multiple wives doesn't mean God approved of polygamy, if their sad stories are any indication. Some scholars point to the Creation story for evidence of this: "A man leaves his father and mother and is joined to his wife, and the two are united into one" (Genesis 2:24 NLT). There are just two. Jesus later added, "Since they are no longer two but one, let no one split apart what God has joined together" (Matthew 19:6 NLT).

CAMELS: FIRST-CLASS
TRAVELS IN BIBLE TIMES

A first-class seat for travelers in Leah's day was the hump on the back of an Arabian camel. In parched fields, badlands, and deserts of the ancient Middle East, camels were the fastest and most reliable way to get from one watering hole to the next. The Arabian camel could carry 200 pounds (about 100 kg) around 40 miles (60 km) in a day. That's twice as far as most people walked.

Under normal desert conditions, these camels can go a week to ten days without water. They carry extra water in the tissue of the hump on their back. Once they reach a source of water, they can rehydrate themselves with about 25 gallons (95 l) of water in 10 minutes or less.

Jacob owned a herd of camels, along with other livestock common for the day: sheep, goats, cattle, and donkeys. As he approached a tense reunion with Esau, the brother he cheated out of their father's blessing, Jacob sent gifts of livestock ahead of his caravan. They included "30 female camels with their young" (Genesis 32:15 NLT).

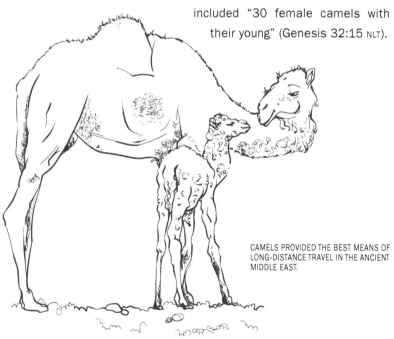

CAMELS PROVIDED THE BEST MEANS OF LONG-DISTANCE TRAVEL IN THE ANCIENT MIDDLE EAST.

There are two main kinds of camels: two-hump Bactrian camels of Asia and one-hump dromedary camels—the Arabian camel of the Middle East. The Hebrews drank camel milk, which is low in fat and rich in nutrients. They used camel hair and hide to make tents, clothes, and other necessities of herders and farmers.

Observant Jews stopped short of eating camel meat. It was against Jewish law, which declared camel meat nonkosher (Leviticus 11:4). Anthropologist Lloyd Cabot Briggs (1909–1975) ate some. He said camel meat "tastes just like rather ordinary beef...[with] a slightly sweetish aftertaste, like horse but not quite so much."

Fiction Author
MESU ANDREWS

Mesu Andrews is a Christy Award–winning author and has received numerous accolades for her other biblical novels. Her deep understanding of and love for God's Word brings the biblical world alive for readers.

Andrews lives in North Carolina's Appalachian Mountains with her husband, Roy, and she enjoys spending time with her tribe of grandchildren.

Nonfiction Author
STEPHEN M. MILLER

Stephen M. Miller is an award-winning, bestselling Christian author of easy-reading books about the Bible and Christianity. His books have sold over 1.9 million copies and include *The Complete Guide to the Bible, Who's Who and Where's Where in the Bible,* and *How to Get Into the Bible.*

Miller lives in the suburbs of Kansas City with his wife, Linda, a registered nurse. They have two married children who live nearby.

Read on for a sneak peek of another exciting story
in the Ordinary Women of the Bible series!

THE ELDER SISTER:
MIRIAM'S STORY

by Tricia Goyer

Miriam watched her mother work the shuttle back and forth on the horizontal loom set up near the front window, closest to the light. Her imma, Jochebed, moved slower now. The baby within grew larger, and the lines of worry on her imma's brow deepened with each passing day.

Imma should have birthed the new babe weeks ago. Maybe it was fear that kept the child inside, safe and protected? Imma and Abba spoke of this baby as a girl. Hope wouldn't let them speak otherwise. But Miriam knew differently. It was an inner knowing that had always been there. A soft warmth that settled in the middle of her chest and a gentle whisper that filled her mind with truth. And the truth was that a boy would soon be born—a brother.

"Just as the Mother Nile brings life to our land, women are honored to bring life to our people." Her imma had taught Miriam this truth since she was a child, but Imma hadn't spoken such things in recent months. Not since the decree from Pharaoh. What good was birthing new life if it would soon be followed by death?

As she found herself doing often lately, Miriam searched for an excuse to leave their small hovel and walk the dirt-packed street along the row of houses. She set down the yarn she'd unraveled for her imma and stood.

"Come, Aaron, let us go see Puah's new lamb. I heard it was a runt brought to her from the fields for extra care."

The dark-haired toddler jumped to his feet excitedly, rising from his spot near their imma's loom. His favorite game of late was claiming pieces of broken yarn and creating river pathways for the straw boat Abba had made for Aaron to sail over their dirt floor.

Like always, after their sparse dinner, Abba had told them stories of their ancestors. He'd invited her to sit beside him or on his lap. As Abba spoke, Miriam would often place her face against his, the feel of his beard against her cheek a comfort.

Last night the tale had been about Noah and his grand boat, even larger than the Pharaoh's royal ship and filled with every type of animal. Yet Miriam's favorite stories were those of Joseph, the slave who became second in command only to Pharaoh. The night he'd told that story, Abba had prayed for such a man to stand at Pharaoh's side and lead their people out of Egypt, just as Joseph had welcomed them in. Miriam had prayed the same prayer ever since. Did El Shaddai hear her prayers? *Their* prayers?

Aaron placed his straw boat near a pile of yarn and hurried to her side, and Miriam imagined a boat filled with her family and friends sailing away to safety up the Nile. *Will that be the way you lead us out, El Shaddai?*

No gentle whisper responded, but the inner urging remained—one that told her to be watchful and to cling to hope that her new brother-to-come would not be fed to the crocodiles. The urging forced her to believe that through prayer and diligence the death wail would not rise in their home as it had elsewhere multiple times a week since the devastating edict had been put in place.

"Imma, I am taking Aaron to Puah's. We will not be long."

Her imma turned her face toward them, offered a half smile and nodded, but from the glazed look in her eyes, it was clear she wasn't seeing her children. Her mind was in a different place, perhaps remembering the first day they'd become aware of Pharaoh's shocking announcement.

It was six months prior, but Miriam remembered the day as clearly as if it had happened yesterday. Fearful mothers calling to their children first alerted her. She had just rounded the roadway, after filling a jar at the river, when she noticed what all the commotion was about.

A chariot had stood in the middle of the narrow street between mud-brick houses, its highly polished six-spoke wheels shining in the early light. One of Pharaoh's Medjay stood beside it, fully armed. His ebony chest contrasted with the bright white of the linen shenti around his waist. The kilt reached to just above his knees and was held in place by a thin strip of linen tied at his waist.

Miriam's knees had trembled as she saw his kohl-lined eyes fixed on two women in the street—the two midwives. Miriam hadn't realized she'd dropped the bucket of water until she felt the coolness hitting her leg, causing the hem of her robe to cling to her.

As she watched, the Medjay pointed to the chariot, ordering Puah and Shiphrah to climb inside. All was quiet then, as everyone held their breaths to watch them go. With a flash of the harness and a shout from the driver, the chariot turned, returning in the direction of the glimmering city of Rameses. Miriam's heart had pounded in her ears, accompanied by the nickering of the enormous brown horses as the chariot journeyed from their world to another.

That day, hours had passed, and Imma had been especially quiet. Had she foreseen the bad news to come? Miriam doubted that. How could one have believed such horror?

It had been just before dinner when the chariot returned, depositing them. Instead of returning home, the younger midwife had walked their direction. Even though Imma and Abba stood in the doorway blocking Miriam's view, she'd heard Puah's sobs fill the air and had also heard what had been demanded of them. All the Hebrew boys were to be killed after birth, Puah had informed them—the midwives had to ensure it was so. It had been a direct order from Pharaoh himself.

Since then, at least twice a week, Pharaoh Amunhotep's desert police—the Medjay—swarmed from the city of Rameses toward the clusters of slave towns on the plains of Goshen.

Once a people from Nubia in the north, some of the Medjay had immigrated to the Egyptian realm during a time of famine or had been captured in war. Yet while the Beni-Yisrael—the children of Israel—found themselves as builders and slaves, the dark-skinned Medjay rose to a place of power by doing Pharaoh's dirty work and using their fierceness to control other slaves, the captive Ethiopians, Cushites, and especially Beni-Yisrael.

When the edict first came, the men of Beni-Yisrael had attempted to protect their newborn sons by refusing to allow the Medjay entrance. But as dozens of men were slaughtered at their doorsteps, Beni-Yisrael had no choice but to submit. That was when the real horrors began. Even as she slept, Miriam could not escape the memories of the high-pitched screams of mothers whose infant sons were ripped from their arms. Their wailing mixed with the pained cries of the infants as they were carried away by a limb and slung carelessly into the Nile.

Numerous times a day, Miriam came up with reasons to leave the house. First to watch. Then to pray. Not too many days ago she'd witnessed the horror of the decree firsthand.

Miriam had taken Aaron for a walk in the cool of the evening, and without warning the Medjay's chariot had rumbled into their slave town. Minutes later it had stopped before a house at the edge of the village. Even though Miriam had turned and rushed the other direction, she had clearly heard the mother's begging and shrieking. Surely someone had told the Medjay where to go, because instead of roaming the houses, they'd grasped up the baby and headed to the Nile. Miriam had hurried Aaron within the reed doorway just in time to see the Medjay's chariot dash away, the guards' deed done.

As her parents talked about it that night, Abba insisted that the baby's presence must have been discovered by an overseer, as surely none of their neighbors would reveal such a thing. But Imma refused to comment. Instead, she'd rubbed her belly in a slow circle and lowered her head in prayer.

Now, outside on the dirt street, the high sun heated the top of Miriam's head. The air smelled of dampness and dust, neither appealing. She took Aaron's hand and paused, looking both ways. Then slowly Miriam released a breath. Everything was the same on their streets. So far, no Medjay today.

She lifted her chin as her eyes fixed on the spectacle in the distance. Beyond their plains, the shimmering city of Rameses rose, nearly blinding in the radiance of the noonday sun. The only thing similar to the great city and Goshen was the wide green of the Nile that flowed through both with barely a ripple, appearing deceitfully calm and peaceful.

Miriam turned away and walked slowly so Aaron could keep pace. Her eyes fluttered closed and then opened again. *El Shaddai, protect us. Keep evil away from our home.*

The words were her father's, but Miriam had memorized them and repeated them often. While many of the slaves who lived and worked near them worshipped multiple gods, her father spoke of only One. While some of the tribes of Beni-Yisrael claimed lesser gods as their own, her father believed that the One who provided a scapegoat for Abraham in the thicket and wrestled with Jacob—El Shaddai—was not only greater than any of the gods, but He alone was to be worshipped.

Above them, a falcon dipped and rose in the arched blue of the sky, and she paused before Puah's door. As expected, Miriam also heard the voice of Shiphrah inside.

"What more can they do to us?" Shiphrah's voice rose. "Pharaoh's counselor has convinced him there are far too many Hebrew males. He claims we are birthing an army to one day overthrow him. The Hebrews have indeed flourished under his oppression, but how is it possible that Hebrew men can rise when they are so beaten down? How can Pharaoh expect us—those who help bring life into the world—to cast these infants to death? I am thankful Pharaoh believed us when we said that Hebrew women birthed their babies before we arrive. I'll have no part of this...."

Shiphrah paused to take a breath, and Miriam pushed aside the reeds hanging in the door, revealing herself and her brother.

The older midwife opened her mouth again and then closed it, holding her pained words inside.

Puah turned toward the doorway, eyes wide. "Is it Jochebed's time?"

"Lamb!" Aaron blurted out the word, and tension eased from the women's faces.

"No. Imma still shows no signs." Miriam pointed to the small white form in the corner. "I wanted to show Aaron Puah's lamb."

"Of course." Puah rose and moved to a sleeping mat in the corner. "I fed him not too long ago, and he sleeps. It's a perfect time to hold him."

Aaron rushed over and sat on the mat, opening his arms wide. "Me do!"

Laughing, Puah placed the small creature on his lap. The lamb wiggled for a moment and then tucked his nose under Aaron's armpit and returned to his slumber. Aaron squealed with delight.

Shiphrah stepped forward and placed a hand on Miriam's shoulder. "We all pray you will have a new sister soon."

Miriam nodded, and she told herself not to argue. All would be revealed in due time. Besides, how could she explain the Voice? Instead, she kneeled before the lamb and ran her fingers through its fleece, praying again that by some miracle her new brother would survive.

A NOTE FROM THE EDITORS

We hope you enjoyed another volume in the Ordinary Women of the Bible series, created by Guideposts. For over seventy-five years, Guideposts, a nonprofit organization, has been driven by a vision of a world filled with hope. We aspire to be the voice of a trusted friend, a friend who makes you feel more hopeful and connected.

By making a purchase from Guideposts, you join our community in touching millions of lives, inspiring them to believe that all things are possible through faith, hope, and prayer. Your continued support allows us to provide uplifting resources to those in need. Whether through our communities, websites, apps, or publications, we inspire our audiences, bring them together, and comfort, uplift, entertain, and guide them. Visit us at guideposts.org to learn more.

We would love to hear from you. Write us at Guideposts, P.O. Box 5815, Harlan, Iowa 51593 or call us at (800) 932-2145. Did you love *The Reluctant Rival: Leah's Story*? Leave a review for this product on guideposts.org/shop. Your feedback helps others in our community find relevant products.

Find inspiration, find faith, find Guideposts.

Shop our best sellers and favorites at

guideposts.org/shop

Or scan the QR code to go directly
to our Shop

Find more inspiring stories in these best-loved Guideposts fiction series!

Mysteries of Lancaster County

Follow the Classen sisters as they unravel clues and uncover hidden secrets in Mysteries of Lancaster County. As you get to know these women and their friends, you'll see how God brings each of them together for a fresh start in life.

Secrets of Wayfarers Inn

Retired schoolteachers find themselves owners of an old warehouse-turned-inn that is filled with hidden passages, buried secrets, and stunning surprises that will set them on a course to puzzling mysteries from the Underground Railroad.

Tearoom Mysteries Series

Mix one stately Victorian home, a charming lakeside town in Maine, and two adventurous cousins with a passion for tea and hospitality. Add a large scoop of intriguing mystery, and sprinkle generously with faith, family, and friends, and you have the recipe for *Tearoom Mysteries*.

Mysteries of Martha's Vineyard

Come to the shores of this quaint and historic island and dig in to a cozy mystery. When a recent widow inherits a lighthouse just off the coast of Massachusetts, she finds exciting adventures, new friends, and renewed hope.

To learn more about these books, visit Guideposts.org/Shop

Printed in Great Britain
by Amazon

49478536R00152